Keeper of the Light

The Three Sisters MacBeith
Book Three

Laura Strickland

ARE YOU SIGNED UP FOR DRAGONBLADE'S BLOG?

You'll get the latest news and information on exclusive giveaways, exclusive excerpts, coming releases, sales, free books, cover reveals and more.

Check out our complete list of authors, too!

No spam, no junk. That's a promise!

Sign Up Here

www.dragonbladepublishing.com

Dearest Reader;

Thank you for your support of a small press. At Dragonblade Publishing, we strive to bring you the highest quality Historical Romance from some of the best authors in the business. Without your support, there is no 'us', so we sincerely hope you adore these stories and find some new favorite authors along the way.

Happy Reading!

CEO, Dragonblade Publishing

Additional Dragonblade books by
Author Laura Strickland

The Three Sisters MacBeith Series
Keeper of the Gate (Book 1)
Keeper of the Hearth (Book 2)
Keeper of the Light (Book 3)

Chapter One

Northwest Scotland, July 1620

S AERLA MACBEITH STOOD poised at the top of the rise overlooking Glen Bronach with her arms spread wide in the sweet morning air. Even though she kept her eyes closed tight, she could see in her mind all the details of this place she knew so well. The great sweep of green that led down from her perch to the valley floor below; the loch that lay glittering in the new light like a precious drop of water cupped in a giant's hand. The burn that led into and out of the loch, deep in its seam. The rough stone dwelling place to her right, which she could see from above.

Home.

A rush of love came up the glen, as if riding on the breeze that flew in from the sea, and suffused her. She treasured everything about this place, from the holy ring of standing stones at her back, to the graves of her ancestors not far away, to the strength of the granite beneath her feet. That feeling upheld her even in such dire times as these.

She opened her eyes and narrowed them a bit against the bright light. Her father, who lay in the cairn not twenty steps away from where she stood, had been their chief, Iain MacBeith. She was the youngest of his three daughters.

She blinked away some of the moisture that had gathered on her lashes. If she focused her gaze and peered far, she could just glimpse a dark blot on the other side of the glen. The keep of Clan MacLeod. Her enemies.

She did not like seeing it there, spoiling this vision of magical beauty. But one thing she had learned—a woman, even a Highland Seer like herself, could not deny what was.

The breeze blew against her a tad more insistently, and she rocked on the balls of her feet. The wind smelled of wild thyme and the far-distant sea, and caressed her skin with warmth.

Standing here so, she almost felt she could fly. Just keep her arms spread like wings, kick up her feet behind her, and soar out over the glen. Leave behind the weight of her responsibilities and her worries. The dread. Soar away into freedom.

The dread, aye, lay like a ball of iron in her gut, tethering her spirit.

"Please," she whispered to the air, to the spirits of those at rest behind her, to the standing stones. To the glen itself. This place that was her strength.

They had lost so much.

That thought had haunted her of late, set up a chant in her head. Even when, as now, she came up here to the place where she'd always found peace to pray and seek guidance, it stole her concentration.

At barely twenty, she had lost so many she loved. Her ma first, to illness. Her big, bright brother, Arran, with his crop of wild red hair, not unlike her own, and smiling eyes. Lost in a battle against MacLeod. Da, cut down just three months ago, also by their enemies. Countless friends and brave clansmen she had known from birth. And now—and now…

Her sister, Rhian.

Och, not that Rhian was dead. no. But she'd been swallowed up in the conflict between MacBeith and MacLeod. Sometimes it seemed to Saerla that Rhian might as well be dead. Lost to her.

Since Arran's death, it had been the three of them, the sisters

MacBeith, standing together against all things. Even when her elder sister, Moira, had taken a MacLeod defector for a lover, they had held, indivisible. With every loss and every blow, they had battled together. Moira on the field as a warrior and in the place of chief. Rhian with her gift of healing, holding them sheltered even as Ma had always done, keeping the fire burning at their heart. Herself with her gift of the Sight rooting them in the magic native to this place and taking her stand also on the field of battle when she must.

Now—now Rhian had gone to the other side of the loch to live at MacLeod. With the man she loved.

Saerla narrowed her eyes again and trained them on that distant black speck—MacLeod's keep. Hard to imagine Rhian surviving there. Alone among strangers, having chosen the man she loved above her sisters and her clan.

Hard, too, not to feel hurt by that. Aye, Saerla understood about the power of romantic love, even if she'd never experienced it. But she didn't realize quite how Rhian had made that choice. She had broken the chain. Now they were two instead of three.

Saerla had come up here, aye, to pray and perhaps seek a Vision to guide them. The bitterness, though, accompanied her. A woman could not present herself to the spirits with bitterness in her heart. A heart that sought a Vision must be calm and open in order to allow in the light.

Only, some Visions were dark.

She pressed her lips together at that, and turned away from the beauty spread out below her. Back toward the stones.

"Da." She acknowledged him with a nod and a touch to one of the stones that formed his cairn. Softly she spoke a prayer for the peaceful disposition of his soul. What would he think of Rhian leaving them?

She could not imagine.

Rhian had left to follow Leith MacLeod, who had been a prisoner here and under Rhian's care. Leith was heir to the place of chief at MacLeod, being cousin to the current leader, a man named Rory.

Saerla's mind flinched from the thought of him. Rory MacLeod. The source of all their trouble. The boggart of Glen Bronach.

Saerla had seen him in the past, of course. She'd caught glimpses of him during battles, a fierce fury of a warrior with flying black hair and feral green eyes. She'd also gained a much closer look at him during the battle not long past when she'd been captured and very nearly hauled away as a prisoner.

She hadn't been hauled away. But only because an exchange had taken place, her for Leith MacLeod.

She'd also Seen Rory MacLeod. In a Vision.

She walked toward the ring of stones, which, as she approached them, towered over her. She was the tiniest of MacBeith's three daughters, and the stones had the height of nearly two men. Some of them had lintels, and formed doorways.

Saerla walked through the nearest of these. Mist frequently collected here, especially so early in the day. It moved about in wisps like trailing spirits. She fancied they greeted her now as she stepped into the heart of the magic.

"Accept me, your daughter."

Softness gathered around her, welcoming. It did not help her mood. The dread inside her expanded.

She wanted to push away the memory of that Vision. But that was the thing about the Sight—it came when it chose. Showed you what it chose. When it did, the images were impossible to chase away.

When first she received this particular Vision, she hadn't been certain about the identity of the man she Saw within it. She'd caught glimpses of Rory MacLeod, aye, in battle. But a madman swinging a sword was a far cry from one looking a woman straight in the eyes. With anger. With longing. With demand.

I want ye, Saerla MacBeith. Ye will be mine.

Nay, she would not. Not if she had to wield a sword or magic in order to prevent it. Not if it meant her life.

But she, a Seer to the bone, believed the Vision. And it had answered a question they'd needed to know at the time—whether, following a grave injury, their enemy, Rory MacLeod, yet lived.

He did. The bastard had survived an arrow straight to his back. He would continue to beleaguer them.

She walked to the center of the stone circle and knelt down. She had told no one about that Vision—och, she'd told them, of course, that Rory MacLeod still lived. Nothing more. But she feared—she feared she must fall into his hands. Into his power. So she brought the dread here, hoping for a measure of reassurance. Of peace.

She bent her head and let the strong morning light beat against her closed eyelids. The power around her, carried in the mist, began to swirl. She fought to discipline herself, her thoughts and her fears. To open the door that would let the light, and the Vision, flow through.

It came suddenly and with a force that nearly knocked her back off her heels. Darkness. Noise. The crashing of arms. Oh God, oh God, it was a battle. And he was near. He was near. She could feel him.

Fear, pure and strong, poured through her, a fear such as she'd seldom experienced. It chased all the breath from her body and sent her mind spinning into a vortex of terror.

Help me. Help me!

Everything stilled. The scene before her inner eye changed abruptly. She saw him again.

He stood before her. A big man he was, a good head taller than Saerla and with broad shoulders. A warrior's body clad in MacLeod tartan. They were in a chamber, one she did not recognize, with stone walls and rushes underfoot. A fire flickered low in a hearth, shedding red light over him, offering her the clearest sight of him since the battlefield.

Black, *black* hair worn long. He must tie it back in battle, for she'd not noticed that before. A face made of all sharp angles. A severe countenance that displayed no mercy. Lips held tight. Green eyes that glittered like hard gems.

Everything within Saerla tightened. She wanted to run. To hide. No refuge from that gaze.

"I hate ye, Rory MacLeod," she told him.

He smiled.

Chapter Two

S AERLA WENT FIRST to seek out her sister Moira and found her in company with her lover, Farlan MacLeod.

Farlan, a big man with a mane of rich brown hair and thoughtful brown eyes, had become a steady if quiet presence in their lives. He did not say much, did Farlan, in company, though Saerla figured he must share his opinions with Moira in private. Whatever thoughts he had, he kept to himself. He knew he was hated here at MacBeith. The enemy. The cuckoo in the nest, as their war chief, Alasdair, put it.

Farlan was detested and mistrusted and had been beaten near death back before he and Moira joined forces. He bore all that for Moira's sake.

Saerla could not say she disliked Farlan. Indeed, in different circumstances, she might have felt respect and even liking for him. But Moira was now her only available sister. And he took up Moira's time.

She found them having breakfast together in the chief's quarters, which Moira had taken over when she assumed that place following Da's death. They had all too clearly just climbed from the rumpled bed.

It made Saerla uncomfortable. Aye, she'd had messages from Da's spirit saying that Moira and Farlan were destined to be together. It still caused her to feel uneasy.

"Saerla? Ye are astir early." Moira had a crop of bright red curls that she fought valiantly to discipline, usually to no avail, and dark blue eyes so like Da's, it was uncanny. She was a strong woman who battled with a sword like a man, a born defender, and it still surprised Saerla she had opened herself as she had to a man.

Her enemy, and the very man who'd struck the blow that stole Da's life.

She'd chosen her enemy to love. As had Rhian, after her.

"Would ye like me to go?" Farlan began to get up from his place beside the fire. He had his hair tied back, but the front of his tunic lay open, displaying the broad chest beneath. An attractive man, aye. But worth the risking of all Moira fought to protect?

"Nay." Moira reached for his hand. "There is naught ye canna hear."

Saerla might have disputed that, but aye, this did concern him.

He sat back down.

"I went up on the rise this morn. To the stones. To seek knowledge."

Moira immediately looked concerned. "Is it Rhian? Has some ill befallen her?"

They both worried about their absent sister. The missing third of their hearts.

Saerla shook her head. "Danger. Darkness. A battle. It will come at night." She contemplated the feelings that had possessed her there among the standing stones. "A terrible battle that will change everything."

Farlan made a wordless sound of protest. He and Moira looked at one another.

"Will we lose this battle?" Moira asked.

"I could no' tell. I did not See. Only that it will come at night, and it will be violent. And it will—will spark the beginning of the end."

"The end for us?" Moira had gone pale.

"I swear to ye, sister, I canna tell." Saerla would not share the rest of it, the part of the Vision that had brought her and Rory MacLeod together in a strange chamber. That which played in far too forcefully with what she'd Seen before.

A warning, that must be. For her to stay clear out of his reach. Perhaps she should not take the field in this next battle.

"Ye canna tell when this will take place?"

Saerla shook her head.

"I maun tell Alasdair. We will prepare and be ready whenever he comes."

He. Rory MacLeod. Even in a crowd of enemies, he stood out. Bold, determined, and dangerous.

"It could happen tonight." Moira rose. "I'd best go find Alasdair straightway. He will be on the walls. Or the training field, even as he should no' be, given that grave wound o' his. Sister, come."

Eyeing Saerla, Farlan spoke softly. "My love, I think your sister needs to sit down a moment or two."

Moira looked at Saerla through narrowed eyes. "Are ye unwell?"

"Here, sit." Farlan rose and guided Saerla to her sister's place. "Finish Moira's breakfast. Ye be in need o' restoration."

Funny, his knowing that. The Sight took much out of Saerla, a thing she'd believed only Rhian understood. Now she beheld a measure of Rhian's kindness in Farlan's eyes.

"Aye, stay here," Moira said. "I will talk wi' Alasdair." She stopped abruptly en route to the door. "You say Rory has overcome that injury o' his? That you Saw him fighting in this battle that is to come?"

Saerla nodded. Moira cursed bitterly and went out.

Saerla and Farlan sat in silence for several moments after Moira had gone.

"We knew this maun come," Farlan said then. "That Rory would no' give up on his efforts to seize the glen. 'Twas but a matter o' when he would move."

"Tell me about him." Better the boogeyman you knew than the one you imagined. Rory had once been Farlan's best friend. There could be no one better to tell her the truth.

"Ah. He is the most stubborn man I ha' ever known. And he is angry. Angry at me for daring to turn my back on him. Angry that he has no' been able to walk over MacBeith and defeat the clan he always considered so weak." Farlan shook his head. "He will no' give up."

Saerla's heart sank. "He wants revenge?"

"He wants revenge and he wants conquest. He wants victory and to be the cock o' the walk here in Glen Bronach."

"He—he sounds like a terrible bad person."

Farlan shot her a close look. "He is no'. Not all bad, by any road. He has his faults, as do we all."

Ah, and would Farlan still defend the man? After Rory had cast him off, deprived him of his very name?

"He appears to ha' more faults than most."

"Perhaps so. He was born ambitious. And 'tis difficult to ever convince him he is no' in the right."

Saerla snorted and asked what had been most on her mind. "How d'ye think he will treat Rhian?"

Farlan's gaze softened. "He is ne'er harsh wi' women." His lips curled in a rueful smile. "Of course, he does no' credit them wi' much either. He has ne'er met women like the sisters MacBeith."

He would meet her, Saerla. It had been foretold. Did she have the strength to endure such a meeting?

In the past, she'd defied her fears. She had taken the field when she was afraid. She'd sought Visions when she was afraid. She'd carried on without Ma. Without Arran. Without Da and now Rhian.

Why did the thought of facing a single boogeyman frighten her so?

Because she sensed he threatened all she held dear. All she was. The light she carried within.

The gods help her, she must be strong enough. Because if Rory MacLeod overthrew the magic of this place, it would destroy them all.

Chapter Three

RORY ROLLED FROM his bed with a groan. He no longer rose of a morning as he used to do, bounding up on a wave of vitality he could barely contain, eager for the day and all he might accomplish during it.

Too much had happened. Too many wounds, both emotional and physical, including this accursed one to his back.

He'd discovered if he trundled from the bed where he either slept far too deeply or not at all, the pain was less than if he flexed his back to stand. Very nearly bearable.

He straightened and breathed deeply, trying to discipline his agony. A young man, and one well used to having his body at his command, he rebelled at this. He needed to conquer it. This was merely pain.

A warrior suffered such as a matter of course. His body carried any number of scars, old and new. None like this.

The healers said he was fortunate to be alive. The arrow he'd taken in the back during that skirmish at MacBeith had been well placed and penetrated between two of his ribs, done some kind of damage to his lung that still made it hard to breathe. But the blow had missed his heart.

The damned arrow had turned as it went in so that when his men got him home and into the healers' hands, the points had caught on his ribs and refused to come out again. The way he understood it—for he'd been half senseless then and raving with pain—they'd had to cut the thing out.

It had left a great, gaping hole in his back. An ugly one by all accounts. He, to be sure, could not see it himself, but he gathered much from the expressions on the faces of those who could.

He stood there beside his bed thinking about it, still trying to breathe. He slept wearing as little clothing as possible because clothing hurt. The room felt cold, as he rarely bothered with a fire at this season, and his skin pricked all over.

Nothing had gone right so far this year. First the death of his father. He still flinched inwardly at the thought of that. Camraith MacLeod had been a legend, a strong man and a wise chief who had somehow managed to combine a measure of mercy with his ability to lead.

Rory puffed out a breath. Mercy. It was for fools and weaklings.

Which did not mean he hadn't admired his father. He had. And he missed him every day, even though they'd disagreed fundamentally on many matters.

Such as ownership of the glen.

Rory steeled himself, ignoring the pain, and stepped to the pile of clothing he'd discarded last night. He'd told Da, and told him again, that Clan MacLeod had business to finish here in Glen Bronach. Their ancestors' business.

Long ago, generations ago now, a branch of their powerful clan had come to this beautiful place. A brother had broken off from another, so it was told—they'd been headstrong even then. Claimed new land inhabited by members of a smaller clan, here before them.

The MacBeiths.

Thinking on it while struggling into his sark, Rory sneered over the name. Those ancient MacBeiths had been few in number but had been well dug in over across the loch. It should have been easy for the MacLeods, filled with ambition, to chase them out. The work of a single bloody summer, perhaps.

Yet they remained.

Some said they had magic on their side. They did have that circle of stones up behind their keep, atop the rise. But he did not believe in such nonsense.

They'd merely gained strength and numbers during his da's time as chief. For Da, even though his clan possessed the greater numbers, had refused to launch a campaign that would completely destroy his neighbors.

Och, there had been raids, to be sure. Running battles. Men had died—the MacBeith heir had. That was what warriors did. They fought and died for their cause.

He had argued endlessly with Da about that. Charged him to finish the job those first MacLeods began. Now Da was gone, leaving a hole that felt bigger than the one in his back. And Farlan—Farlan was gone.

He paused in the act of lacing up the front of his sark, his fingers faltering. Farlan had been raised alongside him following the death of the lad's father in one of those battles. He'd been like a brother to Rory, closer than he could rightly express. The three of them—himself, Farlan, and Rory's cousin, Leith—had gotten into more mischief growing up than he could likely recall.

And this year…this year, Farlan had betrayed him.

He could barely stand to think about it. Because his best friend, the man he'd thought he could trust in all things, had turned his back on Rory and renounced his birthright as a MacLeod.

For the sake of a woman.

Even now, it made Rory want to spit.

He did not know when he'd experienced such anger. Such hurt. He liked women, aye—when he had the time for them. But this woman, to add insult to injury, was a MacBeith, and, following her father's death, had set herself up as chief of that clan.

He finished dressing, shrugging away the resultant pain, just as he shoved away the thought of Farlan.

Farlan was gone, living at MacBeith with his woman, having chosen her over his fealty, their friendship, and his name.

And Leith…

His cousin was his heir, being the son of his father's sister. Rory had no issue. He supposed he would have to fulfill that duty someday, the sooner the better. For just days ago, Leith had returned from captivity at MacBeith, badly injured. And he'd been followed—by a woman. Another of the old Chief Mac-Beith's daughters she was, the sister of the very woman who had set herself up as chief after her father. And stolen Farlan.

He crashed from his chamber and strode down the corridor, buckling on his sword as he went. He did not understand it, no he did not. In his estimation, women were for breeding sons—and daughters. They were for being treated gently and protected.

The MacBeiths sent their women to war. The new female chief fought on the field on a regular basis. Indeed, he'd glimpsed her in numerous battles, including the one that had taken the life of her father, the old chief, without realizing she was a woman.

And he'd seen her sister fighting too—not the one Leith had invited in, for there were three of them, but another. He'd even had her in his hands briefly, a captive.

Nay, he did not understand it. How men could allow such women to endanger themselves. It made no sense.

Outside, the sky had just begun to expand with light. It never truly grew dark at this time of year, but now dawn flooded in, contesting with the aged gloaming for dominance.

All quiet last night. His pulse beat in time with the rhythm of this place. He would know if aught went amiss.

Besides, MacBeith seldom attacked. They were a tribe of defenders. He scowled. Except for that war chief of theirs, Alasdair. He was a right bastard. But Alasdair had been badly injured in that last battle—gutted, if Rory was not mistaken. And that could change everything.

He reached the door of a certain dwelling and pounded upon it, smashing his fist against the boards. His impatience and his aggravation sounded in every blow.

It did not take long for Leith to swing the panel wide and blink at him.

His cousin, a big man, stood half-naked, clearly just arisen from his own bed. Leith had height and a broad chest sprinkled with sandy hair, a wild mop of the same color on his head, and an ugly wound high up on his right arm.

That wound had nearly cost Leith the use of his sword arm. Command of it returned to him, but slowly, and he'd not yet regained the dexterity needed to take the field. That would require work and determination.

Accordingly, Rory spat words into his cousin's face. "I need ye on the practice field. Now."

"Christ, Rory. I am scarcely out o' my bed."

Rory could see that. In fact, behind Leith, in the dusky chamber, the woman—Rhian MacBeith—even now slipped from their bed and drew a robe about herself.

Rory scowled at his cousin, who swiftly considered his disposition and backed down.

"Verra well. Gi' me a moment. Come in."

Rory had no desire to enter the chamber. He chose to have as little interaction as possible with Mistress Rhian MacBeith.

Not that she wasn't beautiful. He could see the attraction. Take now, for instance. She'd come from the bed with her hair hanging loose and wild. Deep red it was, and full of curls. She had a strong, bonny face, beautiful, dark blue eyes, and a lush, womanly body that might make any man take a second glance.

Rory stepped into the chamber and scowled at her before turning his eyes sternly away.

"Good morning, Master Rory," she said.

There was something about her voice, a low huskiness, that set him on edge. A healer she was, and Leith insisted she would be of great use to the clan someday, once she'd settled, tending the wounds her own people inflicted on his men. He wondered how she would countenance that. How might she provide such service?

For love. All these sacrifices for the sake of love. He'd be cursed if he understood.

Chapter Four

R ORY SPOKE LONG at the meeting that followed the practice
session. He and his warriors met in the open, it being a fine
day, and him disliking being confined inside. He'd called in
certain senior members of the clan along with his war chief,
Murgor, a contemporary of his father's whom Rory would
nevertheless pit against any younger man for toughness. For
savagery. Rory needed savagery.

To be sure, he did not need to discuss his plans with anyone.
He made the decisions here at MacLeod. His aim was to whip up
fervor for another attack against their enemies.

The past few had gone very badly. So he tested the waters
and perhaps himself, though he would not readily acknowledge
that.

The training session had been lengthy and agonizing. He
would not spare himself, even though each movement hurt, and
the weight of his leather armor on his back prompted agony. He
could not falter. If he could not endure a mere practice session,
how would he endure battle?

Endure battle, he must.

His men all listened to him, standing in a rough circle beneath
the sun, most still carrying their weapons. Once he'd outlined a
plan for attack—which, he declared, should come just at
nightfall—they continued to gaze at him. No one spoke a word

until one of his warriors, Mathis, said, "When, chief? When will we launch this attack?"

"Tomorrow night. There is no moon. We will row across the loch and march in under cover of the gloaming."

He cast a look at Leith, watching his cousin's face closely. If protest were to come, he figured it would stem from him. Since Leith had returned home, he'd done naught but bleat about peace, talking of striking a treaty with Farlan and his woman.

Striking a treaty would not gain Rory the glen. He wanted it all, from one steep slope to the other, and the stones over on the far rise.

To his surprise, it was his war chief who spoke. "Chief Rory, would it no' be better to wait a time?"

Rory focused his glare on the man. "Wait?"

Murgor gestured at Leith. "Master Leith here works to regain use o' his arm, but he is no' there yet."

Aye, Leith had worked hard toward that goal today, and it had cost him. And aye, Leith had always been valuable in such battles. Though he lacked what Rory would call a killer instinct, his great strength made up for it, and Rory had always felt confident handing him control of one flank.

The three of them, himself, Leith, and Farlan had battled well together. Now he faced the prospect of cutting Farlan down in any encounter. His best friend.

Former best friend.

Making his mind up swiftly, he declared, "Leith will no' come wi' us on this attack."

"Wha'?" Leith chirped.

Rory treated him to a glare but said nothing more. The men all looked at one another.

"And ye?" Murgor said.

"Eh?" Rory switched his glare to the man.

Murgor rarely looked uncomfortable. He did so now. "Tha' wound in your back, chief. Are ye sure ye be ready for hard battle?"

"Will ye tell me I am no'?" Rory drew himself up.

"Well—ye did nearly die o' that arrow, seated so deep between your ribs."

Rory spread his hands. "As ye can see, I did no' die, and stand here before ye, fit to fight."

Again, the men exchanged glances.

"Forgive me sayin'," Leith put forth, "but we all saw ye at practice. Saw what it costs ye to swing a sword."

For an instant, Rory went stone cold. He would not accept disrespect—or pity—especially from his men.

He tossed his head. "There are costs in battle. I am willing to pay mine."

"All I am saying," Leith persisted, "is mayhap wait a wee while before resuming the campaign."

The other men nodded.

"Allow yoursel' to heal a bit more, and me also, before taking the field."

"And waste valuable time this season?" He'd be cursed if he would. Following Da's death, Rory had vowed this would be the summer of conquest. They'd waited long enough to fulfill the intentions of those who had come before them.

If only one thing, one *damned* thing, would go right.

Something flickered in Leith's eyes. "This season. Next—"

Rory pressed his lips together. No matter how the hole in his back pained him, he would not relent. "What sense is there in waiting till that war chief o' theirs is back up on his feet? He is laid up now, and so now is the time to attack. We go tomorrow night. Ready the men," he told Murgor. And, with another glare, "Leith, ye come wi' me."

Leith did not look pleased with the command. No doubt he wanted to hurry home to his woman, to her tender care.

Not just yet.

Rory led his cousin to the hall where the warriors drank, to a shadowy corner where they might sit alone and speak in private.

Leith downed his first mug of ale in one go and eyed the

second one Rory set before him.

Rory longed to do the same, to let the fine brew dull the edges of the pain. He said instead, "We need to talk."

"Aye?" Leith picked up the second tankard but did not drink.

"About yer loyalties, and where they lie."

Leith stared at him, appearing stricken. He put the tankard down again. "Ye question that? Ye question me?"

"I maun know I can trust ye before we go into battle together."

"I am your cousin. Your blood."

"Aye, that. And yer loyalties are tangled, given the woman who followed ye home."

"Her name is Rhian."

"I ken it fine."

"Then ye will call her that, wi' respect."

The anger inside Rory flared. "And there ye ha' it—the reason I question ye."

"Ye question me because I demand a measure o' decency for the woman I will wed?"

Rory flinched. "Nay. Because ye feel the need to upbraid me—your chief—over it. Is yer loyalty to her, or to me? Before we tak' the field together, ye will answer me that."

Leith rarely grew angry. That was one of the things Rory valued most in him. Though a big, powerful man who'd outstripped both him and Farlan as they grew, he neglected to use that power, preferring laughter to anger and strife.

Yet Rory saw him kindle up now. The anger looked so strange in Leith's mild gray-blue eyes that it made Rory sit back a mite on his bench.

"My fealty belongs to ye, my chief. My heart is hers."

Rory held the furious gaze steadily. "That may be a problem."

"How so?"

"Wha' if we meet someone dear to this woman o' yers on the field? One o' her sisters, mayhap. They both fight, do they no'?" Rory could not hold back a sneer. "Their men allow them to risk themsel's that way."

"The twa sisters both do tak' the field, aye, bein' the old chief's daughters—"

"As is your woman." Rory added deliberately, "Mistress Rhian."

"Aye. One o' them, Moira—"

"Farlan's woman," Rory stated with great distaste, and added, "I just want to mak' sure I ha' it right."

"Aye. The way I understand it, Moira stepped into the place of her brother, Arran, after he fell. Just as she has stepped into her father's place now."

"And the other—"

"Saerla. The youngest."

Saerla. He, Rory, had briefly had her in his hands. He still recalled the shock he'd felt when, staring into her face, he'd realized she was not a youth, as he assumed, but a woman. She might have remained his prisoner, only they'd agreed to a trade, had the MacLeods. Traded Leith for her.

"They are strong-headed women," Leith explained. "No one tells them wha' to do, nor makes them tak' the field."

A mad state of affairs, and further proof MacBeith needed overthrowing.

Rory gave Leith a grim smile. "Here at MacLeod, I mak' the decisions, and I say ye will no' tak' the field tomorrow night." Not till Rory was sure he could trust this cousin of his.

But he wondered…he wondered, would he ever see Saerla MacBeith again?

Chapter Five

"I miss Rhian."

The confession came from Saerla unwillingly, the last thing she'd meant to say. Her heart, so it seemed, would not heal from this latest wound. How could it when Rhian, with her gentle, competent hands and comforting nature, had always been the one to do the healing? Rhian was not here.

When Ma had died some six years ago now, Rhian had softly and silently stepped into her place, become the one to light their fires, cook their meals, and provide them with a soft place to fall.

Losing her felt like losing Ma all over again.

Moira, to whom Saerla spoke, glanced at her. They'd met, this second evening after her Vision, up on the battlements just before nightfall. The soft shadows of the gloaming filled the glen. It would be a dark night with no moon.

"Rhian is no' dead."

"She is no' here, either."

Moira sighed and tossed her head. She was strong. Yet Saerla found it hard to believe she did not feel the wound they now shared. One of their three, gone.

"She made her choice."

"Do ye think we will ever see her again? Her, or her bairn?" For Rhian carried Leith MacLeod's child, one of the reasons she'd gone after him to live among her enemies.

"If we can wrangle a peace—"

Moira stopped speaking abruptly and stared out into the dark glen. She stiffened in every limb. "Attackers," she half breathed. And then she hollered it. "Attack! Attack!"

Saerla came to attention also, flooded with alarm. Staring out over the stonework, she could see nothing, so she closed her eyes, hands resting on the top of the parapet, and sought to See instead.

Sure enough, the images came flooding upon her. A horde of men, dark figures moving like mere shadows through the deeper darkness. At the waters of the loch. A cluster of boats ready to launch.

Boats. Water. Men. *Rory MacLeod.*

Horror and dread suffused her so she could not move. He would destroy her.

When she opened her eyes, beating back the images, Moira had gone, running off like other members of the guard. Preparing to fight.

Och, might all the gods and all the powers protect them from what was to come.

She must go don her armor. Find her weapons. She stood here on the wall as a woman. A Seer. She could be neither now. She had to transform herself into the small whirlwind she became on the field, one rarely touched by any weapon. A being with no past and no future.

By all that was holy, she did not want the future that had been foretold. It terrified her more than any battle.

She ran down the stairs from the wall. Confusion raged around her—men running and shouting, gathering arms. She did not know where Moira had gone, but she caught a glimpse of Ewan, the senior member of the council that had opposed Moira at every turn, already clad for war. Differences did not matter at a time like this. There was just the loyalty of the blood.

She hurried to her chamber and changed her clothing, struggling with ties and buckles, her fingers gone clumsy. Hastily, hastily she braided her cap of wild red-gold hair in order to fit it under the leather helmet. When finished, she resembled a slim youth. One bound to fight.

Not till she reached the forecourt where the warriors mustered did she mark the absence of Alasdair. It was he who usually organized them, called them to order and calmed their fears. Alasdair must still be back in his bed—pray God so. If this came to his ears, *when* this came to his ears, he would try to rise. She doubted any power on earth could keep him abed then.

But marching out, taking up a sword, could cost him his life.

It struck her then—Rory MacLeod must know this. He must have seen Alasdair wounded during that last battle. It was why he moved now. She knew it as well as she knew the thoughts in her own mind.

How would they ever survive this battle without Alasdair?

Like an answer to the question, Moira strode out into the forecourt with her sword in her hand and Farlan at her side. Not for the first time, Saerla wondered how this must be for Farlan, marching out to face his friends, his relations, his own men. What if he was called upon to battle his former chief and best friend, Rory?

What if *she* was? Would killing Rory negate what she'd Seen? Aye, surely so. Because a Vision gave a glimpse of but one among what might be several destinies.

All Saerla had to do was take the field and slay Rory MacLeod in order to save herself.

That thought gave her courage. She listened as Moira began to speak.

"We will march out from the stronghold and meet this threat. Some o' the attackers may circle round and seek to cross the burn at one o' the fording places higher up. That will tak' time. The others will ha' to disembark from their boats and make it ashore. We will be waiting to slaughter them then."

This, Saerla knew, had been tried before without success. They seemed to fare best when they defended their walls. But this was Moira speaking, her sister, who was a born defender. If she said to march out—

An interruption came then in the form of a large man hobbling out into the forecourt. He wore a rough blanket around his shoulders and leaned for support on an ash plant. His face writhed in a scowl, betraying his agony.

Moira ran to him, even as the warriors stared. Saerla followed. They intercepted Alasdair just outside the door.

"Alasdair!" Moira exclaimed. "Get ye back to your bed."

"I will no'! D'ye mean, lass, to march out wi'out me?" Alasdair, always careful in how he addressed Moira, never called her "lass." It spoke to his state of mind that he did so now.

"I go at the head of the men," Moira told him, steel in her voice, "wi' Farlan at my side."

Alasdair only stared. Judging by his pallor and the crease between his brows, Saerla could not say how he had walked all the way from the healers' hut.

She laid her hand on his arm, as she knew Rhian would have done, had she been here. "Alasdair, we need ye on the field, aye." She could barely imagine heading into battle without him. All she'd ever seen when on the way to fight was his broad back. "But we need ye well and strong still more. Please go back to your bed."

"My bed!" Bitterly he spat the words. "If I am to die, Mistress Saerla, it will be wi' a sword in my hand."

"No' this time," she told him softly. "No' this fight."

She looked around wildly. All the warriors stared, at a loss. She caught young Calan's eye and gestured him over. "Please, Calan, escort Master Alasdair back inside."

Alasdair glared at her. He glared at Moira and the unfortunate Calan in turn.

"Alasdair," Moira said so low only the four of them heard, "ye can barely stand. Wha' use will ye be to me in battle?"

"Let us carry this fight," Saerla begged him swiftly. "Let us defend the place we all love."

She would take a place at the forefront of the battle, among the first to meet the men coming ashore. All she had to do was locate Rory MacLeod and kill him.

RORY, BALANCED WITH his feet wide in the lead boat, listened to the creaking of the oars and the silken splash of the water on the hull. He'd ordered silence, always essential during a raid. So far his men made a fine job of it.

The scent of the loch rose all around him. A familiar scent, bred into his bones. His limbs twitched, ready to launch him forward as soon as they hit the far shore. The hole in his back screamed at him, though, more than he would have thought possible.

Do no' think o' that. 'Tis just pain. Pain could be dismissed. His intentions could not.

He kept his eyes fixed on the MacBeith stronghold ahead, situated halfway up the opposite rise. No matter who might be in charge there, they were no fools. Men would be on watch.

His approaching forces, no matter how quiet, would soon be spied.

He knew the moment it happened. He could not hear the cries go up, the distance being too great, but torches bloomed all along the battlements and then out in what must be the fore-court. He could almost see dark figures running hither and yon.

Would they march out to face him? Or would they stay behind their walls and defend? He scowled over the question. He'd not had any luck breaking through their defenses. Still, his men who'd gone around by the burn brought a battering ram.

They'd almost had success with that last time. Before he'd taken that damn arrow in the back.

"They've seen us." The mutter spread from man to man and boat to boat, little more than a breath of wind. Rory steeled himself. Not all these men he'd brought with him would make it home again. At least, not alive.

He always tried to collect as many of his dead as possible. To be sure, sometimes they had to be abandoned. Left lying on foreign soil.

He'd feared Leith dead, following that battle in which he'd been injured. The flank had taken a pounding that night, and—

His boat grounded on the shore, and he left off thinking. The instant his foot hit that soil, he left off being a man, and became a warrior.

No mercy. No quarter. And no regrets.

Chapter Six

THEY BURST OUT of the stronghold in formation, with Moira at their head, Farlan and Saerla just behind. Moira had tried to persuade Saerla to stay back and oversee the defense of the keep, as she had at times in the past. Saerla, her sword already drawn, refused.

How could she slaughter Rory MacLeod if she did not face him in battle?

So Moira assigned Farlan the task of keeping close to Saerla's side. Saerla had one glimpse of them sharing a fervent embrace before they marched out—warriors instead of lovers.

They did not know whether they would return together. None of them did.

For the first time, Saerla was glad Rhian was safe at MacLeod. At least she would survive. And her wee bairn, not yet born. Because everything within Saerla insisted this would be a dire battle. A costly one.

She ran off anyway into the dark with her fellow clansmen—men she had known all her life and with whom she'd trained—thundering around her. Driven by the fear inside her, fear of what could be so much worse than this battle, she would not hesitate.

Find Rory MacLeod. Kill him.

The loch side came in sight with boats ranged all along the shore. More boats still floated their way in. Saerla heard Moira's voice up ahead. She had engaged the enemy.

Please to all the gods. Perhaps Moira would accomplish her task for her. Because Moira was as much a warrior as any of these others around her, and Rory MacLeod would likely be among the first ashore.

Someone touched her on the arm. Calan, having caught up after taking Alasdair back into the stronghold. They often fought near each other in battle and, indeed, had been together when Da took his death wound.

Now he cried, "We are to fire their boats! Come wi' me!"

Aye, a group of them had brought torches. It made a good plan, but she shook her head.

And ran on.

Later she would wonder what would have happened had she followed Calan instead. Destiny laid out more than one path. A woman had to choose.

Chaos and slaughter already possessed the loch side. The crashing of arms. Wholesale battle, cries of anger and pain. Every instinct bade her retreat from that. She ran into it instead.

She did not know why she'd never taken a dire wound in a battle. Only mere slashes, a cut to the arm, a slice to the fingers. She was quick, aye, but not half so strong as her opponents. 'Twas as if she were charmed, protected. And aye, she spoke charms, whispered them under her breath now. Most everyone did.

Despite the torches, which circled behind the MacLeod forces, she found it hard to see. The colors of tartan faded in the dark. Men seethed together. How was she to find Rory?

He'd be at the center of things. The spearhead. The place where death shone brightest.

She must take herself there.

Though she'd never been badly wounded in any battle, that did not mean she would not meet death this night. As she advanced, delivering blows right and left when she saw a face she did not know, the threat of death increased. She could feel it.

A man twice her size engaged her. She had one glimpse of a snarling face before she whirled, faster than he expected, and sliced him across the belly. Not waiting to watch him fall, she rushed on.

She caught sight of Moira up ahead and fighting well. Could this be her sister? She looked like any other warrior. Saerla could not see Rory, but she heard shouting, hollering, roars of hate and demand splitting the night.

She had nearly reached the water. Boats, aflame here and there, provided a weird, orange radiance, against which…

She saw him. Rory MacLeod.

He stood like a wolf at bay, a number of MacBeith warriors ranged against him. One or two of his own men fought at his back, virtually in the water. Not Moira—nay, her sister was not here, and Saerla had outdistanced Farlan.

Killing Rory MacLeod was up to her.

For an instant only she eyed the man, taking his measure. A big man, and lithe with it, he had a flying mop of black hair, his face fixed in a savage grimace.

A sword came at her from the left. Almost without thinking, she knocked it aside, her eyes still fixed on her prize. Without hesitation, she ran forward, howling.

RORY FOUGHT WITH the single-minded concentration that always possessed him on the field. Figures rushed at him out of the dark. He took them down as swiftly as he could, not allowing himself to be caught out.

He had three goals. Take out the MacBeiths' war chief, if he had somehow dragged himself onto the field. Take out the woman who had set herself up as chief—Moira MacBeith. After that, the third goal, breaching their walls, should be easy.

He had to find those two targets first. And these bastards just kept coming at him.

He answered the blows with efficient ones. To the belly. To the throat. At his back, many of his boats had been set afire. It did not matter. Once he took the stronghold, he would use it for a temporary headquarters.

Mayhap he'd live here for a time. Fulfill the dreams of his ancestors.

A blade came at him. He ducked and whirled and took out its owner. Time to move forward away from the water and—

A shadowy form flew at him, erupting out of the darkness. It moved with unusual speed, soaring over the turf with a bright sword in its hand. Before Rory had time to blink, the warrior was upon him, nothing more than a slim figure with furious eyes.

Acting on pure instinct, he raised his sword. The MacBeith warrior whirled, his sword becoming a blur, and swung at Rory.

Aiming for his head.

With no hope of blocking such a blow in time, he stumbled back, his shield flying from his arm. The point of his enemy's sword caught his left cheek and laid it open from his ear to his nose. He did not feel any pain, but aye, he faced his own death squarely in that moment. Wondered if it had come.

His opponent gave a cry—not like the bellows he heard all around him. This sounded high, like the scream of a hawk—and whirled away again.

Off balance, Rory did not give him time. He leaped and tackled the MacBeith warrior from behind and, rather than raising his sword, caught the man against his own body with his shield arm wrapped tight.

Which told him his opponent was, in fact, not a man.

He believed he knew her in that instant. For she'd been in his possession once before, if only briefly. She felt small, held there against his body. Small and full of desperate fury.

His sword came up of its own accord. He could lay it against her throat, could hold her fast. But he could not kill a woman.

In that mad instant, he forgot his intention to do just that, to slay the infernal woman who'd set herself up as chief. She, being a chief, did not seem like a woman by any account.

This person in his arms, this woman who'd tried to take his life, did.

"Be still," he growled into her ear. "Be still! I do no' wish to hurt ye."

She either did not hear him amid all the clashing and screaming, or failed to heed. She struggled like a fury in his grip, and he could feel her, by God he could. The flex of her lithe body. The heat coming off her skin. The hate that was not hate so much as focused terror.

He lifted her off the ground. It was not difficult, since she weighed less than half of what he did. She kicked her feet wildly, bashing him in the shins. In the thighs. Between, which forced a grunt from him.

The MacBeith warriors all around had stopped pushing in upon him. The battle slowly died and a preternatural sort of silence fell.

A warrior—the female chief—came racing out of the fighting to face him. She bore a scar on one cheek, and her left arm ran with blood. She looked furious enough to gut him.

"Let her go!"

Not a plea but a command. Yet Rory saw the terror in her face. Three sisters MacBeith, Leith had said. One of them was already at MacLeod. Another—Farlan's bitch—stood before him. Did he hold the third in his arms?

He gave a harsh laugh. "Nay."

"Ye will let her go!"

Farlan came running up, skidding to a halt in the wet, bloodied turf. He appeared incredulous at what he saw.

"Rory—"

The last person Rory wanted to see. He pressed the sword tighter against the throat of the woman in his arms.

"Mistress Saerla!" someone called out.

Aye, so, Saerla was what Leith had called the one sister. The one he claimed was a Seer, of all things. Rory had garnered a prize, indeed.

And this time, this time he had no intention of letting her go.

Chapter Seven

SAERLA CLOSED HER eyes against the sickening fear pounding through her, the horror and dismay. Och, what had she done? In trying to slay her enemy, she'd gone and placed herself directly in his hands.

She'd meant to behead him. To remove him as a threat.

Perhaps she still could.

She opened her eyes and looked at her sister. Moira stood poised before them, her stained sword in her hands and stark terror in her eyes. She did not know how to handle what she saw in front of her.

Her sister in the monster's hands.

Could Saerla break away? Could she, while he remained distracted? He was strong, *strong*. Strong enough to lift her without effort. And furious. She could feel that in every muscle, every sinew pressed against her back.

She could not break away, but she might be able to trick him.

Her dirk lay in a loop at her belt. Her fingers searched for it, and Moira, catching the movement, sought to engage the monster's attention.

"Leave her go, or I swear by this holy ground on which we stand, ye will regret it."

The man holding Saerla—Rory MacLeod—huffed a breath. A scornful laugh.

"Leave her go," rasped Farlan, his heart in his eyes, "and tak' me instead."

Rory's voice rumbled up through his body, and Saerla's. "Why should I want ye? When I ha' one o' MacBeith's daughters." He snugged Saerla closer to him. "I will tak' her home. That will mak' two o' the three at MacLeod."

Saerla swung up the dirk in an arc, clutched tight in her fingers. So swift was the motion, her captor did not catch it in time. Stabbing blindly, she drove the blade into his right shoulder, to the hilt.

He bellowed, and everyone there cried out. For an instant, his grip on Saerla weakened. She threw her weight against his restraining arm and felt the blade of his sword connect with the skin at her throat.

"Nay!" Moira cried.

And then, with preternatural speed, Rory MacLeod recovered. His grip once more tightened, and he lifted Saerla clear from the ground, leaving her feet reaching desperately for the turf.

The circle around them broke and contracted. She saw Moira's face coming at her, full of agony. Moira cared naught for her own safety. Saerla felt herself falling, falling even though Rory MacLeod held her still in his arms. She saw her mother's face and the view over the glen from the holy stones up on the rise. She heard the clash of weapons resume, and someone screaming.

It sounded like her own voice. A blow took her hard on the head, turning the screaming to silence, and the darkness came down.

"Is she dead?" someone asked.

In a distant sort of way, Saerla thought she knew that voice. Male. Not anyone close to her, nay. But it chimed through her mind, arguing she'd heard it before.

Another answered it, a grunt of sound that sent fear rushing through her like flame through straw.

"I do no' think so. Help me wi' this, Leith. The bitch left her dirk in me."

Leith. Aye, that was his voice Saerla recognized. But—he was not at MacBeith. He had gone back to MacLeod, and Rhian after him.

Och, by the gods, was it possible she was no longer at Mac-Beith?

Alarm sent her eyes flying open. She stared into the dim air of an unknown place and fought desperately to orientate herself.

She lay on her back on a pliant surface. Still clad as she'd been for battle, she seemed to be. Unhurt except for a dire pounding in her head and a sickness in her gut prompted by—

That second voice. Harsh and brutal. She remembered it rumbling up through her. Rory MacLeod. How could she be here, where he and his cousin Leith spoke together? Was this a Vision? Or—

Or was she caught in events foretold by a Vision already Seen?

She began to tremble violently where she lay. The two men, surely no more than a pace or two away from her, ignored her as if they believed her senseless.

She lifted up her pounding head just enough to see.

A fire burned on the far side of the chamber, silhouetting the two men. They seemed to struggle together. It took Saerla an instant to realize that the bigger of them—aye, he was Leith MacLeod—stripped the battle armor off the other in order to examine his wounds.

Neither of them so much as glanced at Saerla. But aye, this must be real and not Vision—she must truly be here, since Leith had asked whether she lived or not.

"The bitch tried to kill me. Twice," Rory muttered.

The bitch was her. She had tried to kill him. She had failed.

"Is she badly hurt?" Leith asked. Saerla heard caution in his voice.

"Nay. Hit in the head during that last crush o' the battle before I could get her awa' to the boat."

The boat. Away. Where was she?

"Should ye, cousin, no' be more worried about me?" Rory growled.

"Ye? Ye're a bull. If that arrow in the back did no' kill ye, naught ever will. Who won the battle?"

Rory did not answer at once. Further grunts ensued as he stripped down. Saerla, from her place on her back, could see little more than shadows shifting.

"No one," he said at last. "They burned most o' our boats. We could no' retrieve all our dead. But"—a modicum of satisfaction oozed into his voice—"ye can see I managed to tak' a fine prize."

Leith said nothing.

"Wha' d'ye think her sister the chief will give to get her back?"

"Ye mean to trade her back, then, Rory? Nay to hold her? Nor slaughter her?"

Footsteps sounded on a stone floor. Saerla, squinting her eyes closed again, sensed he stood over her—Rory MacLeod. The monster. Examining her, his gaze sharp as his sword.

"I do no' murder women, Leith. Ye ken that."

Now Leith grunted.

"Wha' should I ask in return for her? Such a bonny thing."

Saerla stiffened with alarm. With an utterly primal dismay.

"D'ye suppose she'll surrender? Quit the fighting and deed the glen o'er to me, to keep her sister safe?"

Saerla stopped breathing. It had come true anyway, despite all her prayers and dread. The Vision she'd seen had found her, for all her fighting.

A destiny lay before her. A path she did not want to take.

Chapter Eight

RORY SAT BESIDE the fire in his chamber where he'd ordered the female captive brought, and brooded. Och aye, he had no other word for his state of mind. Once again, in a battle against MacBeith, things had not gone well.

Or mayhap they had.

He flicked a glance at the small figure that lay upon his bed, here in this safest of places where she might be most securely held. He did not comprehend much of what had happened during the past hours, but he did know he had to keep her safe and secure.

The battle, the details of it, would not leave his mind. Aye, it always took him a while to wind down following combat. This time, though, the sensations remained with him all too brightly. The clashing, the hollering, and the blood.

The feel of the woman in his arms.

She'd tried to kill him there in the heat of that battle. He'd seen the intention in her eyes when first she flew at him, swinging her sword. His death had been her one desire.

He'd known her despite the tight-fitted leather helm that covered her hair. Despite the clothing that made her into a slim lad. He'd known those eyes, so full of desperation and hate.

Because he'd had hold of her once before and had traded her away. For Leith.

He still had difficulty accepting that the MacBeiths risked their womenfolk in that way. This woman, but a tiny thing, weighed almost nothing in his arms.

Yet she was dangerous. She'd done her best to slaughter him.

Saerla. A Seer. And a warrior. A bewildering combination.

The wound she'd inflicted upon him hurt more than it should. The woman's dirk, a small one, had done limited damage, despite the force with which she'd driven it into him. He should barely be able to feel it, given the searing agony of the hole in his back.

Yet he could.

Another bit of torn flesh. What was that? He'd been taking such wounds since he was sixteen.

Leith said he should call in one of the healers to look at him. He'd even offered his Rhian, though Rory could not imagine the woman would relish the task.

The clan healers were busy tending other wounded. Besides, Rory dared not let them see…

He dared not give them another look at the condition of his back.

The man who'd been in charge of his care after the remnant of the accursed MacBeith arrow was removed from his back had advised against resuming training so soon. Against returning to battle. But he was the point of the spear that was MacLeod. Without him, where would they be?

Nay, he did not want the healer to see him again. And as if he'd place himself in Rhian's hands! She wanted him dead as much as her sisters did, no doubt.

Leith had suggested letting Rhian see the lass he'd captured also. Her sister. The one who now lay on his bed.

He wondered whether he should, if she did not awaken. The blow she'd taken to the head might have done real damage. Bringing her sister in would be better than letting the other, heavy-handed healers tend her.

He remembered the agony of that arrow coming out of his

back. It had taken two healers to draw it out and two other men to hold him down. He'd been unable to keep from hollering.

Nay, he would not let them touch his prize.

But he did not necessarily want her sister fawning all over her either. The two of them scheming together. He needed her isolated, frightened, so he might get valuable information from her before he bargained her away again.

Slowly, he walked to the bed, wondering for the first time where he'd sleep this night. The captive lay atop the counterpane in her filthy battle armor, and he eyed her carefully from head to toe.

That close-fitting leather helm—had it protected her head? A pale, almost ridiculously bonny face streaked with sweat and dirt. Brown lashes in fans on her cheeks. A small, compact body that, nay, did not look much like a woman's. Slender, narrow hands, almost delicate to the eye, and tiny feet encased in leather boots smeared with mud.

She was tiny, aye, but he could not fool himself. She made both a threat and a powerful weapon.

He would wield her against her sister. If she ever came awake.

His stomach clenched on a sudden surge of disquiet. What if she died without waking?

He bent closer, watching her carefully. "Mistress Saerla. Mistress?"

SAERLA LAY WITH her breath caught and her eyes tight shut, very much awake. She listened to the man moving about the chamber after Leith left.

Leith—would he go and tell Rhian that she had been captured? Would Rhian come? Could her sister do anything to save her?

Naught could save her, if her Vision proved true.

She heard it when the man—Rory MacLeod—stirred up the fire, and she caught the flare of brightness against her closed eyelids as the fire leaped up. A clang as he no doubt set his weapons aside. The scrape of a chair against the floor. Did he sit? Another as he got up again.

He approached her. She felt him draw near, sensed the coiled energy of him poised, close at hand. He stood gazing at her.

She knew what the man looked like even though she'd only ever glimpsed him in battle. In his armor. He'd, aye, held her once before, or his fellow warrior had, when he demanded Leith's return.

But she'd Seen him, aye. In the Vision.

"Mistress Saerla. Mistress?"

That rough voice speaking her name. She'd heard that too, in the Vision. The foretelling. The terrible, terrifying one where he'd grasped her in his arms, green eyes blazing, and told her, "I will ne'er let ye go."

Ah, she should have better heeded the warning contained in that Vision. She should never have entered the battle, should have kept clear away from him. She should never have tried to kill him, only…

Dead, he could not threaten her and all she loved.

Now her skin pricked all over at his nearness. She could hear him breathing. By God, she could smell him.

The boogeyman, the boggart.

"Saerla." He spoke her name again, sibilantly. A demand.

She opened her eyes.

He stood above the place where she lay, directly above. Lit by the dancing firelight, she could see his face better than ever before. A hard face made up of all planes and angles, it bore a scruff of black beard, and an equally dark scowl.

He wore no sark, his broad chest bare. Saerla's eyes flew instantly to the wound she'd made with her dirk, high up near his right shoulder. She'd stabbed blindly, hoping to take him in the throat.

She'd failed.

She fought to keep her dismay over that fact from showing on her face. She dared give nothing away. This was a powerful man, sculpted in muscle, and she lay at his mercy. He was dark in appearance and spirit, as the boogeyman should be. His hair, still ruffled no doubt from the removal of his helm, shone black as the wing of a crow. His eyes—but she could not see them well. She did not want to look there.

Gathering all her strength, she scuttled away from him on the bed. Aye, she lay atop a bed—they were alone together in a bedchamber.

What did he intend to do?

If he tried to ravish her, she'd fight. But he made at least two of her in size and would be able to overpower her with ease. Aye, but she would damage him before he got what he wanted. She would strike out with everything in her.

"Stay awa' from me."

She barely recognized her own voice. Hoarse with fear.

He drew a breath that expanded the broad chest—she heard the air surge into him. The fire rimmed him in golden light. A devil.

He raised one hand in a soothing gesture. "Do no' be afeared."

She reached the far side of the bed and drew her body up tight, knees bent and arms wrapped around them. Her mind raced and her heart galloped. There must be weapons here in this chamber, if it was his chamber. The man was all about conquest and death, and would not be without a surfeit of arms. If she could slide off the side of the bed and dodge him long enough to get her hands on a knife or sword…

But she did not know for sure that her legs would hold her.

"Keep awa'," she repeated in a croak.

He lifted both hands this time, perhaps showing her they were empty of weapons. He did not need weapons, though. His hands looked as strong and merciless as the rest of him.

"I ken who ye be. Rory MacLeod."

"And I ken who ye be. Saerla MacBeith. Are ye hurt bad?"

She shook her head. A lie. Her skull pounded twice as hard now that she was upright.

"I am Rory MacLeod," he granted, in a deep rumble. "And ye be here at my keep, taken awa' out o' the battle. My prisoner and my prize. Let us see what yer sister will bargain for ye."

Chapter Nine

H E MEANT TO send her home. He held her here at MacLeod, aye, a place she'd seen scores of times from a distance yet never visited. But he intended to make a trade, as he had done for his cousin, Leith.

Relief surged through Saerla in a staggering wave. For an instant she wanted it so badly—longed so intently to be home— that she feared a sob would escape her throat.

She could not let this monster see her cry.

But for whom might he trade her? Farlan? He'd sent Farlan away. Banished him, in fact. His best friend.

For *what* could he possibly exchange her?

She wished he would don some clothing, that he did not stand there before her half-naked, looking so—so threatening. It put her entirely too much in mind of the Vision.

But…but if he meant to bargain her away and send her home, why had he told her in the Vision, *I will never let ye go?*

She shook her head in confusion. If only it would stop pounding long enough for her to think.

He stood where he was, making no move to go around the bed and intercept her. "Ye be the sister o' the woman who has set hesel' up as chief o' yer clan, aye? Wi' Farlan at her side."

Moira was chief of the clan, but with Alasdair at her side, as the council insisted.

"She will want ye back."

She would. Poor Moira must be frantic with two of her sisters gone from her. Both of them here at MacLeod.

"So I will keep ye here safe till she and I ha' the chance to bargain."

And then you will send me home? Saerla ached to ask but would not let herself utter the words that sounded far too much like begging.

"Why am I here in this chamber?" she asked instead.

He took a long look at her before he replied, "I needed somewhere safe to stow ye."

"Is this to be my prison?"

"Nay. Wha'ever ye may think o' me, I will no' put a woman, even a captive woman, in a cell. Though I ha' to say, ye be right handy wi' a sword. And"—he shrugged his shoulder—"a dirk."

"Then what is this place?"

"My bedchamber."

She stiffened in every limb. "I will no'—"

Another searing look. "Wha'ever ye may think o' me," he repeated with deliberation, "I am no' a ravisher o' women."

Welcome words, if she could believe him. Was she to believe that this man who'd attacked them again and again without mercy, who'd banished his own friend, possessed any real honor?

Before she could ponder the question as it deserved, he turned away from her. The firelight washed over his naked back as he moved. She saw—

Och, heavens, such a wound!

They had known of it, to be sure. They'd seen him take that arrow in his back at their gate. Seen him carried away by his men. Had speculated over the damage and hoped he would die.

Aye, she'd hoped he would die—but known he hadn't, when she'd Seen him in the Vision.

Eyeing the wound in his back, she did not understand how he was on his feet, let alone marching out to fight on the field.

A great, ugly thing it was, halfway down the lean, tapering

expanse of his back. A dark hole, the flesh still torn around it. He wore it uncovered like some hideous badge of valor.

She could not keep from gasping.

He glanced at her over his shoulder. His black hair was long enough to brush his shoulders when he moved his head. His expression turned rueful.

"One o' your archers marked me."

How could he fight in such a condition? Even think of going to battle? No wonder he did not wear a sark when he could get away with it. Even light wool would weigh heavy against such a wound.

"I suppose ye hoped ye'd killed me?" He stood at a table against the far wall, where he poured some drink into a pair of mugs.

"We did." Why should she lie about it? Simper or seek for favor? She would fight him to her last breath.

"I am no' so easy to kill as all that."

The wound in his back did not look easy. Saerla did not say so.

He crossed back to the bed and extended one of the cups across it. "Here."

When she remained where she was, arms wrapped tight, he said, "'Tis no' poisoned. See?" He drank from the second mug thirstily, draining it dry.

She accepted her mug, sure not to let her fingers touch his.

The monster offered her hospitality. She needed to go carefully and accept it. For she lay in his power, much as she might detest the fact.

She took a cautious sip. Not ale. Something harsh that burned on its way down.

He went and refilled his cup, affording her another look at his back.

What if she could get her hands on a weapon? Bung it in just there, where his back was torn.

Gods and spirits of the air, help me. Make me as strong as I need to be.

"I wish to see my sister."

He spun around to face her.

"My sister, Rhian. She is here. With Leith."

His lips tightened. "She is." He strolled back to the bed. "Ye do no' make demands, Mistress Saerla."

Setting his mug aside, he sat on the far edge of the bed. Saerla's alarm spiked.

"Ye will see yer sister. When ye deal honestly and readily wi' me."

What did that mean? What did he want from her, precisely? He said he did not intend to ravish her—and despite that accursed Vision, she wanted to believe him. To trade her, then—for what?

She lifted her chin. "I am an honest woman."

"That is good to hear. If ye be also a careful and a prudent one, things will no' go hard wi' ye here."

Saerla drew a breath. "Ye intend to hold permission for me to see my sister over me like a weapon?"

"I ha' said ye will see your sister. But ye maun accept, Mistress Saerla, ye lie in my power now, and that it will happen only by my leave."

Saerla wanted to spit. She wanted to hurt him enough to wipe the confident smirk from his face. She wanted the return of her dirk so she might, aye, plunge it into that hole in his back and take him down.

Instead, she met his gaze head-on. "We ha' heard much about ye, Rory MacLeod, from Farlan. From your cousin, Leith. Dire stories that support what your actions cry aloud. Ruthless. Wi'out mercy. Stubborn. I ha' to say now, the truth o' ye proves all that and more. That the gods should let such a man as ye draw breath is an abomination."

Once more he leaned toward her. "The gods ha' naught to do wi' it."

Saerla's eyes narrowed. "Are ye certain o' that? Because for all your efforts, Master MacLeod, ye ha' no' succeeded in overthrowing us. MacBeith still stands strong."

He lifted wicked black brows. "All that will change now that I ha' ye in my hands. Ask yoursel', Mistress Saerla—wha' will your sister no' do to get ye back safe again?"

Aye, that very question had been swirling through Saerla's mind. Moira was a clever and careful woman. One who almost always put MacBeith first.

She had let her emotions get the better of her when it came to Farlan. In this situation, would she do so again?

Saerla closed her eyes and whispered a swift prayer. *Do no' do anything foolish, sister. Because MacBeith is far more important than me.*

When she reopened her eyes, Rory MacLeod still watched her, his gaze hard and a whit curious. Softly, in almost a croon, he said, "Ye will see your sister if—and when—I say. Do no' try to escape. The door will be barred, and 'twill be the worse for ye, if ye try."

He moved around the chamber, collecting any stray weapons, she realized, when he stowed them about his person. Would he overlook any? Unlikely, since this was his space and he knew it well.

He shot her one last warning look before he went out, taking the weapons with him. A measure of relief flooded through Saerla, along with a terrible weight of dread.

"Curse ye, Rory MacLeod," she whispered. "Curse ye to your bones."

Chapter Ten

"I WANT TO see my sister! At once!"

Rory looked up from his place on the settle when the door of his study crashed open. He'd been forced to take refuge here, since his own bedchamber had turned into a prison, and tried to find some comfort, knowing he must spend the night. There was no way to make his back stop paining him on the hard settle. He wanted his bed and had told himself for the past hour that mattered little. For he wanted to defeat MacBeith far more.

And now he found himself beset by yet another of MacBeith's daughters. By God, they were no end of trouble and caused more grief than they were worth.

Leith's woman, Rhian, stood framed in the doorway facing him. Stiff in every limb, white of face and fiery of eye, she appeared enraged enough to strike him down. No one on earth displayed anger like a redhead. At the moment her very hair seemed to bristle around her.

Rory got to his feet. He would not like to admit it, but the woman possessed a power of her own. Like a mother standing in defense of her offspring. For just an instant, he feared for his life.

"Saerla. My sister, Saerla. You ha' her here somewhere."

"I do." Undeniable. The word would be all over MacLeod by now. He felt surprised it had taken Rhian this long to descend upon him.

"I will see her. At once!"

Rory wondered how Iain MacBeith had gone about raising these daughters of his. With insufficient discipline, quite evidently. They thought they could do what they chose, state what they desired, and in general behave like men.

They did not look like men, though. He remembered the small female perched on his bed, grubby and clad in leather armor, who for all that possessed a delicate beauty and a quite obvious strength.

And this woman—no one could deny she was a lush beauty. No wonder Leith had succumbed.

As if thinking his cousin's name had summoned him, Leith materialized behind Rhian and seized her by the shoulders.

"Now, Rhian, let us discuss this calmly."

"Calm? If he harms a hair on her head, I swear I will kill him."

In that moment, Rory believed her.

So must Leith, for he wrapped his good arm around Rhian from behind and said, "Yelling at him will do no good."

Leith had the right of that. Rory detested being bawled at, especially by a woman.

"Come in and shut the door," he told Rhian, "unless ye wish to raise the whole keep."

Drawing away from Leith, she stalked in like a wildcat on the prowl. Rory speculated as to whether she had a weapon about her person. How swiftly she might leap for his throat.

"Your sister has been taken captive, aye," he told her sternly. "Seized on the field during battle. She is here in the keep, perfectly safe."

"Where?" Rhian had eyes the color of sapphires. At the moment, they looked equally as hard. "Where in this keep?"

Rory hesitated. Did he really want her making a scene pounding on the door of his chamber? Perhaps murdering the guard he had stationed there?

Leith crossed his arms over his chest. Even that limited movement revealed that his right arm, the one that had taken the injury, still did not serve him altogether well.

Rory felt a flash of disquiet. Saerla MacBeith was right. Things had not been going easily for him during this campaign.

He made a sweeping gesture toward the settle. "Please, Mistress Rhian, sit down."

"Not until ye answer my question. Where are ye holding my sister? If ye ha' her in some squalid pen—" Disturbingly, tears suddenly flooded Mistress Rhian's blue eyes.

Rory shot a look at Leith. If there was one thing worse than a screaming woman, it was a weeping one.

Women, in his opinion, should know their place. They should prove obedient and allow their men to protect and care for them.

The sisters MacBeith did not fit this expectation.

He said to Rhian, "Wha' do ye think o' me that I would shut a woman, captive or no', in a filthy pen?"

Her eyes narrowed. "Ye do no' want to know wha' I think o' ye."

"She is comfortable. Safe and in good quarters."

Leith glanced around the study. "Since ye be here, ye maun ha' decided to keep her in your own chamber."

Rory could have throttled his cousin. Instead, he gave Rhian a stiff bow. "The best chamber o' the house."

Mistress Rhian did not appear mollified. In the past, Rory had seen his aunt, Leith's mother, in a fury over some prank they had pulled. Naught to rival this.

"Sit," he suggested again through clenched teeth. "We will discuss it reasonably."

One of her eyebrows quirked. "Reasonably?" she repeated scathingly. "But ye are no' a reasonable man. Ye be a monster."

"Ye ha' a right, mistress, to yer own opinion o' me."

"'Tis everyone's opinion. And now Saerla—precious Saerla!"—her voice broke—"lies in your hands."

A telling reaction. He hoped the chief, Moira, shared it.

"Is she hurt? Was she injured in the fighting?"

"I do no' believe she has taken more than a scratch or two."

"Ye maun let me see her. I am a healer."

Aye, and Leith had recommended her for this damn hole in Rory's back. As if he would allow her near him now.

"No' yet."

"What?" The word flew from Rhian like a hurled rock.

"Ye may no' see her just yet. Later, mayhap. If she deals co-operatively wi' me."

Rhian seemed to expand where she stood. Rage illuminated her. "Ye would keep me from tending my sister's hurts as a means of coercion? Who are ye to do so vile a thing?"

"I am master o' this place. The Chief MacLeod."

She sneered. For an instant, he was certain she would spit on the floor. Apparently she had too much dignity.

Instead, she took a step toward him. In a voice that quivered, she said, "Ye be naught. Naught, do ye hear me? No' worthy to lick Saerla's boots. No' worthy to breathe her air. We shall destroy ye. Ne'er doubt it. We will tak' ye down to blood and bone."

"Leith, curb yer woman!"

"He does no' own me! And he does no' command me, Rory MacLeod."

Rory narrowed his eyes at her. "I would be careful if I were ye, Mistress Rhian. Ye find yersel' alone here, among enemies."

Leith stepped swiftly in front of Rhian, his gray-blue eyes, so often lit with laughter, becoming dangerous slits. "She is no' alone, cousin. And if ye threaten her, ye threaten me."

Curse all women and the influence they put upon men!

Rory whipped a look over Leith, up and down. "Ye do no' want to tak' me on."

"Nor you, me." Leith's gaze had turned to steel.

Christ! It was madness. "I ha' no quarrel wi' ye, Leith." Rory switched his gaze to Rhian. "Ye will be allowed to see your sister. When I say."

Pure hate stared at him from her beautiful eyes.

"Ye will regret this, Rory MacLeod."

He already did. But he sensed that Saerla MacBeith was important. Quite possibly the key to his ultimate victory. The one missing piece he'd needed all this while.

Kin of the MacBeith chief. A Seer. Beloved. Saerla MacBeith might allow him the leverage for which he longed. The outcome he owed his ancestors.

"Leave me," he barked at Rhian.

"Rhian," Leith said, "let us go. We will seek out your sister in the morning."

"Aye, the morning," Rory agreed. Anything to get rid of the woman now. He was weary to the bone—sick to death of the carping—and he hurt.

They left, Rhian directing one last glare at him that could have flayed flesh. He closed the door behind them and leaned against it.

He needed rest. If only that could be found by such a man as he.

Chapter Eleven

S AERLA DOZED FITFULLY atop the comfortable bed, not quite able to give way to proper sleep. Every sound, whether it be a footstep in the hallway beyond the closed door or a log shifting in the fire, brought her sharply aware, sending alarm through her again.

She'd performed a search of the chamber after Rory departed. He had many possessions. Garments in the clothespress. Boots tossed against the wall. Books and a jumble of empty flasks. The table held several sheets of foolscap with scribbles on them. The man had terrible handwriting that she could not puzzle through.

He was not particularly neat, but he was careful. She'd begun to despair of finding any weapon—her own having been stripped from her upon capture—until she rifled through a chest at the foot of the bed. There she found more garments, one with something hard concealed in its folds. A pocket contained a sgian dubh.

It now rested in the pocket of her own sark, and her fingers frequently revisited the antler bone handle for reassurance. She'd peeled off most of her leathers, dragging the helm from her head and unbraiding the bloodied hair, mostly for the sake of comfort.

Comfort, however, did not ensue. It resided at MacBeith, the stronghold she knew so well. It dwelt on the rise above the keep, with the standing stones where she so often sought refuge.

If she closed her eyes, she could almost imagine she was there.

She dozed and dozed again.

She thought of those at home worrying about her. Moira would be frantic for her safety and wild to get her back.

Would she be so foolish as to launch an attack against Rory MacLeod's stronghold? Moira, a born defender, rarely took such a step. Indeed, nor had Da. The only time MacBeith raided MacLeod was in an effort to get back their stolen cattle, and mayhap a few extra head.

She was no cow. But, aye, Moira would be mad to try to take her back.

And what of Alasdair? The big man had been sore hurt in the fight that saw Leith traded away. A strong bond existed between her and Alasdair. What if her capture caused him to rise from his bed before time? What if that, in turn, cost him his life? Alasdair was only slightly less than a brother to her, but far more than a friend. Being the cause of further harm to him would pain her beyond bearing.

Would he blame himself for her capture? Alasdair never said much, but he did tend to hold himself responsible when a battle went awry. Regret might be enough to make him take a risk he should not—not only arise from his bed and march out, but challenge Rory to single combat.

Alasdair, aye, was a mountain of a man. He rarely showed distress. That did not mean he failed to experience it, and the wound he'd taken to the gut had very nearly killed him.

She thought again of the man who'd stood before her in this very chamber, half-naked. An impressive specimen of a man, also, was Rory MacLeod. He did not have Alasdair's size. Few men did, though Rhian's Leith came close. And he too bore a terrible wound. But Rory's body looked like a weapon, honed and shaped for one purpose. Saerla had seen the man fight on the field. Lethal.

Ah, but she was creating fantasies in her head, scenes and

situations that might never come about. Even the terrible Vision might never come true. Destiny presented possible paths, as she well knew. It was up to her to choose the way.

Still, she shivered where she lay, shivered with dread, and let her fingers brush the handle of the sgian dubh once more. She dozed and then roused to a furious pounding on the door, accompanied by raised voices.

She was on her feet without knowing how she'd gotten there. Because she knew one of those voices full well.

Rhian.

"Ye will open this door at once and let me in!"

Rhian rarely sounded imperious. A calm and biddable woman for the most part, she went about her tasks and duties providing comfort to others. Indeed, what she gave was felt most in its absence.

She sounded imperious now. A queen insulted. An outraged mother denied access to her offspring.

The unseen guard who'd been stationed outside the door all night replied, a muffled protest.

"Ye will move aside and let me in. That is my sister in yon chamber!"

"Mistress, please. I do no' wish to harm ye. I was told to let no one in."

Saerla pressed herself against the inside of the door. "Rhian?"

"Saerla! Be ye hurt or harmed, lass? D'ye need me?"

Nay, she was not hurt—not much, anyway. Aye, she needed her sister. Sudden tears filled her eyes.

"I am no' bad hurt."

"Mistress, I maun ask ye to leave—"

"Do no' touch her." Another voice rumbled dangerously. Leith. "Or ye will deal wi' me."

"I do no' want to harm her, Leith. But the chief gave me orders. 'Tis his own chamber. No one goes in. Or out."

"Stand aside," Leith said. "Let me lift the bar. I will deal wi' the chief."

"Do ye speak o' me?" Yet another voice. This one raised the anger in Saerla's breast, a staggering wave.

"Open this door! Let me see my sister."

"I told ye we would discuss this come morning."

"It is morning."

"Barely. Leith, I told ye to curb yer woman."

An unholy sound ensued. Saerla, with her cheek against the door, defined it as a cry of rage from Rhian. "Am I a hound to be curbed?"

"Leith, I swear to Almighty God—remove her or there will be harm done."

A scuffle followed, brief enough. A growl came from Leith. "Let her in to tend her sister's hurts."

"Nay."

Rhian, who must have pushed past the guard, pounded on the outside of the door. "Saerla?"

Sudden fear for Rhian closed Saerla's throat. Rhian carried a child. What if Rory did something to her out of anger, pushed or knocked her down? Aye, Leith was there with her, yet his right arm served him but poorly.

She did not know whether Rhian and Leith had told Rory that Rhian carried a child, the heir to MacLeod.

She once more threw herself at the door. "Step awa', Rhian. Do no' allow that monster to hurt ye." Though she wanted her sister's presence more than anything, ached for the comfort of Rhian's arms around her, she forced herself to say, "I am well enough. Please go."

A muffled conversation sounded in the hallway outside the door. Rhian called, clear, "I will be back, Saerla. He will no' be allowed to keep ye!"

They left then, all of them, so far as Saerla could tell, except possibly the guard. Saerla remained where she was, leaning against the panel, tears running down her cheeks.

RORY VERY NEARLY choked on his aggravation as, sometime later, he retraced his steps back to his chamber. He felt beyond exasperated with the situation. Rhian MacBeith looked to prove troublesome, all too determined to fight on behalf of her sister. He did not understand how a strapping man like Leith could fail to keep her in line.

Of course, there was something to be admired in anyone who stepped forward to battle for her kin. Even if she fought only with a pair of furious blue eyes.

At his back walked a servant—an older woman—with a tray containing the prisoner's breakfast. He would not be accused of mistreatment. Mistress Saerla would be provided the best his stronghold could offer.

His gaze met that of Seumas, who had been on guard all night. Seumas, an earnest young man, had expressive eyes, which he now rolled.

"All quiet?" Rory asked him.

"Aye, Chief Rory."

Rory jerked his head. "Get ye off. Find someone to tak' yer post."

"Aye, chief. That woman—the one who was here before— she would ha' gutted me if she had a weapon."

Aye, so she would. Anger, as Rory knew, made a sharp enough weapon on its own.

He wondered what his reception by her wee sister would be when the door opened.

Ah, and was he afraid of a mere woman?

Chapter Twelve

S HE STOOD IN the very center of the chamber between Rory and the bed, and the sight of her stole his breath. He'd been picturing her all the night long as he'd last seen her, clad in a warrior's leathers. But she'd stripped most of those away.

To be sure, she had.

Her hair—

Her hair!

He'd caught glimpses of her before on the field, when he'd not paused to think she could be a woman rather than a lad. He'd had her once before in his very hands. And they'd brought her all the way across the loch from MacBeith yesterday. Unconscious, she'd been then.

He'd never seen her like this, her form looking small and vulnerable, her hair a cloud on her shoulders.

Such hair!

Aye, her sister, Rhian, had a crop of it, all dark red and wild with curl. From what he'd seen of her, she kept it mostly confined and plaited.

This…

It made a halo around Saerla MacBeith's face, red-gold, shining like something precious, lit by the sun coming through the slit window behind her. He'd never seen such hair, that a man could get lost in if he took her to his bed of a night.

And her face—strong with determination and resolve not to let him cow her. Yet delicate at the same time, with a point to the chin, wide eyes, and lips the color of rosebuds. He wondered what color her eyes were. He had not yet been near enough to see.

All the things he'd meant to say flew out of his head. He said instead, "So ye think me a monster, do ye?"

Her gaze met his. The pointed chin flew upward. "Aye."

The serving woman walked past Rory and set the tray on the table. She went out without a word, shutting the oak panel behind her.

"Wha' sort o' monster am I? A kelpie? A sea serpent?"

"Nay. I ha' always imagined kelpies as being pleasant for the most part."

"I am no' pleasant."

"Nay. Ye be a boogeyman."

"Why that?"

"They love to frighten people. Those weaker than themselves."

Something within Rory sank with dismay. It could not possibly be his heart. Did she think he would hurt her and take pleasure in it?

"Would a monster bring ye breakfast?" He nodded at the table.

"I do no' want your food. I wish to see my sister."

"All in good time."

"Another healer, then."

He stiffened. "Are ye indeed hurt?"

She turned and showed him the back of her head, matted with blood.

"Ye told me last night—ye told yer sister this morning—ye were no' hurt."

"I did no' ken how bad it was till I stripped off the helm. And then I did no' wish to worry Rhian more than she already was. She—" Saerla broke off suddenly.

Rory lifted an eyebrow.

"She was already upset enough."

Rory drew a breath. He remembered the small whirlwind of a warrior flying at him on the field, trying to cut him down. He remembered her being clubbed by one of his men. Unconscious after.

Yet—she was on her feet. Talking to him. Making sense.

"I will fetch you a healer. Is there aught else ye need?" He let his gaze trail down over her. She wore a lad's leggings that defined her slim legs in a way that no respectable woman would condone, and a soft woolen sark not unlike his own, which hung loose. "Clothing, mayhap?" A woman's clothing, he meant. What a decent woman would wear, though—he sensed she was decent to her soul.

"Nay."

"Please." He gave her a bow as if she were a grand lady. "Eat your breakfast."

He went out and barred the door from the outside, then leaned against it for a moment. What had that been? He did not understand his own reaction to this woman. She was a bonny wee thing, aye. But just a woman.

Still, he should have made certain last night that the blow to the head had done no real damage.

He wondered which of the healers he should fetch. Bann, who had treated him, was heavy-handed, as Rory could attest. To be sure, most of their men were heavy-handed.

There were the midwives who treated the women in labor. That would not do.

There was Saerla's sister.

He scowled to himself, still leaning against the door. He did not want to give in and let Rhian MacBeith have her way. If he did, there would be no end to the demands she thought she could make.

Nor did he want to think of Bann's hands in Saerla's hair.

With a grunt, he went off to his cousin's quarters.

Rhian was on her feet and pacing when Rory reached Leith's door. She did not appear quite as angry as she had earlier, but when her gaze lit on Rory, the hate came pure and strong.

Leith shot her a glance before he turned to Rory. Indeed, Rory hoped he'd had words with his woman when they returned home. The scene outside his bedchamber had been unacceptable.

"Wha' d'ye want?" asked Leith, not looking particularly happy to see him.

"I would like Mistress Rhian to come wi' me."

Leith's eyes narrowed. "Why?"

Rory turned to Rhian. "Bring your healer's supplies, if ye will. I wish ye to tend the prisoner."

"Saerla?" Rhian whispered. "Wha' ha' ye done to her?"

Aye, they both thought him a monster.

"Naught. She took a blow to the head in yesterday morning's battle."

"And ye let her suffer so long?" Rhian cursed, turned away, and began collecting things from the chamber.

Rory's gaze met Leith's for an instant. Leith looked...not sympathetic, but Rory saw a guarded understanding.

"I will come." Rhian stood before Rory, eyes ablaze. "Tak' me to her."

The reunion, as Rory acknowledged later, would have moved a stone. As soon as his chamber door opened, the two sisters flew at each other, meeting a few steps inside his door and embracing most fervently.

Rhian's hands fluttered over her sister, patting and checking for wounds. When they found the crusted blood at the back of her wild head, she drew away and shot a glare at Rory that near pierced him.

"Beast!" she tossed at him before turning back to gaze into her sister's face. "'Tis well now, Saerla. I am here. I am here."

Neither woman wept. Watching them from the doorway, Rory figured them too strong for it. Too strong and too angry.

"Be ye hurt any place else, besides your head?"

"Nay. A few cuts, slashes to my fingers. Naught to signify."

"I ha' some supplies here." Rhian turned again and spoke to Rory as she might a servant. "Bring hot water. Now."

"I will go," said Leith, who lurked in the hallway behind Rory.

"Ye may leave us also," Rhian barked at Rory.

"I do no' think so."

"I wish to be alone wi' my sister."

Rory wondered if it was worth an argument. He did not back down from much in life, especially females.

Sometimes, however, it was wiser to retire from the field. He turned from the door of his bedchamber and went.

Chapter Thirteen

FEW THINGS HAD ever felt so good to Saerla as the refuge of Rhian's arms. Comfort flowed from them and threatened to undo her hard-held resolve to remain strong. She would not weep. *She would not.*

She took deep breaths over Rhian's shoulder as they clutched one another tight. "Och, I am that glad to see ye!"

"Has he hurt ye, the monster?" Rhian backed off just enough to gaze into Saerla's eyes, her own blazing with protective rage.

Saerla had never seen her sister look like this. It both comforted her and brought an increased awareness of her predicament.

"Nay. He has no' hurt me. But—" Saerla licked dry lips. "I fear he may." Could she confide in Rhian now about what she'd Seen in the Vision that beset her? Dared she? Nay, for describing it might make it real.

"Rhian, I maun get awa' from here." *Away from him.* "Back to MacBeith. Is there aught ye can do to help me?"

"I ha' been thinking about that. Moira will no' stand for leaving ye captive here. Nor will Alasdair—"

"Alasdair is still hampered by his wound, though he will never admit it." Worry poured through Saerla in the wake of all the other emotions. "Ye do no' think Moira will launch an attack in an attempt to rescue me, do ye? Rhian, I think that is what he wants. To use me as bait."

Rhian bit her lip. "Who can say? But I do no' see Moira sitting back and leaving ye in Rory MacLeod's hands."

"Ye maun help me get awa' out o' here before she does aught so foolish."

"But how? The place is swarming wi' warriors. There is no chance—"

Saerla glared into her sister's eyes. "We maun kill him. We maun kill Rory MacLeod. D'ye no' see?" Saerla hurried on in a hushed voice for Rhian's ears alone. "There is always more than one path forward fro' any destiny."

"So ye ha' told us, but—"

"I feared being brought here. Rhian, I knew I would be brought here one day."

Rhian caught her breath. "This? This is what ye Saw?"

Saerla nodded solemnly. She need not tell her sister the rest of it. Not if she still might keep it from coming true. "Wha' if I've been brought here in order to kill him? To end all the madness and bring us peace."

Rhian blinked rapidly. "I do no' see how."

"I ha' a sgian dubh. I will plunge it into his heart."

An indecipherable expression flooded Rhian's eyes. "Such a thing, here in the center o' MacLeod, in his very lair, could cost your life."

"Aye, I ken." Saerla faced that squarely as she had during the night just past. "But perhaps I am meant for that."

"Nay. Dear one!" Rhian caressed her cheek. "Ye are a creature o' magic, meant for fine and beautiful things. For prayers and Visions, and holding the ancient light of the first MacBeiths."

"Mayhap. Mayhap I did that for a time. But there maun be a reason also I learned to tak' up a sword, aye? Learned to fight and kill." Saerla drew a breath and said starkly, "I am willing to spend my own life, if I can end his."

"By God, Saerla!" Rhian whispered in dismay. "Do no' say such things. Wha' if someone were to hear? Sit down. Sit down for now. Let me care for ye properly. I do no' ken when he will let me see you again."

"Can ye find me another weapon? Smuggle it in, perhaps? Somewhat better than this wee sgian dubh, which I admit is better than naught. Bring me one o' Leith's swords, if the monster lets ye see me again."

"Ye expect Leith to hand over a weapon that ye might use to slay his cousin and dear friend?"

As if Rhian's using his name summoned him, Leith came in the door, which still stood ajar, followed by a serving woman carrying a basin of steaming water. He closed the door behind the woman when she left and looked at Saerla doubtfully.

"Are ye bad hurt, mistress?"

Rhian answered him. "Bad enough. This wound has bled much. Leith, wha' can we do for her? Can we get her awa' out o' here?"

Leith's expression turned grim. "I do no' see how. Rory kens full well he has a prize."

Saerla met Rhian's gaze. She willed her sister not to speak of her desire for murdering Rory.

Rhian said, "Speak to him, Leith. Tell him 'twould be an act o' good faith to return Saerla home. 'Twould go far to make Moira agree to negotiate wi' him. Negotiate a peace."

Leith laughed harshly. "He does no' want peace, my love. He wants conquest."

Rhian clenched her teeth. "Sit still, Saerla." She applied the dampened cloth to the back of Saerla's head. "This might sting."

So it did, but Saerla sat quietly beneath Rhian's ministering hands. She'd always believed there was healing in Rhian's touch, and more than a little magic.

Two of MacBeith's daughters here at MacLeod. What did it mean? Surely there must be a power in it, and the two of them might act together to bring Rory MacLeod down from within.

Then—then she could go home. To her circle of standing stones. To the serenity of being there among them. To the beauty of watching clouds sail down the glen from the direction of the sea. To blue sky and green turf and gray stone. Och, she ached for all of it.

But if she had to sacrifice her life…

She closed her eyes for an instant and called upon the spirits. *I pray thee, give me the strength to do as I must.*

"Am I hurting ye, my dear one?" Rhian asked softly. "I am almost done."

"'Tis naught I canna bear."

A woman could bear much, if she loved.

RORY PACED THE forecourt with doubt and determination warring in his mind. He could not help believing it had been a poor idea, a very poor idea, to let the two sisters unite. But what else could he have done? Saerla needed her wound tended. And he could not let his heavy-handed healers, used to treating rough warriors, near her.

He intended to send her back to MacBeith, to be sure he did. But he would be certain to get a high price for her.

He must set things in motion. Moira MacBeith was fond of writing letters. She'd even called upon Farlan to do so when she held him prisoner. So aye, Rory would write to her now. Lay out for her on the parchment just what she would have to do in order to save her sister's life.

He must do that, aye. Go and write the letter. Get shed of Saerla before the two of them, MacBeith's daughters, had a chance to scheme together.

To be sure, Moira would want her sister back. Such an exquisite wee thing with so much… Well, and he could not come up with a word for what he saw when he gazed at Saerla. Wisdom, perhaps. An uncanny sort of knowledge.

The word *magic* presented itself to his mind, but he dismissed it with scorn. A woman might carry many things. Hatred, for he saw that aplenty in Saerla's eyes. Spite. Anger. Disdain. Compassion. Love. Magic was a far cry from any of those.

On the other hand…

She was supposed to be a Seer, was she not? So Leith had said. Rory wondered if she'd foreseen her own fate. Had she known she'd be captured during that battle? If so, why had she taken the field?

Had she known she would be brought here? That she would end in his hands?

In his hands.

He snorted. It was nonsense, all of it. He'd do much better to go and write his letter. Keep away from the woman. Turn his thoughts from her.

And keep his eye on the prize.

Chapter Fourteen

RORY LABORED LONG over his letter, there alone in his study, wanting to get the words of demand just right. He would offer Moira—and that traitor who stood at her side—no options. It would be done this very summer, the matter of who ruled Glen Bronach.

It had been a favorable fate, after all, that brought Saerla MacBeith to him, and a stab wound from her wee dirk a small price to pay. No doubt, though, she'd been aiming for his throat.

And if she'd succeeded there on the field? If she had killed him?

Chances were slim, but it did make a man think. Life could prove fragile. That meant he needed an heir other than his cousin, Leith.

Fond as he was of Leith—and aye, he was tremendously fond of him—he could not say his cousin would make a strong or suitable chief to follow him. Canny as Leith was, and fit as he used to be on the battlefield before his injury, he did not have the steel in his backbone needed to make a strong chief. Just look at how he let that woman of his lead him by the nose.

How could any man who could not render a woman obedient lead a clan?

He, Rory, needed to get himself a son.

Still staring at the letter on the table in front of him, he sneered. A terrible thing for a man of only a score and six years—seven soon, for it was very nearly his birthday—to have to face his own mortality.

Still more terrible to consider entering into marriage with a woman for the sole purpose of assuring the succession.

He had no time for it. Worse, he had no interest. A woman must be wooed. Paid attention to. Even if he'd had the time, he had not the patience.

Still.

There were plenty of single women here at MacLeod. The fighting assured it. Some, widowed already, had bairns that proved they were able to bear.

Like livestock.

Could he go into a marriage with the sole objective of breeding? Nay.

That arrow in his back could well have stolen his life. Naught but strength and determination had brought him out of that. He sat with his hands resting on the top of the desk, running possible mates through his mind.

There was Dairmid's widow. What was her name? She had a lush body that promised sons. He had no time to waste on daughters.

Or Marchan's sister. Peggy. Rory had caught her looking after him with interest more than once. Several women, come to think of it, looked at him that way. No doubt the place of wife to the chief held a certain attraction.

It would have to be a woman he could tolerate. One he would not balk at taking to his bed.

A sudden image arose, blazing through his mind. A cloud of red-gold hair, all wild. A slim, whipcord body. Already there in his bed.

He snorted again, a sound of disdain. He could scarcely have a worse idea. But she would not be gone from his mind, and he felt his body tighten.

It had been far too long since he'd had a woman, that was all.

He could barely remember the last time. It did not do for the chief to walk out looking for a random female willing to relieve his need with no strings attached.

Anyway, he told himself harshly, Saerla MacBeith did not look suited to bearing sons. Too small by half. Those slender hips. The diminutive breasts that barely made a bump beneath the leather jerkin.

As if she'd ever have him. Welcome him onto her thighs. She hated him. He would be the last man on earth she—

A knock sounded on his door. He turned to it with relief. "Come awa' in."

His war chief, Murgor, rattled into the chamber. He looked like he'd come straight from the practice field and still wore his weapons.

"Aye? Wha' is it?" Rory did not get up, wanting to conceal the physical condition that thoughts of Saerla MacBeith had prompted.

"Chief, several o' the guards and others o' the men ha' come to me. They insist they've seen signs o' muster over at MacBeith."

That did make Rory swivel in his seat. "Did ye tak' a look? Is it so?"

"Could be. I thought ye might want to come and look for yoursel'." Murgor measured Rory with wise eyes. He had been a contemporary and good friend of Rory's father, Camraith, and had served him well. The two men had fought together when young. Just like Rory and Farlan. But he pushed the thought of Farlan away hastily.

"D'ye think she will attack, this female chief MacBeith? 'Tis her sister ye hold, is it no'?"

"Aye." He may not have time to send his letter. "She'll want the sister back."

"Ye mean to bargain over her?"

"Aye. Unless she attacks us first."

"Come and see."

Disciplining his body ruthlessly, Rory arose and followed his man.

Considerable excitement reigned on the walls where the best outlook over the glen might be found. A beautiful, clear day it was. Narrowing his eyes against the glare of sunlight, Rory could see movement near the stronghold situated across the loch and halfway up the opposite rise. Mustering for war? Then why be so obvious about it? Putting on a show? Aye, maybe.

Murgor took the place beside Rory and said softly, "She has ne'er attacked before, this woman chief."

"Nay." She defended, and defended well. Rory twitched, remembering the blinding pain of the arrow piercing his back.

"Mayhap she has no' the mind for battle. Bein' a woman and all. I mean to say, any woman will defend her home. Being bold enough to march out is a far different thing."

"True." Moira's father, Iain, used to launch the occasional raid. Both he and Camraith had. Rory sensed it had been like a game to both men, an honorable contest without much animosity behind it. But men had died in those raids. Iain's son, Arran, had. And spilled blood raised it all above the level of a game.

"She'll want her sister." Besides, she had Farlan at her side. Farlan knew how to launch an attack, if he put his mind to it. He knew how Rory thought and how he fought.

If Moira MacBeith attacked MacLeod, that turncoat could make a difference.

He narrowed his eyes still further. "I think she is just rattling her shields—for now. Who d'ye trust to tak' a message?"

"Any number o' men."

"Select a pair. I will ha' a letter ready anon."

Murgor nodded. Rory hurried down from the battlements, trying to convince himself that what he'd just seen was not a bad sign.

In his study, he read the letter once more, contemplated its fierce tone, and wondered what Moira would make of it. When she read it, she would have two choices—meet his demands or march out and attack him.

And he would have a choice of his own then. Sit here and guard his walls against the attacking MacBeiths, or march out and meet her.

He closed his eyes for a moment, striving for a clear mind. He could afford no mistakes. He wanted this strife over and done.

So he could settle down and breed sons upon a woman he did not love.

Chapter Fifteen

R HIAN HAD GIVEN Saerla a draught before she left. For the pain of Saerla's aching head, so she said. It made Saerla sleep, and took her deep into dreams.

She was a girl again, a lass of no more than eight or so, which must mean Arran was still alive. And Ma. And Da. She was running wild with the three of her siblings, always the smallest of the group but fleet of foot and able to keep up without too much difficulty.

They played at some game of hide-and-go-seek out on the green sward of the rise above the glen. When it was Saerla's turn to seek, she found them all easily, just as if she could see them where they hid.

Sometimes she could See things that were not there, though she did not know that then—that the beings and animals were not there, that was. This glen she loved was inhabited by any number of creatures and spirits with whom she might communicate.

No matter, for she found both her sisters, her brother, and their friends also. When it came time for her to hide…

She looked for a very good place, one where no one would be able to see her. The circle of stones up on the rise drew her. The stones always had, because Ma said they were a place of enchantment, of old, old magic.

All Saerla knew was that the light dwelt there. It took many forms, did the light. Sometimes it looked like mist and floated on the air, moving of its own volition. Sometimes it slanted down the glen like a blessing, starting a warm hum of happiness inside Saerla's chest. Sometimes she saw it in the eyes of those she loved.

It would be a fine thing, she decided, to hide among the stones where no one could see her. For even though Ma said to be careful in the stone circle and that she should not go there alone, she sensed naught there that might hurt her.

She scampered barefoot in through the entrance stones that still had a lintel balanced atop them. At once the skin all over her body prickled. Her breath quickened and the mist rushed toward her as if in greeting. It engulfed her, took her strength from her. She fell down.

There were people in the mist, a crowd of them who wanted to tell her things. But they did not speak quite the same language as she, and had to find a way to convey what they wished in another manner.

They formed pictures that appeared directly in Saerla's mind.

She Saw three boys out running on the green turf just like her friends below. The scene looked like the glen—her glen—and yet it did not. A place she had and had not seen before.

The sky overhead was the same. And the loch toward which the three lads raced. Yet the perspective seemed all wrong. And the hills beyond them—

It snapped into place in Saerla's mind. They were the hills on the far side of the glen. Only closer.

The three boys looked all very different. One, taller and broader than the other two, had a head of light hair that shone in the sun and wore a happy, peaceable expression. He and the second lad, whose hair flew behind him in rich brown waves when they ran together, pushed and shoved one another with tangible liking. Good friends, they were.

The third lad—aye, he was as different as ever a young lass of light could determine. Not the tallest nor the broadest, he nevertheless led the other two, and when he called out, they ceased with their tomfoolery to listen.

Let us swim across the loch. I dare the both o' ye.

His companions stared at him. He made a braw sight somehow, standing in the bright sun with his wild crop of black hair gleaming like the wing of a raven.

But, said the lad with the fair hair, *there be monsters in the loch.*

Who told ye such nonsense?

My ma says, and my da as well.

The lad with the black hair tossed his head. *They only tell ye that to keep ye from drowning.*

I do no' want to drown, said the lad with the brown hair. *And 'tis a long way across.*

Besides, protested the fair-haired lad, *'tis dangerous o'er there. We could be kilt.*

The lad with the black hair sneered. *Ye maun learn no' to be afraid. I will be chief one day. Wha' I say goes.*

The other two lads exchanged glances.

Someday, all o' this will be ours.

It had been her first Vision. The first she ever received.

Subsequent Visions, dire ones, far more powerful ones, had thrust it from her mind. Over the years she'd remembered more the unexpectedness of the Seeing than what it had contained. The three lads whom she did not know meant nothing to her.

She'd come to herself, on that warm summer's day, to the sound of her name being called.

Saerla?

Saerla!

Her sisters and her brother called her name, upset because they could not find her, and it had ceased to be a game. They could not find her because she hadn't been there in the stone circle. She'd been on the far side of the glen. But how could she have forgotten?

She awoke now from the haze provided by Rhian's draught

to find herself lying flat on her back upon the bed in her prison. Just as she'd been lying in the stone circle that day, when her loved ones called for her.

On that day, the mist of light had surrounded her, borne her up, carried and perhaps consoled her. A curious thing to be there in one place and yet somewhere else in spirit. Able to See with the mind's eye. Or perhaps the eye of the spirit.

She knew the three lads now, to be sure she did. They looked quite different from what they had but still, in a curious way, the same. Farlan with his brown mane and the somehow curious look in his eyes. Leith with a face made even then for laughter.

Rory MacLeod. Imperious. Handsome. With his world held securely in his two hands.

Why would she revisit that first experience with the Sight? And why See those lads again?

They'd been running and playing on the green turf just like she had with her brother and sisters. But it had turned dark at Rory's direction. Had they ventured into the water? They might have drowned.

They had not.

She closed her eyes once more and drew a breath. They'd been close back then, the three lads. She'd been able to feel the bonds between them.

For Rory and Farlan, those bonds had now broken. A deep wound, that had to be. But Rory MacLeod was not an easy person—that was clear enough from her limited encounters with him. Perhaps the break had always been destined.

Perhaps it followed that she, Saerla, was here for a reason. To, as she'd told Rhian, kill Rory. But killing that lad she'd just Seen seemed a far cry from slaying the man.

The boy had been bossy and arrogant, aye, yet there had been something about him, a strength far beyond his years. An indomitable spirit. A—a dark sort of light.

She would not want to have harmed that boy, to still the blood that beat so wildly through him. The boy, surely, existed yet within the man.

Or perhaps not. Mayhap the boy had already died.

She sat up on the bed, trying to gather her scattered energies before climbing to her feet. Still unsteady, she walked to the chamber's single window.

High and narrow, it would not afford even her slight body an escape. Indeed, it offered only a sliver of a view. This must indeed be a fine accommodation, for it faced out over the glen. She could see bright green turf, the blue glint of the loch, the hills beyond.

Home.

For an instant, she ached so that she did not think she could bear it. She caught herself up sharply. Just as Rory was no longer a lad, she was no longer a wee lass caught in her first Vision.

She was a Seer, aye. She was a woman also.

The path she must now choose might well be strewn with blood.

Chapter Sixteen

RORY WATCHED THE messenger's party out of sight, squinting against the radiance of the afternoon. Having found men suitable to carry his letter to Moira MacBeith, Murgor had presented an argument for making the party more than two or three men.

"A wee show o' strength," he suggested, "as she may be mustering. No' enough to present a threat, but enough to show we are no' afraid."

Rory did not fear Moira. He harbored many other emotions toward her, including disdain and impatience. He wanted this over and done.

She would, aye, want her sister back. She would reply with a full capitulation.

Or she might slay the members of his party, if she wanted to provoke him. And if—if she trusted him not to slit Saerla's throat in return.

Nay, and nay. He would get the response he desired.

And how to fill the time till he received his answer? He should be organizing the men in case Moira's response was an attack. He should don his armor and gather his weapons.

His back protested the very prospect.

He could go and see Saerla MacBeith first.

The thought appeared whole in his mind. He tried to view it

dispassionately, to come up with reasons he should deny the urge. It did not seem an entirely emotionless prospect, nor one devoid of reason. He had reasons to see her, and reasons to stay away.

She was a valuable prisoner, the best weapon he had to force Moira MacBeith's hand, and he would do well to make sure of her. When last he'd seen her, she'd been suffering from that wound to the head. Should she once more fall unconscious and die…

It would be a bad, bad outcome. One that started dread in the pit of his stomach. His best weapon, lost.

Yet he'd left her in the care of her sister, who, Leith insisted, possessed considerable skill as a healer. Surely the sister had treated Saerla and made her better.

He could go make sure.

Indeed, he had a right to venture anywhere in this fortress, and the chamber where she dwelt was, after all, his own. He could claim to need something that remained there. If he needed an excuse. Which he did not.

His feet carried him even as the thoughts circled in his mind. The guard, a young man named Donal who looked quite bored, lounged outside the door of the chamber. When he saw Rory, he sprang to attention and brightened.

"Chief. A grand day outside, is it no'?"

And he was stuck here in a windowless corridor guarding the door of a single prisoner.

"I hear we will soon be at war," the young man continued, not without excitement.

Rory eyed him. "How did ye hear that?"

"Seumas came by. Says MacBeith is mustering for attack."

"Maybe so, maybe no'. All quiet here?" Rory jerked his head at the door.

"Och, aye. Quiet as the grave."

That caused Rory a quiver of unease. He jerked his head again. "Off wi' ye. Send someone else to spell ye."

"Aye, chief." The young man ran off without a backward look. Rory stood for a moment eyeing the boards of his own door, wondering how best to go on.

It would be a courtesy to knock. To treat the woman therein with some respect. She was a woman, after all, and a high-status captive.

Accordingly, he raised his knuckles and rapped. "Mistress MacBeith?"

No sound from within.

"I be coming in."

He lifted the bar, his ears still reaching for any sound. What if he found her lying on the floor? Head wounds, as he knew, could prove treacherous. And she'd been struck hard.

If she died, her sister would want his blood. Both of her sisters would.

The chamber came into view, filled with afternoon sunlight. Saerla MacBeith stood at the window, her arms wrapped around her slender body, and her hair a nimbus of red-gold.

By God, what a mane the woman had!

She turned when the door swung open and looked at him. Her eyes…

He got his first good look at them, her face flooded as it was with light. Blue they were, but not a deep blue like those of Leith's woman. These were the color of the mist that gathered over the loch on a frosty morning. Framed by thick brown lashes, they seemed to look not at but into him. Past skin. Past bone. Past the man he presented to the world.

A breath whispered into his chest. At least he found her alive.

"Mistress."

She finished turning toward him, one of her hands moving to wriggle inside her shirt. "Wha' d'ye want?"

Her voice carried an edge, aye, and also a thread of something more. Longing, perhaps. Had she been standing at the window wishing for home? He told himself he did not care. She was a commodity only. He had no time for soft feelings.

He stepped in and shut the door behind him. "I came to see whether ye ha' benefited from your sister's visit."

"Aye." She tipped up her chin. It was small and pointed. She looked like one of the magical beings from the old stories he'd heard when a boy—a fairy, maybe. Fairies, as he remembered, were often treacherous. "Will ye allow me to see her again?"

Rory did not know how he might prevent it. Rhian would make a terrible fuss. So would she, no doubt. Saerla.

"Saerla." He said it aloud.

She raised her eyebrows, the expression in her eyes turning to ice.

"I will no' keep your sister fro' tending ye. The wound on your head—how dire is it?"

"Dire?" she repeated. "D'ye care, Master MacLeod?"

"Chief. I am Chief MacLeod. And to be sure, ye be a captive o' some worth. 'Tis the other thing I came to tell ye. I ha' sent a letter to the Chief MacBeith, stating my demands."

"Your demands."

"Aye. Wha' I require in return for your release. I ha' no doubt she will respond soon enough, and ye will be turned free out o' here."

"Wha' demands are these?"

"That remains between the Chief MacBeith and me."

She drew a breath that expanded her narrow chest. "And if she does no' meet your demands?"

"She will." For just one blessed moment, he let his gaze rove over her. The cloud of hair. The delicate face. "She will want ye back." Anyone would.

"My sister, Master MacLeod, is devoted to her clan and will act for the greater good o' all."

"She will not." The woman must be in a fine panic, having her sister snatched into the hands of the monster they all deemed him. He expected full capitulation by morning. Then he would send Saerla MacBeith away. He might see her again, aye, when he took possession of his new holdings. He might even live at

MacBeith for a time in order to exert his control. Allow them to learn their places.

He would see her then.

"They say ye be a Seer." It was not what he'd intended to remark. It just came out of him without warning.

She gave a hard, grudging nod.

"I do no' believe in such things." He'd not meant to say that either.

She lifted her brows again. "I am no' surprised. It takes faith to believe. And it takes, in turn, belief in somewhat greater than onesel' to ha' faith. Ye clearly heed only yoursel'."

He felt as if he'd been cut to the bone, so sharp and complete was her disdain. It seemed she had pulled out a knife from somewhere and slashed him deep.

"Ye suppose ye know me, do ye?"

"Your every action has taught us what ye are. Bent upon your own goals and no' caring who gets trampled on your way. Even your best friend receives no notice from ye. 'Tis all about what ye want."

"Farlan is a traitor."

"He is a fine man, as I ha' had the opportunity to learn full well. He has made a choice for reason, for mercy, and for love. It is a strong choice."

"Love," Rory scoffed. So she admired Farlan, did she? And despised *him*.

"To be sure," she scoffed in return, "ye would no' credit such a soft emotion. Yet, Master MacLeod, 'tis the strongest force on earth."

Aye, mad she was. A typical woman, prating about emotions. If he gave her half a chance, he wagered she'd speak about magic also.

"No' so strong," he told her, "that it canna be put to the sword and vanquished by death."

"Is that wha' ye think? And wha' makes ye suppose love does no' continue beyond the grave?"

Frustrated and impatient, he met her gaze. In her eyes he saw…

The swirl of mist on the shoulders of the mountains. The glitter of hoar frost on a winter's morning. The slant of light streaming down the glen. *Eternity.*

He backed up a step and growled, "I ha' no time for this nonsense. Prepare yoursel' to leave here. I expect your sister's reply by morning."

"Och, I shall just pack up all my belongings, shall I?" One eyebrow lifted this time.

Rory MacLeod, who never ran from anything, backed out of the chamber. She thought him a fool.

For the first time in his entire life, he conceded it. Perhaps he was.

Chapter Seventeen

"HE SAYS MOIRA will reply to his demands by tomorrow, Rhian. He sounded verra sure o' it. Wha' might those demands be?"

The hour had grown late, and Rhian had come to tend Saerla before retiring to bed. Beyond the slit of a window, the soft gloaming had settled. Clear summer air trickled in, smelling sweetly of the far hills.

Rhian had lit a taper in order to examine Saerla's head wound. Her hands, parting the red-gold hair, were gentle.

"I do no' ken. I think Leith may know, but he will no speak o' it to me."

"Can ye no' persuade him? I ha' a terrible bad feeling about it."

"Ha' ye Seen—"

"Nay. No' that." Saerla frowned. "I had a dream about when we were all small. The first Vision I ever received."

Rhian said nothing. She understood the vagaries of the Sight, how it might be sued but never controlled.

"Moira must be half out o' her mind, wi' me gone."

"Aye."

"Rhian." Saerla turned to face her sister. "I fear him. I fear Rory MacLeod."

Rhian studied her kindly. "Of course ye do. I think we all do."

"Nay, I do no' mean in an ordinary fashion. I fear him. *Here.*" She clutched her hands to her stomach just below her heart. "I did no tell ye—I dared no'. That Vision I received back home concerned him. I Saw mysel' in his power."

"And now here ye be. Och, love!"

"Aye, but 'twas no' just that. He—" Saerla met her sister's gaze and fought through the fear, the dread. "He desired me."

"Was that wha' terrified ye so?"

"Aye." Yet even that was not all of it. What had most terrified Saerla was that she'd wanted Rory in return. Even while she hated him.

"I maun get away' out o' here."

"Listen to me. Moira is clever. And determined. She will find a way to get ye free. Farlan knows Rory well and stands at her side. Ye maun believe."

Just what *she* had flung at Rory.

"Meanwhile"—Rhian lowered her voice, even though they were alone, with no one to hear—"I ha' this."

From the bottom of her basket she retrieved a knife with a honed blade. Only a bit longer than a man's hand, it was nevertheless a better weapon than Saerla's small sgian dubh. This might not just wound, but kill a man.

"Take it."

Saerla did, by reflex. "Is it Leith's?"

"Aye."

"Does he know ye ha' it?" And that Saerla would use it to kill his cousin, his chief, if she could?

Rhian shook her head.

"Then…" Rhian betrayed him by giving Saerla this.

"Sister, I will no' leave ye defenseless. If he touches ye in the way ye fear—well, he will no' expect ye to be armed, will he? And ye be quick. Stronger than he knows. Ye can ha' this at his throat before he can force ye."

Saerla's fingers tightened on the hilt of the knife. "Aye." It would be a good means of getting near enough to inflict a wound, by seducing him. Yet she did not know how to seduce a man.

And it seemed a sort of betrayal to try. As she saw it, desire was all about love. Love, in turn, was all about trust. The kind Rhian and Leith had found for each other, that lent Rhian the courage to leave home. The trust Moira had for Farlan, so steady at her side.

How could desire exist without that?

"Saerla." Rhian caught her sister's shoulders between her hands. "Ye ha' the courage ye need."

Did she? Aye, it was easy to be filled with strength while standing on the rise back home, up among the stones. A little harder when taking the field with a sword in her hands.

Here?

She drew an uncertain breath.

An end to Rory MacLeod could mean an end to warring in the glen she loved. Leith—Leith would make a far different sort of chief. And there were already differing paths ahead from which to choose.

She raised her eyes to Rhian's. The strength there allowed her to draw a still-deeper breath. "Aye, ye be right."

"Pray on it," Rhian urged. "Pray for Moira to ha' the wisdom she needs, and ye the courage."

"Aye," Saerla said again, wondering if she could find the refuge of her prayers while in this place.

"Och, I near forgot." Rhian turned and retrieved a bundle she'd set beside the door when she came in. "Clean clothing. Yours is all smeared wi' blood."

Saerla took the garments into her hands. "Are these yours?"

"Aye. I altered them. See? There is a pocket in the skirt. Or, if ye prefer, I ha' stitched in a loop beneath where ye might secure the dirk. And see, ye can kilt up the skirt if ye need to run." Once more, Rhian's gaze met Saerla's. "Ye maun promise me ye will try to get awa' once ye—once ye do wha' must be done."

Kill him. Kill Rory MacLeod.

"Ye can run verra fast when ye choose. Go to the loch. There are always wee boats—"

Slowly and regretfully, Saerla shook her head. "I do no' think I will get awa' out o' here after. There are too many guards. Once they ken he is dead—"

"But they will no' ken at once."

"Still, they know me for a prisoner. They will no' let me walk or run awa'. I expect, sister, that I will die here."

"Nay," Rhian said fiercely. "Nay, ye will no'. At worst, they will hold ye. And bring ye before the chief, the new chief. That will be Leith."

"Rhian, Rory is his cousin. He will ha' no choice but to retaliate against me."

"He wants peace as much as I do. He wants it for our bairn."

"Aye, so." Perhaps. Saerla thought of the three lads she'd Seen in her dream. So close in friendship and in spirit. As close, in their way, as she was to her two sisters. Could such ties be completely severed even by anger or betrayal?

"Still, I am certain Leith harbors strong feelings for his cousin. And in such a situation, he will act as his clan expects."

"He will act as a new kind o' chief, Saerla. One who has already an agreement wi' Farlan. Saerla, a new age can begin for Glen Bronach."

Begin with her performing a heinous act. For whatever Rory MacLeod's nature or his intentions, he was a man. Slaying him in cold blood and not in battle would violate all she believed in.

And yet…

Mayhap it would not be in cold blood. If what she'd Seen in the Vision came true, it would be very hot indeed.

She shuddered.

"Pray on it," Rhian urged again. "And get what sleep ye can."

"I will."

"I maun go. Be strong." Rhian embraced her fiercely. Saerla clung to her for one moment before letting her go.

She must let it all go, she thought as she watched her sister slip from the chamber. She had always been a woman of faith.

One who harbored magic. She must now place her fate in the hands of the spirits who had always gathered around her. Who had comforted and advised her. She must have faith they would direct her to the right path, the one her feet needed to tread.

She shed her filthy, tattered clothing and donned the garments Rhian had brought, which smelled wonderfully of her. Herbs and comfort. She stashed both her weapons carefully about her person where she knew she could reach them if Rory returned. Then she curled on the bed and imagined herself not at home in her own chamber, but up on the rise, safe in the light.

Chapter Eighteen

B Y FIRST LIGHT, Rory stood on the ramparts straining to gaze across the glen. A familiar view was this, one he saw every day. A position of strength that usually calmed his doubts and assured him he held a measure of power.

He had never been a man who experienced much in the way of self-doubt. Instead, he knew things. He'd known all his life that his clan, Clan MacLeod, should hold all the glen, as his ancestors had intended when they arrived here generations ago. He knew he'd be the man who would make that come true. He'd been impatient with his father, who refused to move upon the notion, despite MacLeod's superior numbers over MacBeith.

To be sure, he'd known other things as well. That he could trust his best friend, Farlan, to the death. That naught so fragile as the fancy of love could come between the three of them—himself, Farlan, and Leith.

Now just look at them.

Love, as he told himself even while he strained to see out over the glen in the first gray light of morning, was just a pretty word for lust. One meant to persuade a woman into a man's bed.

His war chief, Murgor, came up beside him.

"See aught?" Rory demanded, not sparing a greeting. "Are they still mustering?"

The party of messengers he'd sent out had not returned. That might be a good thing. They could be awaiting Moira MacBeith's decision, which she would send back with them this morning.

Or they could be dead.

"We think they are still mustering, aye." Murgor leaned on the battlements beside Rory. "The men caught glimpses o' movement overnight. O' course, it may be anything."

Rory narrowed his eyes and grunted in frustration. The man on watch beside him, named Alec, gave him a sharp glance. Alec had been a particular friend of Farlan's. He'd been markedly cool toward Rory since Rory dismissed Farlan as he had.

Banished him from the clan.

"Why," Rory muttered more to himself than to the two men who flanked him, "would she continue to muster when her reply to me may make it unnecessary?"

Neither man replied, though Alec shifted uneasily. Moira would continue to muster if she meant to reject his offer. If the party he'd sent was dead.

If that were her answer. Hers, or Farlan's? Farlan stood at the woman's side. Did he want to retaliate against Rory? Would he bargain away scores of lives to do so?

Rory did not think he would. Despite the breach between them, he knew Farlan. None better. A reasoned, careful man he was, not the sort to give in to the lure and heat of revenge. At least, he never had been.

For an instant, a stab of longing, mixed liberally with regret, pierced Rory's heart. There had been strong comfort in sitting with Farlan over a flagon of ale and discussing the future. Talking over battle strategies and eventualities. Farlan had balanced him well, the calm against the desire to act out of hand. Would he do the same for Moira?

It did not matter. For those days of companionship were long gone. And he, Rory MacLeod, was a man who did act out of revenge.

"'Tis set to rain," said Murgor morosely. "'Tis hard to see aught that is going on."

To be sure, heavy clouds lowered over the glen, obscuring the tops of the hills and blending with the gray morning. In the distance, toward the sea, Rory could see a curtain of rain that would all too soon sail down the loch and move in upon them.

Would she use the cover, the obscurity of the rain, to attack? Would Farlan?

"Is there no way," Alec asked, "to avoid more war?"

Rory glanced at him in surprise. He'd had no idea the man harbored such feelings. It made him wonder what other warriors felt. Of course, Alec was not other warriors. Likely he did not relish meeting his friend on the field.

Nor did Rory, truth be told. It had not happened yet. But if he found himself facing Farlan in a battle, if it came to kill or be killed, could he do what needed to be done?

Aye, indeed. He was Chief MacLeod. He could not allow himself to falter.

"Any sign o' our party returning?" he asked.

"Nay," Murgor grunted. "No' that I can see."

"If she sends a message, if she replies as she aught," Rory said to Alec, "'twill mean an end to the battles." Oh, there would be pockets of resistance when he and his men moved in to take over MacBeith. Soon quelled.

Despite the heavy cloud, the morning grew stronger around them. It was a leaden sort of light that turned the loch to steel feathered over with white foam.

"There," Alec said suddenly. "Is that our party moving out?"

Rory, his muscles bunched as he gripped the battlement and leaned out dangerously far over the stone, squinted. "Maybe. Only three o' them."

"Mayhap she keeps one o' our men back as hostage?"

Rory huffed impatiently. He did not want to play at games sending messages back and forth. He wanted this done.

He wanted Saerla MacBeith out of his keep, if only for his own peace of mind.

They watched the tiny figures of the party moving slow as

ants from the distance, set out from MacBeith toward the loch. Three of them, aye, when he had sent four. Before they had gone far, the skies opened and a deluge descended.

Rory swore bitterly. "Muster the men," he told Murgor. They would not be happy about it. "We will stand in readiness. I will march out to meet our party."

"D'ye want for me to go wi' ye, chief?"

Rory thought on it. "Nay. I will tak' Leith."

He hurried down from the battlements and ducked inside out of the rain. A vile morning and no mistake. An evil omen, if he believed in such, which he did not.

Everyone he met on his way to Leith's quarters asked him the same thing. *Are we bound for war?* The order for muster had been given. It did not take long to spread.

He passed the door to his own quarters. The guard stationed there asked, "Are we marching out, chief?"

"Mustering for it. Stay where ye be."

What had Saerla heard from within? He had no doubt Rhian had been to see her. What did she think?

He told himself it did not matter. She would be soon enough gone.

He pounded on Leith's door, and the man himself opened it. Hair in a tangle and the front of his sark hanging open, he stood but half dressed. Had he been making love to his woman all morning?

Rory sneered. "Come wi' me."

Leith stared at him. When had the expression in his cousin's eyes changed? Blue-gray eyes they were, and what Rory would once have called *merry*. Leith, by and large, had been a pleasure to have for a companion. Always with a laugh or a quip. Able to make even him, Rory, smile.

Now his eyes had gone cold like the loch out beyond the fortress. The woman had changed him, Rory told himself. Or mayhap, in truth, he had. Leith had not looked at him the same way since he'd banished Farlan. Certainly not since he'd returned from imprisonment at MacBeith.

"Come?" Leith did not budge from the doorway. "Where?"

"We march out to meet the messengers. I want ye wi' me."

"Gi' me a moment or two."

He ducked back inside, leaving the door ajar a crack. Rory could hear the rumble of his voice speaking to the woman. The lighter tone of her reply.

She came pushing out first, fully clad and with her hair hastily bundled at the back of her head, a basket clutched in her hands.

"I will wait wi' my sister."

"Ye will no'." Rory did not want the two of them conspiring together against him.

She drew herself up. Tall for a woman, she nevertheless had to glare up at him. "Stand aside."

"Ye will stay here in Leith's quarters, mistress. We may fall under attack. Yer sister is safe enough under guard."

"Her head wound needs tending. I will no' leave her wanting." She started to push past him. Rory put his hand on her chest to keep her back.

The door flew open. Leith stood there, eyes blazing. Rory did not think he'd ever seen such a look in his cousin's eyes. "Tak' yer hand from her."

"Eh?" Rory let his hand drop.

"Touch her again and I will hack yer arm fro' yer body."

Rory's ire kindled. No one, including his cousin, spoke to him in such a tone. Through gritted teeth he said, "Go carefully, cousin."

"Nay, *ye* go carefully. Rhian is under my protection. I will let no one on earth harm her."

Taken aback, Rory said, "I ha' no intention o' harming her. 'Tis safest for her to wait here for your return. Once we ken whether MacBeith has accepted my terms, we can let her see her sister."

"Wait here, *mo chridhe*," Leith bade the woman.

For an instant, Rory thought she would refuse despite the

endearment. But she nodded and withdrew into the chamber.

Rory gave a grunt of satisfaction. A small victory, but he'd take them where he could find them.

Chapter Nineteen

BEYOND THE WINDOW it rained in a torrent, rendering even Saerla's narrow view nothing more than a blur. She could feel, though, that something had happened out there. Something beyond the torrents of rain. The very air of the place had shifted and quickened.

She'd had little sleep. When she did fall into slumber, she dreamed of battle, of chaos, of darkness and despair. It did not bode well for this new day that might bring so much change.

Her release. Rory MacLeod's death—by her hand.

Had Moira replied to his letter? Had she decided on some mad scheme of rescue instead? Saerla prayed that someone would come and tell her.

But no one came. No guard or servant bringing breakfast. Not Rhian. Not Rory himself. Her prayers, increasingly desperate, dangled like ribbons in the wind.

Beyond the window, the rain continued to fall, and the air coming in grew chilly.

She spoke to them, those spirits of the air drifting in. *Bring me knowledge.* She spoke to the spirits of the fire when she kindled it, thinking of her ma all the while, and her sister, Rhian. *Bring me action. I canna stand being trapped here.* She spoke to the droplets of rain that flung themselves through the window. *Let me accept whatever my fate may be, and let wisdom flow to me.* She spoke to the stone itself, the walls of her prison. *Root me in my faith, my strength. Let me believe that where'er I am, my spirit is home.*

When she finished, she felt stronger. She might be far distant, aye, from the standing stones upon the rise and the magic that dwelt within them. But there might well be a worthy cause. For here, she began to learn that the magic dwelt within her. It abided like a steady light wherever she might be.

RORY WENT WITH Leith and two guards, all of them thoroughly miserable before they'd made a hundred strides. When it chose to rain in Glen Bronach, by God it rained. The hills wept, silver tears flowing down. The sky threw sharp daggers that pricked the skin. Rory's hair, fully beaten, clung to his skull and water sluiced down his back inside his clothing. His boots squelched with every step.

They did not attempt to speak to one another over the crash of raindrops. He had a feeling—a bad feeling—that a horde of MacBeith warriors would follow their returning party, bent upon attack. And here was he with but his sword, two warriors, and a man who could barely hold a weapon well enough to fight.

He hoped he had not made a fatal mistake. He did not know Moira MacBeith, but he'd met her two sisters. Strong women. Extraordinary women. If she was anything like them…

To be sure, she must be. She'd stepped into the place of chief. She'd won Farlan's heart.

After the death of Farlan's young wife, Ainsley, Rory had not thought his friend would ever mate with another woman. Ainsley had been Leith's sister, and so Rory's cousin—a bright, luminescent lass who, like her brother, loved to laugh and brought beauty to the world. Almost too young to wed she'd been when they joined in marriage. Too young, as it proved, to safely bear a child.

Farlan had been devastated when she died, and the wee lad

with her. Rory had never seen his friend so, and for a time had not thought he would survive the loss. He'd never believed Farlan would open himself to its like again.

Now, walking through the rain, Rory wondered: what if it came to battle? What if he, Rory, faced not Farlan but this Moira MacBeith and slew her? What if he took from Farlan his second chance at love?

Love. Och, had he not assured himself he gave no credit to that notion?

Farlan did. He'd sacrificed everything to be with this woman. For the first time, Rory, marching through the rain, considered the courage of that. Not that Farlan had defied Rory, but that he'd found the fortitude to take a chance and risk his heart again.

Rory swore bitterly. Deep down, he still cared about Farlan. He did not want to, but—

They reached the loch and halted. He would wait here and let the party row across to him, using the tiny boat they'd taken yesterday. He would not relish the task of rowing the distance in this downpour.

It took so long that he began to fear the party had been lost out on the wild water. That they'd overturned and drowned. He could not display his uncertainty to his companions, and stood like a rock, the rain pelting his face.

Clouds rolled across the loch toward them. No small party came out of those clouds. By God, an entire army might erupt from cover, and here he stood like a fool.

He was about to give an order for retreat when a creaking of oars reached his ear. The boat appeared with three men aboard. Rory and his companions ran to the shore and hauled the vessel from the water.

Rory swiftly inspected his men, who looked half drowned. Two of his younger warriors, dependable men Murgor had chosen, and a slightly older warrior.

"Where is Kevan?" he shouted against the rain. It had been Kevan whom he'd entrusted with the letter.

Bodach shook his head, gestured with his hands. Despair lay in his eyes. "They kept him."

"Eh?" Rory's heart fell. Aye, he had expected this when they spied only three men returning. He'd hoped he was wrong. For this—Moira MacBeith keeping back a hostage—meant she had not agreed to his terms.

"Wha' happened?"

"He is alive," Bodach yelled. "I ha' a letter." He gestured to his jerkin.

"Nay, do no' tak' it out now." It would be unreadable. "Let us get back. There is no' an army on your heels?"

Bodach shook his head once more.

"Then let us get awa' inside."

⋙⋘

THE FIRE IN the hearth of his study felt better than anything had in a long time. He sent the two younger warriors off to change into dry clothing and rest. He could see that none of them had slept during their night at MacBeith.

He, Bodach, and Leith stripped down to their sarks and leggings there in his study before he poured drams all round.

Bodach, in the doing, dug out the paper he'd carried and spread it on the table. Though it was only damp and not soaking, the ink had started to run.

Remembering the first letter he'd received after Farlan's capture, Rory glanced at it and froze. Farlan—already a traitor to him—had written that first missive. And this one also. Rory recognized his hand.

They'd spent countless hours together when young beneath the tutelage of a man called Crallan. He'd been a right bastard who liked to smack a lad's fingers with a stick when the student grew restless. Which Rory always had. It was hard to write well with fingers that stung. But Rory's father had believed it important for a man, and especially a chief, to be able to read and write well.

Now, despite the blur lent by the rain, Farlan's letters jumped up at him from the page. He knew Moira could also write—unusual in a woman. Perhaps Farlan's characters were neater. Or perhaps she'd had him write this to send a message that she and Rory's former friend stood united in this stance they took.

Bending over the table, with his hair dripping water upon it, he puzzled through the message. Dismay, like a rock, weighted his chest as he read. He thrust the wet hair back from his face and read it over again.

"Well?" Leith asked, all too evidently on edge.

"The chief o' Clan MacBeith has rejected my terms for the return o' her sister. She offers me a trade o' the captive she now holds, instead."

Chapter Twenty

ANGER, AS RORY well knew, could make a man do foolish things. Cause him to react from his gut rather than his head. Speak words he ought to keep back. Make threats he did not want to carry out.

Such anger had always been a fault of his, one his father had pointed out to him many times. He'd fought the tendency to follow his anger with haste all his life. As a man grown, he believed he'd come a long way toward conquering it.

But now, gazing at the letter spread upon the table, anger flared up, searing his insides. Curse the woman! He'd been so close, so close to what he desired—possession of the whole glen. Given the affection among the three sisters MacBeith, he'd been certain Moira would do anything—*anything*—to win her sister's freedom.

Including ceding to him all her holdings.

How dare she leave Saerla in his hands, where he might do anything to her? Cruel imprisonment, starvation. Torture. Rape.

Nay, not that. He could not imagine sullying that beauty with any sort of violence.

He would never abuse a woman, any woman, unless it be on the battlefield. Moira, though, did not know that.

Unless Farlan had told her. Farlan, who knew him as well as he knew himself. He bared his teeth and growled in rage. He wanted to call up all his men and march out despite the accursed rain. He wanted to attack Moira MacBeith's fortress and tear it to the ground stone by stone. Teach her what it meant to defy him.

Leith, standing behind him, edged forward. "Wha' does it say?"

Bodach moved up also. Though he'd carried the message, he had not read it.

"The Chief MacBeith will no' accept my terms."

After two beats, Leith said, "She does no' want Saerla back?"

He sounded as surprised as Rory felt. "Och, I am certain she does." The decision could not have been an easy one. "She is no' willing to trade awa' her holdings to free her sister."

Leith swore. "Then what?"

"She offers to trade us Kevan instead."

"Och." Bodach stared into Rory's face with steady, dark eyes. "And, chief, will ye?"

How to answer that? Kevan, Bodach, and the warriors had gone to MacBeith at his bidding and in good faith. He could scarcely declare he would abandon one of them there. Or that he valued the captured man less than the woman he held.

Kevan was indeed a valued member of his company. Just…not valuable enough.

"We shall ha' to negotiate further," he said heavily. "She did no' like my terms, and I do no' like hers."

"What will they do to Kevan there?" Bodach asked.

Leith grunted again. "Captivity at MacBeith is no easy thing."

Rory glared at him. Leith had come back from such captivity followed by a beautiful woman, had he not? How difficult could it have been for him to consort with her there?

"Wha' if Moira MacBeith attacks," Leith asked sourly, "while ye be plotting yer negotiations?"

"Then we'll march out and meet her, o' course." If things went badly, that would be the time for him to drag out the bitch's sister with his dirk at her throat.

The defenses stood at the ready. If Moira came, she came.

And Farlan at her side.

Rory had to master his anger. His disappointment. There was more than one way to conquer the glen.

"Go get some rest," he told Bodach. "I'll send orders to Murgor to be on guard."

Bodach went out, leaving Rory and Leith alone.

Rory gestured roughly at the letter. "This is Farlan's influence."

"I doubt it. Ye do no' ken Moira MacBeith. She has a lot o' the old chief in her. She is strong."

"Does she care so little for her sister?"

"She cares. The thing ye do no' understand, Rory: that land over there, and especially the graves and stones up on the rise—'tis sacred ground to them."

Again, Rory bared his teeth. "I will no' raze the stones. I will eventually let them live on their lands in peace. But they will answer to me. There will be but one chief in Glen Bronach."

"Moira will no' countenance that."

"Even if I send her sister back to her slain?"

"Ye will no' do that. Moira kens so. Farlan kens so."

"Curse Farlan!"

"Cousin, ye maun think again."

Rory's anger flared. "Get ye back to yer woman."

"Eh?"

"Ye heard me. Get back to yer MacBeith bitch. I will no' ha' ye blathering in my ear."

Leith went out. Rory heard the door close behind him, though he did not turn around, and kept staring fixedly at the letter. The one Farlan had written.

To deter him.

He must think clearly about what reply to send.

He must go and tell Saerla MacBeith she would not be returning home.

THE RAIN HAD abated from a deluge to a steady downpour when Rory walked upstairs to his chamber. The young guard standing outside the door looked on edge.

As was everyone.

"Go on wi' ye," Rory bade him. "Get somewhat to eat."

He wanted to burst into the chamber. To rail at Saerla about her sister's refusal to behave as he desired. To make her tell him the weak point in Moira's armor where he might insert his sword.

He could not do that. She was a woman and, since she was not at present on the field, defenseless.

He hauled hard on his anger and aggravation and rapped at the door. "Mistress MacBeith, 'tis I, Rory MacLeod. May I enter?"

She must be half mad with wondering. She would let him in.

It took a moment, though, before he heard her reply. "Come awa' in."

He lifted the bar from the door. Entered the chamber.

She had lit a fire in the hearth, and welcome warmth met him. He still stood damp in his sark and leggings, his hair dripping. Beyond the narrow window, rain continued to fall, filling the space with echoed sound. Within the chamber…

Och. He'd expected to find her as he'd last seen her, clad in the remnants of her battered leathers. Instead, she wore a woman's clothing. A pale gray gown loosely belted at the waist, the hem dragging on the floor. A shawl he thought he'd seen Rhian wearing, wrapped around her shoulders. Her hair…

Her hair hung loose, a cloud of red-gold around her face that spilled down her back to her narrow waist. Her eyes, as she faced him, seemed to glow in defiance of the weather outside, with their own light.

She lit the place, she did, filled it with more brightness than the fire.

He'd never before seen her dressed as her sex ordained. Her

beauty made him humble. *Damn it!* Her beauty, along with her bearing, made him want to fall to his knees at her feet, an impulse he'd never in his life entertained.

He stopped where he stood. All the words he'd meant to say flew from his head. He could do naught but gaze at her while sensations, rather than thoughts, tumbled through him.

She lifted her chin. He tried to remember what she reminded him of standing there so, some figure out of the stories his old tutor had made him, Farlan, and Leith read. A queen out of a fairy hill, maybe.

Though, to be sure, he did not believe in such beings. No more than he believed in love.

"Wha' is it?" She drew a breath that lifted her bosom. "Ye ha' news for me?"

"Aye. Your sister has refused my offer to ransom ye for return to MacBeith. I regret to say ye will no' be going home."

Chapter Twenty-One

REFUSAL. MOIRA HAD refused to ransom her. Saerla fought against the despair and disappointment caused by that news and battled to understand.

Aye, she'd known it might be so. If Rory MacLeod asked too much, Moira would have no choice but to refuse.

'Twas her fate to be here at this time, in this place. To take hold of all her courage and end Rory's life.

She eyed him up and down. He had quite obviously been out in the rain. His boots still sopped with wet, and the rest of his clothing, a sark and leggings, clung to him.

She'd seen him in less.

His hair—it clung to his head, sopping, dripping onto his shoulders. She would no sooner touch him than she would a dangerous asp, yet her fingers twitched with the desire to smooth that hair away from his angular face.

She would have to touch him if she meant to put an end to his life. Get close to him. Close enough to sink her blade into his flesh.

His throat would be the likely place. She eyed it—a strong column with a pulse beating, visible to her gaze. He fought some strong emotion in coming here, did Rory MacLeod. Disappointment, maybe, that rivaled her own.

He strode in and closed the door behind him. Went to the fire and held out his hands.

"Wha' did ye demand o' her?" Saerla asked. "Wha' in exchange for my return?"

He made a face, looking at the fire and not at her. "Only that she cede all MacBeith lands to me."

"Och! I could ha' told ye she would no' agree. Even if she wanted to do that—which she would no'—Alasdair would no' let her. The council would no'."

"Council?" He shot her a narrow look out of those brilliant green eyes. "Is her power no' absolute?"

"Like to yours, ye mean? Nay. She is a woman. The council, old men and some younger who were close to my father, do no' trust her yet."

"Yer father—Iain MacBeith."

"Aye. Your scheme will no' work. Did she mak' ye a counter-offer?"

"Aye, to exchange one o' my men—one of the messengers I sent and she has taken prisoner—for ye."

Saerla wanted to laugh but did not. "A messenger who is no' important to ye."

"He is important. Just—"

"No' important enough. Ye will leave him there to die." She meant it as a simple statement, not as a condemnation of him, but he took it for the latter. Turning from the fire, he stepped up to her.

"Is that wha' ye think o' me, Saerla MacBeith? That I value those who are loyal to me so little?"

Somehow she forced herself to meet his gaze. Since he was nearly a head taller than her, she had to tip up her head to do so. A wealth of emotions swam in the green eyes, clear for her to see. Outrage. Indignation. Anger.

Desire?

Nay. Her heart began to pound. *Not that.*

"Aye," she said softly. "'Tis all about loyalty wi' ye, is it no'? That is what made ye cast Farlan off. Or so ye claim. I think 'tis arrogance instead. Ye just canna stand to be crossed."

His lips parted, but he said nothing.

"Now my sister has crossed ye. She has dared. If ye want to kill me in retaliation—to cause her pain—go ahead."

"I do no' want to kill ye."

"Why no'? 'Tis what a bully would do, and that is what ye are. A bully. A—"

"Monster. Aye, I ken 'tis what ye think o' me. But I do no' want to kill ye." He shook his head. Water droplets flew. "I want—"

His hand snaked out and caught the back of her neck. It happened so swiftly that she had no time to reach for the knife in her pocket or otherwise resist.

She saw the flare of desire in his eyes then—clear and bright—and expected him to be rough, violent. To bruise and hurt and harm. Instead, he drew her to him gently, with infinite care, brought her body up against his and bent his head.

She had barely time to draw a breath before his mouth claimed hers. Again, she might have expected—feared—brutality. But his lips were soft, questing. They teased hers, tasted them. Feathered a touch and asked a question.

Her lips wanted to answer his. She could not allow it.

But oh, *oh* the sensations that tumbled through her, not all of them purely physical. She could feel him, aye, his body damp and incredibly hard pressed against hers. She could smell him—the sharp scent of the rain and wet wool and something else beneath the both that wooed her. *Wooed her.* She could taste him when those soft, questing lips urged hers apart and he entered her mouth, breaching defenses she'd never meant to let fall.

More than that, though, she felt the tangle, the swirl of emotions that filled him. Dark emotions—anger and regret. Iron-fast determination. Flaming ruthlessness. A thread of light woven through it all, sparkling like dew on a spider's web.

All of it drew her unexpectedly. The light within him, faint as it might be, called to the light inside her, a wealth of light, and had it rearing up. Was this desire? For him?

Nay, and nay.

'Twas instead her Vision come to life. Rory MacLeod overpowering her. Taking her. Making her his own.

Panic arose, overwhelming all other emotion. Bright and hard as the stones at the top of the rise back home, it surrounded her. She placed her palms against his chest and shoved.

She should not be able to shove him away. She had not been able to, during that Vision. He had the strength in plenty to keep her there, caught fast in his arms. Yet he let her go. Raised his hot mouth from hers, stumbled back a half step, and stared into her eyes.

They gazed into each other's eyes, into each other's souls.

She saw the young lad running with his friends on the green sward. The young man training at arms, his black hair gleaming in the sun. The young warrior, making promises to himself. The man kneeling at the bedside of his dying father.

She felt for him. Even though she did not want to, she did.

He drew a breath that expanded his chest. "Mistress Saerla—"

Her lips felt…not bruised, no, for he'd been too gentle for that. They felt softened, aquiver with the need to feel him again. She licked them tentatively to get the sensation under control, and his green eyes brightened, following the movement of her tongue.

She said softly and clearly, "Stay awa' fro' me."

He lifted both his hands in a placating gesture and took another step backward. Saerla also backed away from him, toward the window.

It would not be now. Her Vision, so it seemed, would not come true now. They would not tangle together, limbs and tongues in helpless passion. Perhaps—so she prayed—not ever.

"My apologies," he said, his voice rumbling through him. "That was—"

She could see the words moving in his eyes. His choices of words. *Unforgivable. Irresistible. Magnificent.*

"—unforgivable," he said, choosing among them. One corner of his mouth twitched. "Even for a monster."

"Ye will no' win this battle," she told him. "Ye will no' best Moira. Ye will no' possess MacBeith—nor me."

"Will ye fight me, Saerla MacBeith? To the death?"

Only then did she remember the knife hidden in her pocket. She should have stabbed him when she had the chance, while he had her so close in his arms.

She had failed.

"If I must."

"I will write back to yer sister. Tell her I do no' find her offer acceptable."

"And leave your man to his fate?"

"Kevan is a warrior and kens fine the risks o' such an assignment. Besides"—he tossed his head—"wi' the way things ha' been, he will likely come home wi' a woman in tow, to whom he will swear his undying love."

"Do ye mock the emotion, Rory MacLeod?"

"Would ye no' expect me to?"

Aye. She would expect him to mock it, spit upon it. And yet—there had been those threads of brightness inside him.

"Do no' forget, mistress, I am a monster."

He gave her an exaggerated parody of a bow, and left.

Chapter Twenty-Two

RORY LEANED AGAINST the wall outside his chamber and tried to catch his breath. No one lingered in the corridor beyond what had once been his own quarters. He'd sent the guard off. Another had not yet come to take his place. Others of the warriors had no call to be here anyway—in such weather as this they would most likely gather in their own hall, drinking ale and speculating over what he would do next.

What *would* he do next?

He could not think. He could not think even though he must.

In the past, only anger had kept him from thinking clearly. And he'd succeeded for the most part in mastering his anger. It was not anger he felt toward mistress Saerla anyway.

It was lust.

That thought shocked him. It had him pressing back against the wall like a man avoiding a blow. Surely not. She was the last sort of woman to attract him. The very last.

He went for women much more of her sister Rhian's bent— lush-bodied women who promised successful childbearing.

A harsh wind might blow Saerla MacBeith away. Only, it hadn't. She was strong, *strong*.

Strong enough to take the field with a sword in her hand.

Strong enough to defy him and call him a monster.

Again, he tried to discipline his emotions. Those that had

possessed him when he held her in his arms. A staggering need to protect. Desire that ran like fire through his blood.

It ran through him yet.

He wanted—

He turned and stared at his door. He wanted to march back in there. Kiss her for a day and a night that lasted a month. Learn every part of her with his lips. Run his fingers through that wild mane of hair and gaze into her eyes and—

He must be mad. That thought came swiftly, followed by another. It must be some dark spell of magic.

That made him sneer at himself. He did not believe in spells of magic. Yet only look at the evidence. Farlan—practical, levelheaded Farlan, of all men—had gone to MacBeith a prisoner and come back so besotted with a woman that he surrendered his fealty and his birthright for her sake.

Leith—who, at his heart, had time for little but foolery and laughter—had fallen with a terrible injury and then fallen again for the woman who cared for him, to the point that he would run a dagger through Rory's heart rather than see him look at Rhian wrong.

Another of Iain MacBeith's daughters.

And now he—he, who had no time or patience for it—found himself attracted in a way he had never been before.

Perhaps they were witches, these three sisters MacBeith. It was dark magic. It must exist after all.

And yet…Saerla MacBeith did not feel dark. She did not, when he held her in his arms. With his mouth on hers, he could feel a brightness. A warmth. A light that lured him irresistibly.

By God, he wanted her so much he ached.

He must put her from his mind. She was a hostage, nothing more. One over whom he must persuade her accursed sister to bargain.

If her sister truly was the chief of her clan, she should put paid to this council of which Saerla spoke. She should tell Alasdair the war chief—who, unfortunately, had survived that dread wound he'd taken on the battlefield—that she made the decisions without his interference. Woman or not.

He must get himself in hand and go take care of his business. He should muster for war, for he was not the man to sit behind these walls if the MacBeiths came calling.

He had regrets about Kevan. He was a fine warrior and a loyal man. But if Moira wanted her sister back, she must give him all or nothing.

Up on the walls, he could see the rain clearing to the west. Black clouds sailed up the loch, darkening great swaths of the glen. His men on watch assured him they had seen no further signs of mustering on the other side.

"Gone back inside their walls, have they no'?" said Tearlach. "Out o' the rain. No doubt their chief does no' wish to get her bonny toes wet."

She would have to wet her blade if she refused to deal with him.

Rory climbed down from the walls and retreated to his study, where he searched in vain for dry clothing. Most of his things remained in his own chamber.

He could return there. It made a fine excuse. He could strip off his clothing and—

Nay. She did not want him. And he had never yet forced himself on any woman.

He did not want to force himself on Saerla MacBeith. He wanted—desperately—for her to want him. Wanted her to cling to him with need. Wrap her arms and legs around him after shedding her clothing without shame. He wanted to see those misty blue eyes heat with passion as she invited him in.

Curse the woman.

He paced his study, unable to think about the words he should write to Moira. His problem was, he needed to spend himself on a woman. A woman who was not Saerla MacBeith. It had been too long. Sheer deprivation had worked its way upon him.

Usually when the need became dire, he resorted to his own fist. To be sure, that would not do now. He wanted the softness of a woman. The warmth. He wanted the smell of a woman.

He wanted her to smell like Saerla.

He could not just walk out and start a dalliance with one of the clanswomen. Not when he had important matters needing his attention.

He did not need a quick tumble, by any road. He needed a wife. One with whom he could get an heir.

He thought of Ratha with her two wee sons. She was not ill to look upon, and had a lush body where he could ease himself. But doing so would set expectations. He would have to court her, God help him, if he decided to wed her.

He could not even imagine it.

A fine-looking woman, Ratha, aye. But she had not a cloud of red-gold hair. Nor a small whipcord body, slim and strong.

He wondered how Saerla MacBeith's breasts would taste.

With a grunt, he went to his desk and forced himself to sit down. He stared at Moira's missive spread out there. Covered in Farlan's neat, careful script.

Suddenly, it all came crashing down upon him. The overwhelming loss. He *missed* Farlan, everything about him, from his slow smile to his steady gaze. He missed his calm, wise counsel. The ease of his company.

He missed his da, without question the finest man he had ever known. Slow to anger. Quick with reason. Everything he, Rory, was not.

Indeed, Farlan was more like Da than he was. Not too surprising, as Da had half raised him, the son of his perished comrade-at-arms. The boy with the mop of brown hair. Da had made Farlan his own.

Rory could never call his da, Camraith, soft. He'd been a strong sword in battle, and strong also in his belief in what was right. But aye, there had been a soft thread running through him.

The same Rory had often sensed in Farlan. The same he felt

when he kissed Saerla.

By heaven, he had to put that away from him. He had to lay aside the maddening thoughts and decide what was best to do. For he would not, under any circumstances, give up on his intentions.

If Moira MacBeith had refused his offer, he must act accordingly. Return a letter, aye. The damn woman liked letters. But saying what? That she could keep his man? The very idea made him prick all over with heat.

He could threaten to kill her sister if she did not surrender her lands to him. He'd already implied that before. He would come right out and say it now.

Your sister's life will be forfeit.

The lines on the page blurred before his eyes. Not that he would ever harm one curl on Saerla's head. One brown eyelash. One freckle sprinkled across her nose.

She had tiny brown freckles on her face.

She was, without question, the most exquisite thing he'd ever seen.

Grimly he pulled a sheet of foolscap toward him, dipped his pen in the ink, and began to write.

Chapter Twenty-Three

"NO ONE DARES guess what Rory will do. 'Tis a matter o' wide speculation. Leith says 'tis all anyone will talk about."

Saerla gazed up into Rhian's face. Her sister stood over her, treating the wound at the back of her head.

A day and a night had passed since Rory MacLeod had kissed her. She had to state it that way in her mind. He had kissed her.

She had most definitely not kissed him back. At least, she did not think she had. Her lips, captured, had merely, well, *responded*. Because there had been something in his kiss, in his touch, that snared her. Made far too many moments tick by before she pushed him away.

Before he let her go.

It was the memory of her Vision that had affected her so. The terror of being in his power. Him, of all men.

Yet it had not been mere terror she felt while in his arms.

"Saerla? Are ye quite well?" Rhian paused in her chatter and gave Saerla a closer look. "Does your head still pain ye?"

"Nay, no longer." Her heart pained her. And—and another part of her body with which she was much less acquainted.

"Would ye like me to mix ye a draught?"

Saerla gazed back at her sister somberly. She'd never seen Rhian look so well. Despite being displaced from home and her own hearth, she was blooming, her body lush and her cheeks full of color. Carrying a child suited her. Carrying Leith's child most of all.

"Rhian, I had a chance to kill him—well, to attack him—and I failed." Saerla had not told Rhian about the kiss, did not know if she could.

Rhian's brow wrinkled in concern. "Aye, well—"

"He stood close to me at one point. As near to me as ye be now. I did no' pull the knife."

"'Tis no' an easy thing to do, to slay a man in cold blood."

His blood had not been cold. It had beat hot under his skin. As had hers.

"It does no' matter. I ha' felled men on the field. Why no' him?" It was that which truly bothered her. Why not him, who most needed to die?

"He is strong and could well ha' overpowered ye once he spied the knife."

"It does no' matter. I should be willing to pay any price in order to wound him." Saerla seized Rhian's wrist. "We need him dead so Leith may become chief, and the child ye carry after him."

"Aye."

She would have to get near Rory MacLeod again, near enough to let his blood. It struck her suddenly that perhaps *that* was what the Vision had foretold. She had been looking at it the wrong way around.

The two of them twined together in passion. The strength of him overwhelming her. Perhaps in that Vision the power had in truth been hers, rather than his.

Mayhap she needed to seduce him.

The prospect made her draw an unsteady breath. Quite plainly, he had an attraction to her, though she had no idea why. A man like him—strong and dominant—could have any woman he chose. Beautiful women. In fact, it astonished her that he had not taken a wife already and gotten an heir of his own.

Perhaps he was accustomed to taking a woman, any woman he chose, and doing as he wished with her. His arrogance would argue it.

It should be easy for her, then.

Panic fluttered up through her, a wild bird trapped in her breast. Nay, it would not be easy. She had never seduced any man, never done more than smile at one in friendship. Could not imagine taking off her clothing for one. Lying down with him. Allowing him to—

Well, but she would have to keep her clothing on, would she not? If she meant to pull a knife from her pocket and slit Rory MacLeod's throat.

She would need to act in that moment of passion before she—or he—removed her clothing.

Heat singed her all over. She saw again the bright gleam of passion in green eyes.

She could not do this. She *must*.

"Saerla, love, what is it? Somewhat bothers ye."

"Moira could muster and attack at any time."

"Aye, so. Leith says Rory's men keep watch continually for any such movement. He has been up on watch himsel'."

"She may persuade the council. And Alasdair. I hope Alasdair is all right. That terrible wound o' his—"

"He should no' march out wi' a sword in his hand, nay. But he is stubborn to the bone."

She, Saerla, must prevent that. She must act, and soon. Before Rory sent his letter and provoked a war. Because she loved them all. Moira and Farlan. All the true hearts who would march to their deaths for her sake. Alasdair.

If she must sacrifice herself, so she would. Aye, surely, so the Vision meant. She had only to find the courage.

IT HAD BEEN two nights since Rory had slept. Even had he possessed a bed—which he no longer did—his thoughts would not have let him rest. When he did ease down onto the settle in his study, which made an uncomfortable roost, he could not so much as close his eyes without reliving it again.

The kiss. Saerla MacBeith.

Aye, he'd decided after hours-long pondering, there must be some magic in it. Given, he had never much in the past lent any credence to magic. Mayhap he'd been wrong.

For she carried a measure of magic inside her, did Saerla MacBeith. An uncommon magic, like light. He'd been able to feel it, aye, when he held her in his arms. To taste it in her kiss.

Why else had the memory, and a brief memory at that, taken such hold of him?

She was but one ordinary woman, after all. Utterly ordinary. Except for that wealth of hair. Those eyes. The very scent of her.

Nay.

Was he a lad, a child, to lose his good sense to such a degree? Yet he could not rest. He could not stop thinking about her. And he could not decide what to write to Moira.

Och, well, he could. He had written three letters. Burned them all. Told himself if she expected a reply from him, the better to let her stew. Dance on the hot coals of uncertainty.

Launch an attack?

She had not done so yet, which argued she would not. Women should not lead. Or was it truly his former friend with whom he contested?

The thought merely served to raise his level of disquiet.

He walked out, paced the ramparts and the grounds, assuring himself all lay in a state of readiness. The weather continued foul, rain moving in successive waves down the glen. The men on watch suffered, as did he.

Because the very sound of the rain made him remember having her in his arms. The rain crashing down outside the window. The sound invading the chamber.

Desire, he assured himself over and over again, was but desire and could be conquered like any other emotion.

He needed to banish her from his mind. A draught of strong ale might help.

The hope of it took him to the warriors' hall, where he soon found himself surrounded, his men asking when they were to fight again. He told them it would be soon and pried himself away to sit with Leith, whom he found at a table against the wall.

"I am surprised to see ye here, cousin." Instead of with his accused woman.

"And I, ye. Does that hole in yer back still pain ye, then?" Leith's blue-gray gaze probed him.

It did, damn it. "Why should ye think so?"

"Because 'tis no' like ye to take to drink in the middle o' the afternoon."

Rory could scarcely admit he needed relief from his thoughts. Instead, he cocked an eyebrow at his cousin. "And ye, Leith? I am that surprised ye ha' torn yoursel' away from your woman."

"She is with Saerla."

Saerla. Rory's gaze flew to Leith's face. "I did no' give permission for that."

"Ye did give permission for Rhian to tend her sister, did ye no', in the capacity o' a healer?"

"Aye—"

Leith pushed a flagon of ale toward him. "Then drink and shut yer gob about it."

"Is Mistress Saerla unwell that she still needs a healer's attention?"

Again, Leith studied him. "I do believe Rhian goes there to check the head wound, where Saerla was clubbed down."

Rory flinched.

"But I freely admit, it may be an excuse for Rhian to see her. Comfort her. They are attached, those three sisters."

"Aye, so."

"And if ye think I will endeavor to keep Rhian awa' for any

reason—"

Rory sneered. "Ye canna even control your woman."

Leith leaned closer across the table. "If ye suppose, Rory, 'tis about control, ye be more the fool than I thought."

Rory did not like being called a fool. He asked, not without sarcasm, "Nay? Wha' is it about, then, wi' yer woman?"

Leith fixed him with an unexpectedly serious eye. "Bonding. Sharing. Give and take in equal measures. A love wrested, Rory, is no' worth the having."

"Love." Rory tried to scoff at it. "A weak man's game."

"Funny, then, cousin, it should require so much sheer strength to keep alive."

Chapter Twenty-Four

O N THE WAY back to his study from the warriors' hall, Rory encountered Dairmid's widow, Ratha. To be sure, half blinded by the rain, he bumped into her, nearly dislodging the pile of clean linens she carried in her arms.

His hands came out to steady her, and their gazes met, she peering out from beneath the hood of her cloak.

Not so much a bonny woman, Ratha, but a lush one, the sort who had in the past always caught Rory's eye. She had a wealth of auburn hair, now caught beneath her hood, and eyes to match. A strong-boned, oval face and a body made for welcoming a man.

She'd been a good wife to Dairmid. Rory had to admit, he knew little more of her than that. Did she like to laugh? Was she bright of spirit? Had she grieved long enough, yet, to be?

"Chief Rory," she exclaimed as he steadied her.

"Forgive me, mistress. I was no' looking where I was going."

"And I could no' see. I am taking these old, washed linens to the infirmary to mak' bandaging."

"Aye, so." And was it a coincidence that Rory had met her this way when she headed his list, more or less, for a wife? "Where are yer wee lads?"

She gave him a smile. "Dairmid's ma has them. They bring her comfort. Wee William, so she says, looks much as Dairmid did when he was small."

"Och, aye." Rory could tell from the sadness tinging her smile that her grief lingered. Would it be an offense for him to say he would like to pay court to her? To wed soon, in order to get a son of his own?

He stood there in the rain staring at the woman, unable to decide. He, a man who rarely had trouble making up his mind about anything, now could not tell what to write in a letter to his enemy or whether to speak to his clanswoman about the future.

She, as his clanswoman, would have a duty to wed with him. In truth, he would give her full choice. But he thought she would agree. And he would perform a duty, nothing more.

Let that fool, Leith, prate on about love as he would.

"Chief Rory?" She now looked at him in concern. "Is somewhat amiss?" Worry gathered in her eyes. "I ha' heard we may come under attack fro' those devils at MacBeith. Is it so?"

"Ye ha' no need to worry. Our walls and our warriors both stand strong."

"Aye, but"—she gave a shiver—"I hate the thought o' more killing. More—more dying."

"When 'tis done, mistress, 'twill be done for good and all."

She said a curious thing then. "My Dairmid followed ye, Chief Rory, and trusted ye also. I maun then trust ye to do what is right for my sons."

Rory felt the weight of that descend upon him like a cloak of iron. He stood there staring at his warrior's widow, thinking— though he needed to spend himself on a woman, it could not be this one. Not now. Not yet. Mayhap not ever.

He gave her a hard nod. "I am honored by yer faith in me, mistress, as well as Dairmid's."

They parted ways as simply as they'd met, and he walked on through the rain, pacing away the afternoon, looking for peace that would not come.

Gloom filled the glen, with billowing rain clouds and driving rain, long before dark came. Rory figured he should get something to eat. The fumes of the ale he'd taken with Leith had long since worn off. He felt raw and hollow.

If he went to see Saerla MacBeith…

Would Rhian be there still? Nay, surely she had long since returned to her man. Saerla would be alone. He could spend a few minutes in her company. Make an excuse to—

What? Speak to her? Touch her?

Aye, both those things.

He needed to keep clear away. He needed to call on his good sense. Keep his eye on his goal, that toward which he'd yearned for so long.

His feet had their own intentions, and carried him on through the gloom.

SAERLA'S HEAD HAD indeed stopped aching, even though it seemed far too crammed with thoughts, with considerations. After Rhian left her, she spent time trying to decide which of those thoughts stemmed from her fear, and which flowed from her Vision. Again and again she prayed for guidance. The magic she so often found back home must remain with her, or so she reasoned, yet it felt so very far away.

When she tired of staring out the slit of a window at the rain, she sat by the fire. A young man had brought her a load of wood earlier, having been admitted by the guard who remained outside. She had plenty of fuel to warm the chamber. But dread, like a chill, crept through her.

She knew he would come even before she heard his voice outside the door, speaking to the guard. She'd felt him growing closer all afternoon. Now, when a preternatural dark dominated the sky, a rap came at the door.

"Mistress Saerla, I wish to come in."

Ah, and was this fate, presenting her with the opportunity she needed? The chance to end the life of this man who threatened everything she loved.

Was this to be the path, the destiny, she chose?

She scrambled up from her place by the fire and onto her feet before she replied. "Aye, come awa' in."

Did the man spend all his time out in the rain? For he came in once more dripping wet. He brought the bar from the outside of the door in with him and paused to bar it again from the inside, his hands glittering with moisture as he performed the task.

Shut in. She was shut in with him. Alone. Helpless.

Only, not helpless.

Her hand crept to the pocket of her gown where lay the weight of Leith's knife.

After she let Rory's blood, once he lay dead, she could lift the bar. She could escape out into the corridor, for he had no doubt dismissed the guard. Rhian had tried to tell her how to reach Leith's quarters, but Saerla had no doubt she would lose her way in this foreign place.

Might she hope to escape? Find her way home? *Home.* Her very spirit yearned for it.

All this she ran through her head, imagining it, as she stared at the man who faced her. He looked overlarge and threatening. She could not let her fear deter her. She had to steel herself and kill him.

Yet—yet he looked so alive. His green eyes studied her, considering, and she could see the vitality flowing through him. Almost as if she could See his spirit.

"Saerla," he said. Just her name, but she could not describe the emotions she heard in that single word. A twisted wealth of them. "Will ye welcome me here?"

Chapter Twenty-Five

RORY MACLEOD HAD not moved from the door and continued to watch Saerla with those canny, bright green eyes between narrowed, wet black lashes. The resolve within her wavered. She commanded it to hold strong.

She did not know how to seduce a man. She had never been that kind of woman. She dealt purely and honestly with the people she knew, men and women alike, and only kept from them the truths she Saw in Visions that she thought might hurt them.

For this, she would have to twist truth and do it convincingly. She was not equipped for it. She had no coquettish ways. No womanly wiles.

Fate had chosen wrong, placing her here.

Why should he believe she desired him? That she might invite his touch? His kiss? Might want him to take her to the bed that lay just behind her, where she might slit his throat?

Get him talking, her inner woman urged. *Make it intimate.*

"Chief MacLeod. Ha' ye word for me about my release?"

"Nay." He still regarded her as if he expected her to attack him. As indeed she would. "I yet prepare the letter to your sister. I seek fro' ye some information."

"Oh?"

"Aye." He did take a step away from the door toward the fire.

Then another. He went and held his hands out to the flames, but he kept his gaze on her.

"Come, sit," she invited him. "I will answer what I can."

"Will ye?" He looked surprised.

"I want to leave here, do I no'? To go home." Her own yearning made that sound all too convincing. "If I can in any way further my release, I wish to do so."

"That is a very sensible attitude."

"I am a sensible woman."

"Aye, then." He sat on the settle that fronted the fire. Knowing she must get closer, Saerla joined him there.

Aye, and being so close made it all too real. No Vision, this. She could not convince herself of that. For she could smell him just as she had last time. The tang of the rain, and leather, and wet wool, and that other scent she'd caught when he kissed her.

Kissed her.

She needed to convince him to kiss her so again. Render him unsuspecting. Then bring up the point of the knife and—

Fear got her on her feet. "Ye be very wet. I ha' a cloth."

It was the one she used for washing and drying. Since she'd found it here, she suspected it was his, after all.

She brought it in her hands, which trembled. Sat back down, closer to him this time. Caught his gaze as she said, in a murmur, "Pray, allow me."

He sat stock-still when she touched him. Like rock when she applied the cloth to his face, gentle as she might touch a child. Like stone as she ran it down across the angle of his jaw and farther—farther, to his throat.

Just there, she would have to place her blade. Pierce the flesh.

The collar of his sark lay open and his skin gleamed wet. A pulse jumped as she plied her cloth there, but naught else moved.

Saerla's head went light, as it sometimes did before a Vision. She felt like another woman, almost. One who had stepped out of herself. One who, the cloth still caught in one hand, used the fingers of the other to pluck at the laces on the front of his sark and untie them.

He drew a harsh breath as she placed her cloth inside his sark, meeting a crop of coarse hair and hard muscle.

"Saerla." It came in a growl as he caught her wrist, his paralysis suddenly broken. And then, in a whisper, "Saerla."

He pulled her into his arms. She had not far to go as she leaned into him so closely. It might have been a chasm, since she crossed her fear, her doubt, and her reluctance.

All that flew away as soon as she met the wall of his chest. Just like before, she half expected violence. As before, he surprised her.

His arms wrapped around her, forming not a prison but a cradle. Not confinement, this, but protection. She felt safe. *Safe.* That allowed the fear to subside even before his mouth found hers and made her forget every other consideration.

The scent of him surrounded her, and she craved more. More. The taste of him flooded her, and she could not get enough. Gentle lips. Gentle hands. They slid up around her and into her hair, holding her carefully as if she might break.

"Saerla." He spoke it into her mouth an instant before his tongue entered her, and her bones turned to water. Aye, on some level she'd wanted this since the last time he touched her. The taste of him. The heat. Why had she spent so long denying it? She'd been born for this.

She abandoned the cloth and thrust both hands inside his sark, meeting hot, hard flesh. He felt wonderful and unlike anything she'd ever touched. Her fingers caressed their way through the hair on his chest reverently, and he made a sound deep in his throat. One of satisfaction.

When he broke the kiss, she wanted to protest. She drew a ragged breath and stared into his eyes, fixed upon her as if he could see nothing else.

"Ye're a bonny, wee thing."

His voice sounded slurred. He was drunk, surely, with the effects of that kiss. She felt the same way. A thought skittered through the mist that filled her mind, that which felt so much like a Vision. Mayhap it would not be so difficult to seduce him.

She wanted to sob and beg him to kiss her again. She need not, for his lips remained only a breath from hers.

She reached for them.

Because she did not want to breathe air. She wanted to breathe him, to take the scent and taste of him inside her. To fill herself with this man's essence, dark and light.

Dark and light.

He cradled her chin in gentle, damp fingers and kissed her more deeply, so she could no longer tell where he ended and she began. When he abandoned her chin and moved his fingers down her throat, she did not protest. She wanted him there. She wanted him everywhere.

She did not notice when he tugged the ties at the front of her gown. She was fixed instead on the sweep of his tongue inside her mouth, like a claiming. But when his hand slid inside her bodice to cup a breast, her entire body took notice.

She drew back from him and found him once more gazing into her eyes. "Saerla. I pray thee."

Did this man ever beg? Apparently so, for he beseeched her now. He sought her permission with his eyes and with his fingers that moved so gently across her flesh. He sought permission. He would not rend or seize.

She gave it with a sigh and the return of her mouth to his. She'd never felt a sensation like his fingers caressing her breast, caressing so gently. Never imagined anything could feel the way it did when his calloused finger tips caught her nipple and a spear of pure desire pierced her to the core.

Now *she* wanted to beg. *Please.*

It would not be difficult, nay, to seduce this man. To shed her clothing for him. To spread her thighs, to open herself, to seek to capture and pull upon the threads of light woven through his darkness.

"Saerla. My God." He'd stopped kissing her again, but his lips did not leave her, nay. They slid from her lips over her jaw to her ear and down her neck. Lower still, they affixed to one naked breast.

Saerla forgot who she was. She forgot what she was, save a woman. She wrapped her arms around his sopping hair and drew him in closer, closer, offering more of herself to the mouth that wooed her.

She arched her body into him and Saw the bright, golden threads within him glow. She could give him this. Defeat the darkness.

"Saerla." When he lifted his face from her breast, he looked like a stranger. Earnest. Humble. Anything but her enemy.

"Please." She tried to urge him back to her breast.

"Nay, I dare no'." His voice came ragged. "I want to lay ye down on that rug. I want to tak' ye. D'ye understand?"

For the first time in her life, she did.

"I dare no' stay."

"Rory." She captured his face between her palms.

He kissed her softly, softly, fleetingly, before pulling away.

"If I do no' leave ye now, I will no' be able to leave ye."

He rose from the settle and went to the door, stood for a moment with his head resting against the panel, then drew up the bar and went out, leaving Saerla with but one thought.

She'd once more forgotten the knife in her pocket, failed to use it to end his life.

Chapter Twenty-Six

THE RAIN HAD fled at last, disappearing up the glen sometime during the night. Rory stood on the battlement gazing out over the land that lay awash with pure golden radiance in the new dawn.

He'd come up here to look for signs of movement at Mac-Beith. To search out danger. To clear his head.

After leaving Saerla last night, he had not slept. He'd tried once again to write a letter to her sister and come up with an effort he thought might serve.

The other thoughts—sensations—had refused to forsake him. All of them were of Saerla MacBeith, and they consumed his mind.

He had wondered how she would taste. Her breasts tasted like honey. And like light.

It was inexplicable to him how a woman could taste like light, but she did. Sweet, sweet and strong. The finest thing ever to meet his tongue.

Kissing her…kissing her was like nothing he'd ever known.

He stood with his hands on the stone of the battlement—hands scarred from fighting, hands blessed by touching her—and tried to make sense of it. There was no sense to be had, and little rational thought. Just pure feeling.

Seldom had he been victim to his emotions, seldom did he

permit it. He thought. He planned. He sacrificed.

He would have to sacrifice Saerla.

In the end, she would have to go back to her sister. In exchange for ownership of the glen.

He let his eyes wander across the land that stretched out in front of him, peaceful in the golden light. A bonny place this was, aye, and part of him, blood and bone. As a lad, he'd intuitively recognized that beauty, being somehow connected to it. Over the years, though, it had slipped away from him, replaced by the need to take.

He'd forgotten why he wanted Glen Bronach. Och, he told himself it was because his ancestors had been bent upon it, and he needed to achieve what they had not.

Mayhap that was not the truth. Mayhap he'd forgotten that the true reason was how much he loved the place.

Something in Saerla's kiss had reminded him of that. For was she not beautiful in just the same way as the glen? A wee bit wild and a wee bit mystical. Filled with the changing light.

That made no sense either, that kissing a woman could remind a man of what had slipped away from him. His feelings made no sense.

He needed to send her back—not only to achieve his goals, but for his peace of mind.

One of the guards on duty came up beside him. "Chief, d'ye think yon MacBeith woman will muster now that the weather has cleared?"

"Quite likely." He would, if his enemy held something of such precious value in his hands.

The man eyed him uncertainly. "Will we be getting our Kevan awa' back home, then?"

"I hope so." He eyed his man in return. "We are ready, are we no'? For a battle? A defense?"

"Aye, chief."

Rory nodded and left the battlements, left the peaceful, sleeping glen, trying to exude an air of confidence he did not actually feel.

He sought out Leith at his chamber, where his cousin was just dressing for the training field. "I need a word wi' ye, man," Rory said, casting a look at Rhian, who eyed him without favor. If she knew what had passed between him and her sister last night, she would glare still harder.

Would Saerla tell her? Would she claim he'd tried to force her? Women did. Yet he had not. She had kissed him just as he had kissed her, and held him to her breast.

For an instant he went dizzy with remembering that, as if all the light of the morning had gotten inside his head.

Leith narrowed curious eyes at him. "Are ye well, man?"

"Aye."

"Is it the wound to your back still? Would ye let Rhian look at it?"

"Nay." For the first time since that accursed arrow had pierced his back, he'd forgotten the wound. "I just need to speak wi' ye. Come to my study."

He went out, loped back to the chamber, the buzz clearing from his mind as he went.

Leith soon joined him. Without waiting, Rory thrust the letter he'd scribed into his cousin's hands. "Read that."

Leith took the sheet and puzzled it out. When he finished, he raised his eyes to Rory's face.

"Wha' will Moira MacBeith think o' that?" Rory demanded. "Or, more to the point, wha' will Farlan think o' it? Who am I dealing wi' there, Leith? Her? Or him?"

Leith drew a breath. "Matters are complicated there at Mac-Beith, and I was locked in a chamber—"

"Yer woman talks to ye, does she no'? She is one o' them— the sisters MacBeith."

"There's a council. Older warriors that stood wi' the old chief, and a few younger bucks as well. They do no' trust Farlan and dislike his standing at Moira's side. They say their war chief— that Alasdair—must mak' all decisions wi' her, for now."

"For now?"

"Till they learn to trust Farlan, I suppose. If they ever do. They say if Moira weds wi' him proper, she maun gi' up the place o' chief. She insists she'll keep both the place and the man."

"She maun be quite the woman."

"Farlan did no' choose her idly. Rory, ye know him. Farlan is a man o' sense. Loyalty—"

Rory scoffed.

"Loyalty to Moira now. He believes she is his destiny."

"Then he is a fool." But Rory thought of the warmth of Saerla in his arms. Of the light inside her.

"Rory," Leith began, and Rory had never seen him so serious, "there maun be a better way than war. The killing. There is a road to peace—"

"I ha' offered her peace. I ha' offered her the return o' her sister. God knows, I want naught more than to send the woman back."

A lie.

Leith wagged his head. "Aye, so. All she has to do is gi' up everything she holds dear, the glen her ancestors settled, over to ye."

"Aye. There will be peace after that, Leith. I will let them live on the land."

"That belongs to them no longer."

Rory shrugged. "Let Moira MacBeith decide wha' means more to her—her sister or her lands."

"Wha' I am trying to tell ye is, that choice is no' hers to make."

"Let her fight out that battle wi' her council. Is she chief, or no'?"

Leith shook the sheet of foolscap at him. "Ye ha' given her ten days. Then you say her sister's life will be forfeit. Would ye truly do it, man? Saerla is a sweet lass wi' a valiant heart. The gods speak to her—"

"The gods," Rory scoffed again.

"Aye, so believe it as ye will. Would ye anger the very gods that protect her?"

Rory said nothing. He meant to force Moira's hand. And Farlan's.

"Wha' o' our man, Kevan?" Leith asked then. "Will ye refuse to trade for him? Leave him there among strangers to die?"

"'Tis war, this, just in another settin. He would ha' gone to die on the battlefield, would he no'?"

Leith backed off a step. Rory did not like the look he saw in his cousin's eyes.

"List to me, Leith. I want ye to tak' this letter to MacBeith."

"Aye? So I can be captured and killed in turn?"

"She will no' harm ye. No' a hair o' ye. Not her sister's man."

"I canna. I will no'."

Not words Rory wanted to hear, especially now when he felt his back to the wall.

"Leith, man, ye swore fealty to me. When my father died, ye did."

"Aye, so." Leith's blue-gray eyes grew hard. "A lot has changed since then."

Pain slammed through Rory, shaking him. Shaking his world. "Will ye turn on me? As Farlan did?"

"I am no' sayin' that."

"Let us get this settled, Leith. Once 'tis done and the lands are mine, ye'll be able to live wi' yer woman in peace."

"Let me talk it over wi' Rhian. She may ken better how her sister will react."

Rory wanted to sneer. Wanted to deride his cousin for being under a woman's thumb.

Thinking of Saerla MacBeith, he kept silent.

Chapter Twenty-Seven

AFTER RORY LEFT her, Saerla could not rest. She had not a hope of sleeping and could not make herself lie in the bed. Instead she paced from the fire to the window and back again, cursing herself.

What had come over her? She did not know the woman who had been in Rory MacLeod's arms. How could she have invited him to kiss her the way she had? To touch her the way he had?

How could she have forgotten—forgotten completely—to plunge her knife into his neck when she had the chance?

It was madness.

She rubbed fitfully at her head as she paced and tried to deny what she had done. What she had failed to do. Mayhap the blow to her head had affected her. But nay, that was not it. *It was him.*

Remembering made the breath come short in her lungs and made her fingers tremble. She'd set out, aye, to seduce the man. She'd succeeded so well, she'd seduced herself also.

Morning came and bloomed through her slit of a window, finding her exhausted and still on her feet. The rain had fled, and golden light washed upon her. She wanted to be home, up among the stones. Away from all this.

Away from him.

She'd always feared him, on some level. The boogeyman. The monster. Now she doubly feared him for a new reason. He threatened her self-control and all she believed about herself.

She tried to look at it dispassionately, there in the light of the new day. Rory MacLeod was a fine-looking man. Indeed, despite the terror he instilled in her, she did not think she'd ever seen finer. Those canny green eyes of his. The way he regarded her with them. The fall of black hair and—och, by the powers, the wiry black hairs on his chest. The sharp planes of his face that spoke to her—spoke to her in a way she did not understand. Of longing. Of something so right she could scarcely comprehend it.

She'd expected him to be a brute. When he'd touched her, he was not brutal, not at all. Gentle, his touch and his lips. On her lips. At her breast.

Who would have thought such a sensation could exist? She had to stop thinking on it. She would lose her mind if she did not.

Had she not forgotten what she was about when he kissed her, he'd be dead by now, her mission done. Leith would become chief, and Rhian's son after him.

How could a man's kiss distract her from all that?

Would he return? Would he come back expecting more kisses and to be held again at her breast?

She could not bear it if he did, could not bear it if he did not. He would not return. He had taken himself away saying that, in essence, he could not trust himself to remain near her. That he wanted to lay her down on the rug before the hearth and take her as only a man could take a woman.

If he did…if he did, he would kiss her everywhere. Move above her. Move inside her. How easy would it be to take him unawares then and plunge her knife into the place where his pulse beat so strong?

She needed to seduce him. And, aye, that would be distressingly easy, if she let herself. She needed to kill him.

She did not know that she could perform the act. Either of the acts. She sat down at last in the sunlight at the window and began to pray.

RORY SPENT THE day at the training field working his men and himself till the pain of the wound in his back roared at him, and he wanted to drop. He would not consider returning to see Saerla MacBeith. But all through that day, in a curious way, she accompanied him.

The memory of a red-gold curl clinging to his fingers as he plunged his hand into her hair. Warm silk. The way she tasted, lips and breast. The way she'd trembled with urgency in his arms.

Urgency. She had wanted him just as much as he wanted her.

That thought—and the truth of it—distracted him so badly he almost had his head taken off by one of his own men. She might try to deny it. He had felt the truth.

He needed to see her again. He could not.

He took himself back to his study, aching for his own bed and Saerla in it, only to find Leith there ahead of him, waiting. Pain and frustrated impatience made him snap at his cousin.

"Well? Ha' ye made up yer mind?"

Leith, who'd been sitting in the chair by the table, got to his feet.

"I am sorry, cousin. I canna take yer letter to MacBeith."

The last of Rory's forbearance fled. "Canna, or will no'?"

"I canna."

"Yer woman," Rory sneered, "will no' gi' ye permission?"

"'Tis to do wi' Rhian, aye, but no' her permission. Sit down and let me explain."

"I ha' no time for yer mewling explanations. Ye ha' left yer balls back in yer quarters, in her keeping."

Leith did not flare to anger. He rarely did. But his gaze turned to ice.

"Leave off wi' being a bastard, Rory. Sit ye down and listen to me."

Rory sat, but only because the pain in his back demanded it.

After giving him a narrow look, Leith poured a whisky and slid it toward him.

"Drink that."

Rory did. The fiery liquor helped, though it did nothing to soothe the other blaze that raged inside him.

Leith came and sat opposite him, lacing his hands together between his knees. Rory could not help but notice that Leith's injured arm served him better than it had.

"Speak, then," Rory tossed at him. "Tell me why ye withhold yer loyalty."

"I canna go to MacBeith because I canna leave Rhian."

"She will no' allow it?"

"Nay. 'Tis no' that. This is my decision and mine alone. I canna leave her alone here among enemies. Not while—"

"I am here, am I no'? D'ye think I will not protect my cousin's woman?"

"I am sure ye would. But should the council at MacBeith decide to hold me in a bid to win Saerla's freedom, I could be separated from Rhian a long while. And she—Rory, she is carrying my child."

"What?" Rory stared at him, his eyes narrowed. "Ye canna know such a thing. 'Tis far too soon—"

"She knows. I know." Leith slid forward on his seat. "Rory, I believe there is some magic in it. She is magic. I canna explain."

Rory thought of Saerla in his arms. Of tasting the light that dwelt inside her. He pushed the memory from him.

"Do no' be a fool. She tells ye. It does no' make it so."

"Rory, she carries my child. 'Tis a boy. The heir to MacLeod."

That hit Rory squarely between the eyes. All the air went out of him in a rush.

The heir to MacLeod. Not his son. Leith's. From a MacBeith bitch.

"I do no' believe it," he declared. But he did. God help him, he did. Having held Saerla in his arms, he believed the three sisters MacBeith possessed some wild magic.

Leith believed it also. Rory could tell by the steady light shining in his eyes.

"How could she know so soon?" A woman, so he supposed, might tell anything about her own body. But that the child would be male?

"The spirits, they speak to the three sisters MacBeith in differing ways. I am convinced they make Moira strong. They whisper to Rhian o' healing and such like. Saerla—Saerla is verra special. Rory, ye canna harm her. She is the gods' own."

"Then go to MacBeith and convince her sister to deal wi' me. I will set Saerla free as soon as Moira agrees to my terms." Watch her walk away from him. Could he do that?

Slowly and with regret, Leith shook his head. "I canna leave Rhian. I urge ye, Rory. Send Saerla. Send her back wi' a letter asking for peace."

"Peace." Rory surged to his feet. "I swear, Leith, if ye do no' cease in prating about it, I will kill ye mysel'."

"Go ahead, Rory. 'Tis the only way I will leave Rhian."

Fury rose in a bubble to Rory's head. "Fine, then," he spat. "We will risk another messenger. And his blood will be on your hands."

Chapter Twenty-Eight

THE HEIR TO MacLeod. Leith's son. Not Rory's own.

The thought chased its way through Rory's mind like a snake twining through tall grass, while he watched another party leave for MacBeith the next morning. While he went to the training field after and worked himself hard in an effort to still the emotions inside him.

Anger. Doubt. Envy. Lust. A terrible mixture, seared by regret.

He had been a fool, and that was one of the last things he'd ever wanted to be.

He should have taken care of the succession. The thought of it had been always in the back of his mind. He'd thrust it away from him, not wanting to deal with a woman and reasoning, always, that there was time.

There still was time. Unless he fell in the next battle, or the one after that. He'd been so focused on conquest, he'd neglected the fact that securing the succession had a part in it.

He grunted to himself as he left the training field, hesitating over whether to join the rest of the men in the warriors' hall. He'd rather be alone.

He'd rather be with Saerla MacBeith.

"Chief? When d'ye expect the messenger to return?" Murgor stopped him with a hand on his arm.

Rory met his war chief's worried gaze and shook his head slowly. Why pretend confidence he did not feel? He had stated clearly in his letter that if Moira did not return his man and cede all her lands to him, Saerla's life would be forfeit.

The way he saw it, even with Farlan talking in Moira's ear, insisting Rory would not actually kill a defenseless woman, she could make but one answer. She, like her sisters, considered him a monster. Could she take a chance that he would not act upon his words?

How long a reply might take, he could not tell. According to Leith, she would have to convince this council. And Alasdair, if he still survived.

"I ha' given her ten days," he told Murgor tensely.

"And after that, chief?"

"After that, we attack."

"Aye, so." Murgor's gaze moved over him slowly. "And that wound o' yourn—will ye be fit to fight?"

Rory straightened indignantly. "Did ye no' just see me on the training field?"

"Aye, chief, I did." Murgor's gaze did not waver. "'Tis why I ask. Master Leith's arm does no' yet serve—"

"I will be ready to lead the men when the time comes."

"Chief—"

"I will be ready."

"Aye, so." Murgor did not appear convinced.

Rory tossed his head. "I will be in my study betimes."

He marched off, aware that he'd just added outrage to the morass of emotions inside him. How dared Murgor imply he was not fit? He could disregard the pain. He could disregard everything besides his goal.

At his study, he called for hot water and, when it came, barred the door, stripped down to his skin, and washed away the sweat and grime, wishing he could shed his aggravation with it.

"Nearly there," he growled under his breath. He almost had all he wanted in his hands. What he should do was dress himself in clean clothing, go out, and pay a call on Mistress Ratha. She was his best choice, after all. He could deal honestly with her. Tell her plainly what he was about. She was a practical, sensible woman. She'd loved Dairmid and would not insist on a love match in remarriage.

If he explained to her that he needed sons—sturdy ones like she'd borne Dairmid—surely she would understand. For him, it would be a duty like any other he owed MacLeod. For her and Dairmid's wee sons, it would provide security.

Evening dimmed the sky when he finished his ablutions. He dressed himself in clean clothing, dragged a comb through his hair, and tied it back. Strictly disciplined his emotions.

Or thought that he did.

Ratha still lived in the small hut she'd shared with Dairmid. Rory had directed his feet there before they stopped suddenly of their own accord. He stood where he was, gazing out over the glen.

The sun sank in the west through a bank of cloud that looked like mist. It looked like the mist in Saerla MacBeith's blue eyes.

Rain by morning. He knew the signs. He had lived here all his life and loved this place with every part of him, to the bone. He lived for MacLeod.

What, then, did these emotions inside him mean? The longing, the desire that poured through his blood?

He wanted to go to Ratha, aye, and see to his duty. He would, anon.

His feet took over then, moving in accordance with the longing in his heart. They turned him around and back inexorably to his chamber, where he dismissed the guard with a jerk of his head.

He raised his hand to knock and called instead, "Mistress MacBeith, I desire—I desire to come in."

As soon as Saerla heard Rory's voice outside the door, her heart began to pound. She'd been seated at the window catching the last of the light. Rhian had brought her a spindle and wool—something, so she said, to keep Saerla's fingers busy and her mind sane.

Such work might well keep Rhian sane, but Saerla fumbled the task over and over again.

Now she leaped to her feet, and the mess of wool slid from her lap. The spindle hit the floor with a bright clatter.

Her fingers flew to the pocket of her skirt and tested the weight of the knife there. Fate had given her another chance.

This time, she could not fail.

"Come in."

Her voice did not sound like her own. And what a foolishness that she should give him permission, that he should ask for it. This was his chamber, his stronghold. His land. She lay in his power. All she had was the tiny sgian dubh in her shoe and the knife in her pocket. Those, and her intentions.

The door opened to admit Rory, large and dark and lethal. He did not look at her, not at once. Instead, he placed the bar on the inside of the door and stood for a moment staring at the panel as if warring with himself.

After she killed him, she could lift that bar—it would make no barrier—and escape.

She had only to kill him.

He turned. He faced her with heavy emotions in his eyes.

Saerla did not expect to see those emotions. Rory MacLeod was composed for the most part. His feelings did not escape him. Except for that passion last time.

He lifted his eyes and regarded her. His gaze touched her hair, her shoulders, the bodice of her gown. Her hands.

Och, what if he'd come back for more of what he'd had before? What if he expected kisses and for her to open her bodice to him?

Then she would. Because she needed to seduce this man. And

leave him lying in his own blood.

"Mistress Saerla. I came…I came to inform ye of where ye stand. I ha' sent another letter, this day, to MacBeith. To yer sister."

"Ah." So was it that had brought him here to her, and not desire? She did not believe it, because she could see the desire bright in the green eyes that regarded her so intently from between black lashes.

"I ha' given her ten days to respond. If she does no' cede all MacBeith lands to me by then, I ha' told her your life will be forfeit."

Saerla began to tremble. A monster, aye, and so he was. How could she have imagined differently?

She lifted her chin. "I am glad ye ha' told me."

"Are ye?" His gaze did not waver from her, and the breath came more quickly, lifting his chest.

"Aye. 'Tis best, is it no', to be prepared for such an eventuality? To ken fine how much longer I ha' to live. So I can make my peace wi' the spirits and call upon my ancestors to welcome me."

"Ye do no' believe, then, your sister will do as she must to save your life?"

"I do no'. She canna. But if ye harm me, Chief MacLeod, ye will ha' an unholy war on your hands."

"Aye. I ken."

"'Tis one ye just may lose. Moira will avenge me. As will Alasdair." For an instant, she longed for the both of them so strongly she could not breathe.

Moira was a warrior, Alasdair, the ultimate warrior. She had once fought alongside them. Now she must battle here, instead.

In the only way she could.

Chapter Twenty-Nine

RORY HAD BEEN harsh—overly harsh, maybe. He'd told Saerla straight out that she would die if her sister refused to deal with him. He'd done that in an effort to quell the emotions that rose inside him at the sight of her.

Emotions he did not know how else to master. If he was harsh with her, he could be doubly so with himself.

He'd needed an excuse to see her, even this excuse. Now that he stood here, he felt himself coming apart inside. All his resolution, his anger, his frustration—it evaporated at the sight of her standing there facing him so bravely, fragile and yet strong.

He wanted so desperately to touch her that it made him start to shake. He wanted to protect her from all harm. Even while he threatened to end her life.

Such a mixture of courage and femininity was Saerla Mac-Beith. For he could see the fear in her eyes. And the determination. Both swirled there together in a haze that hinted of enchantment.

But he did not believe enchantment, in magic, did he? He'd sneered at Leith over that.

He took a step farther into the room. "I thought…ye might tak' a part in yer own salvation. Send yer sister a letter o' yer own pleading for your life." How could Moira refuse such a plea? Even the council could not. "Can ye read and write? If no', ye might speak the words to me and I will write them down."

Her chin jerked up still farther. "Ye expect me to plead? To beg? I will no'."

Rory had a sudden vision of her lying beneath him on the bed. Naked. Those misty eyes wide with desire. Begging him. Begging for him inside her.

He wanted to hear her plead. For him.

"Why should Moira believe any words that come fo' me in your hand? Why should I believe ye would write what I say, for all that?"

Aye, for she thought him a monster. A brute. A tyrant.

He could not ask her to trust him. Not after he'd told her that her life hung in the balance.

A lie. For he could not—ever—harm one hair of her.

It was an empty threat. But he could not confess that either.

"Mistress Saerla—my attainment of MacBeith lands is inevitable. Control o' all Glen Bronach will come to me."

"Says who? You? My ancestors were here already when yours arrived. They lived but lightly on the land. Took care always to honor what they found up on the rise. Sought always to preserve what is there."

"Wha' is there?"

"Magic. Aye, ye might well scoff at it. Ye being what ye are."

"A monster."

"A MacLeod. The breed that came to this land wi' swords and devastation on their minds, seeking to conquer and destroy all that lay here. Ye do that yet."

Despite her hard words, he took another step toward her, unable to prevent it. By God, he could feel the magic inside her. It drew him like nothing he'd ever known.

"Let us deal together, ye and me."

"Deal together?" She lifted her brows. "How? I am your prisoner."

"Ye be but an honored guest."

"One ye mean to slaughter if my sister does no' meet your

demands. Rory MacLeod, d'ye take me for a fool?"

"Nay. Let us sit down together, ye and me. You explain it to me—what is up on that rise. I will mak' a promise to ye to preserve it. When I seize MacBeith lands, I will leave the stones up there be. Nae harm will come to them."

"Stones. And graves. There were graves there long before my ancestors arrived. And my own folk are buried there as well."

"Nay harm shall touch that place. Or ye. I vow it to ye." What was happening to him? In her presence he could scarcely think aright. He wanted to touch her, defend her. He wanted to kneel at her feet.

By God, if there existed some enchantment up on the rise, if she perhaps kept a part of that within her, it must be a powerful magic indeed.

Her chin jerked farther upward. Her eyes glowed like the mist that rose from the loch of a morning. Cool. Soft. Mystical.

"That," she said softly, "is a bargain I may be willing to make."

THEY SAT TOGETHER on the bench that faced the fire, half facing one another, their knees a short distance apart. Saerla kept her hands twisted in her skirt, the right one tucked into the pocket that held the knife. She had only to await the moment when he seemed distracted. Incautious. He was much stronger than her, true. But as she'd learned on the battlefield, she was much quicker than her opponents and carried a kind of blessed protection that kept her mostly unscathed.

As it was, fear quelled the breath in her lungs. She fought that fear back. She must remain focused. She could, aye, end it all now.

"Tell me," he said, "o' this magic."

She weighed him silently. Did he play with her? Did he scoff?

Knowing she believed, did he seek to use that belief against her?

The green eyes appeared guarded, but she glimpsed the stirred emotions there all the same. A certain wildness. Precious little scorn.

"'Tis ancient. As I say, 'twas there long before my ancestors found this glen. As were the stones. This is—and always was—a gey special place."

"Aye."

Even a brute like him must be able to sense that. No doubt it had a part in making him desire ownership of the glen, even if he did not realize as much. Those who did not understand magic sought to control it.

"Glen Bronach," she told him, "is sacred ground, and that up on the rise doubly so. Blood should no' be spilled upon it, though far too much has been."

"Why then, Mistress Saerla, d'ye tak' the field wi' a sword in yer hand?"

"Something so precious maun be defended. Protected. I would give my life to do that." She added softly, "I will."

Something moved in the wild green eyes, a shadow stirring in the vibrant, dangerous depths. "This magic—d'ye own it or does it own ye, mistress?"

A curious question, and one that surprised her. "No one can own magic, Chief MacLeod. No more than one can own the light that floods through the glen at sunrise." Would he, could he, understand? "'Tis there and yet 'tis no'. Ye can feel it, but ye canna capture it in your hand."

"And it visits ye, does it? This—this light. The magic. It blesses ye."

If it did, would she be here, captive? Aye, maybe so. Because this was her chance. Just as when she stepped on to the battlefield, she could fight the darkness for the sake of the light. Here and now.

Her fingers caressed the hilt of the knife in her pocket—Leith's knife. As it had been foretold. She had Seen herself in this man's arms.

Terrifying as that Vision had been, she must make it manifest. This very night.

She leaned toward him. "The spirits tell us, Chief MacLeod, that all is a battle, a contest between the dark and the light. Much ugliness exists in our world." She eyed him for a moment. *Including you.* "And much beauty. I will do aught I can to preserve the beauty existent up on that rise."

"Anything?" His hand came up—one large, scarred hand—and cupped her cheek. He touched her but lightly, the whisper of skin on skin, yet the effect pierced Saerla like the kiss of lightning. For an instant her vision wavered. She Saw…

The two of them twined together, naked in the bed that lay just behind her. Moving, moving in complete and total accordance, she giving, he taking, flesh upon flesh. A consuming fire in green eyes.

Her blade at his throat.

"Saerla." He leaned forward and whispered the word just an instant before he took her lips. "Show me. Illuminate my darkness wi' yer light."

Chapter Thirty

FIRE, SAERLA THOUGHT, her stunned senses struggling to fight through the enveloping heat of that kiss. Fire brought light. Fire *was* light. Even the ancients knew that. Yet unleashed, it could also bring destruction and consume everything in its path.

The fire Rory MacLeod brought to her now was like that. Because it called up an answering flame inside her, one she was not sure she could control.

As he had before when he'd touched her, Rory did so gently, his lips questing on hers, soft and supple. It did not matter, because the passion had a life of its own. It came. It manifested. It left her defenses devastated.

She never knew whether he moved toward her or she slid across the bench to him. It did not matter, for she came up against the hard wall of his chest and the flames broke around the both of them. No escape from it.

No hope of escape.

"Saerla." He spoke her name into her mouth, which had opened for him. No preventing that either. She could not possibly deny him entrance, because in a curious way, he was the light. Even though he was the darkness.

This time she remembered the knife in her pocket. Indeed, her fingers remained curled around the hilt till she withdrew them, worked her arms around his neck, and dug the fingers into the black silk of his hair.

Saerla. *Saerla*. This time she heard her name only in her mind. Her spirit rose and expanded when he called to her. Threw its arms wide to him.

The light—brought in the fire—united them. It flowed from his mouth to hers and back again. They kissed while he held her ever more surely. While he threaded his fingers through her hair. Until he broke off, gasping.

"Saerla." Burning green eyes stared into hers. No demand in them. This had gone far past the point of demand.

He slid from the bench onto his knees and caught both her hands in her lap. "I maun have ye. Please."

He pleaded. For what only she could give. What she could not withhold.

"Aye."

He lifted her from the bench and carried her to the bed behind them. He did it carefully, effortlessly, as if she weighed nothing. Setting her just as carefully on the counterpane, he gazed at her before he reached for the ties at the front of her gown.

Those hands. Those hands.

Some mad part of her remembered the knife then. She would need the knife before this was done. She needed to retain her clothing, then.

She had to have him first. The light inside her must consume the darkness. Yet…the darkness would not remain defeated. It never did.

"Wait," she told him, and stripped off her own gown while he watched with an avid gaze. She bundled the garment beside the bed with the slit of the pocket uppermost. Her chemise followed, and she—who had never been naked before any man—barely noticed for the heat of it.

With his gaze still upon her, he stripped off. She'd already seen the muscled torso, the brawny shoulders, and the terrible wound he bore. The rest of him, equally formidable, should have terrified her. But she could not look away.

She'd been taken before by the magic, possessed by a Vision. Would this be like that? Irresistible. Transformative. Glorious.

She made a sound in her throat, and in response he came down onto the bed.

"Saerla. Lass. Let me worship ye."

Had those words truly come from him? The brute who knew only conquest and demand? Who knew naught of mercy?

She reached for him, wove her fingers into his hair, and brought him to her breast. Lost even before his mouth closed upon her, her soul launched.

And flew.

It was impulse that took hold of her and moved her beyond herself in that flight. Flame, and the taste of him, aye, still on her tongue after those kisses, and the scent of him all moved with her, even as the air streamed past her wings.

His lips felt hot when they left her breast and traveled over her skin. Worshiping, just as he'd promised. Everywhere. At the pulse that leaped in her neck and down both arms in turn. Kisses pressed into the palms of her hands. Onto her knees. Up onto her thighs. His large, scarred hands parted them ever so gently, and he kissed her between.

Unthinkable. Unimaginable. An act she should not permit. One, just the same, she had not the power to refuse.

He laid his mouth upon her, slid his tongue inside her, and the fire leaped up so fierce and bright that she clutched his hair and threw herself wide to him. The pleasure hit, convulsed her. A wild vortex it was of yearning, rippling sensation that lifted her high. She lay there open for him. She let him in as she had no one else ever, save the light.

When he removed his mouth, slid up her body, and returned his lips to hers, she welcomed it, unable to give enough of herself to him. Even as his tongue entered her mouth, he pierced her below, causing only a pinch of pain, almost lost in the rise of the flames once again.

They rode the glory of those flames, the two of them together, not two bodies but one.

The fire died but slowly, with small bursts of light like tiny explosions against the inside of Saerla's eyelids. She came to herself with equal slowness, only then realizing in full what she had done.

Let the conqueror inside. The man she needed to defeat at all cost.

He lay half atop her, his weight pressing her into the counterpane, and his warm breath against her neck. When the last of the sparks faded and she opened her eyes, she had a close-up view of him. So close. Close enough that he might be still inside her.

Eyes closed. Thick black lashes on cheeks bronzed by days spent on the training field. He was a warrior, this man, to the bone. Except with her. With her he was…

She did not have words for what he was. Gentle. Yearning.

He opened his eyes. The intensity of his gaze pierced her once again, started up the heat.

Nay. And nay. She needed to end this. Finish it. Complete what had begun in the Vision.

"Saerla."

His hair had come loose from its tie during the madness that possessed them and fell like silk against a cheek rough with stubble. He reached for her. "Bonny lass."

He wanted her again. He did not have to tell her that. She could feel it in the heat of him pressed against her and the flames leaping up through her own flesh. Something in her responded to something in him, and likely always would.

It did not matter, for now—this moment—presented her with her best chance. While he reached for her lips with his lips. While he thought only of stoking those fires and mating with her again. Flying, flying on the strength of the light.

She could not let herself fail. Much as she wanted to wind her arms around his neck, to give herself to him again, she reached over the side of the bed instead.

Her fingers tangled in soft wool. The fabric of her gown. They could not find the opening. The pocket where lay the knife.

Rory lifted his lips from hers and half propped himself on one forearm, gazing into her face. The green eyes between those spiked lashes had gone soft with mist. In that instant, she caught no hint of darkness.

"Saerla."

Her entire body desired him. Without her permission, her lips parted. Her legs spread wide, offering him admittance. Her fingers, on their deadly mission, froze.

He kissed her. His lips asked a question even as his tongue slipped inside and his body slid into position between her thighs, ready to enter her. Every part of her wanted him inside her, even as her fingers returned to life, dug through the fabric, and located the hilt of the knife.

He lay upon her, poised to enter her, his mouth fixed to hers. As vulnerable as this man would ever be.

Saerla drew the knife from the fabric and brought the point of it up, up over the side of the bed and directly to the pulse that beat at the side of Rory MacLeod's neck.

Chapter Thirty-One

I**T TOOK A** moment, the span of perhaps twenty heartbeats, for Rory to register the prick of cold at the side of his neck. He thought only of kissing Saerla. Of the sweetness of her mouth and the heat of her below. He wanted to be inside her so intensely, nothing else existed. He wanted only to fly with her, fly and fly on the wings of light.

She was of the earth, of the ground and the rock that made up this glen he loved, and yet she was not. She was of the air. The light.

She could make him believe in magic.

He had only to slide into her again, her sheath made for him where he had always, always needed to be.

Then she went still beneath him. Utterly still.

He stilled also and stopped breathing, because at that instant her breath supplied his own. Through the fog of rapture came a sharp point of pain.

"Do no' move."

She spoke into his mouth, so close were they to one another. She had no need to tell him. He could not move, seized by disbelief.

Her eyes stared hard into his. Wide, blue, no longer filled with mist, they looked sharp enough to glitter. The eyes of a warrior. On the battlefield.

"I am sorry," she whispered. "I am sorry."

The sensation of a blade entering his flesh cut through all the others and brought him to life. His reactions had always been quick, and now served to save his life. He jerked away with a grunt. Felt the hot blood start at the side of his neck.

Saerla skittered away from him, slid off the bed with the knife still clutched in her hand. He blinked at her in dawning horror and clapped a hand to his neck. It came away wet with blood. She had attacked him.

Nicked him only.

Another moment, a tiny bit more pressure, she would have ended his life.

That truth crashed upon him even as he continued to stare at her standing there naked at the side of the bed. The place where they'd just made love. Where another splash of blood among the tangled sheets proved she'd been untouched before he took her.

His. *His*.

She'd tried to kill him. Och, God! Och, God, och—

"Gi' me the knife." His voice did not sound like his own. A stranger inhabited his body. Another stranger looked at him from Saerla's eyes.

She shook her head. That glorious red-gold hair of hers tumbled across her shoulders. Covered her breasts.

Breasts he could still taste. Och, God! But there was no God. There could not be if the most beautiful thing he'd ever known, ever held in his hands, someone in whom he'd almost, almost believed could betray him so.

"Come," he told her. "Ye ha' made yer bid. Tried to kill me." The words tasted bitter on his tongue, which had so recently known wild pleasure. "And failed. Ye canna get away."

She shook her head again, the knife still outstretched toward him. As if she would fend him off. He, who had already been inside her.

"Be reasonable," he said, as if she had not heard him the first time, "Ye canna get away."

"Let me go."

"I canna do that. I canna let ye go." Among the truest words he'd ever spoken. Even now that he knew—knew that what she'd offered him had been false. A ploy. A means to get near enough to hurt him, for, och, aye, he saw that quite clearly. He did not feel anger, not yet. The other pain flared too bright to let him feel anything else.

"So." Tears began to trickle down her face. "Ye will kill me now."

He could not do that either. Kill her. Harm her in any way. He'd as soon lay waste to this glen he loved.

He moved swiftly, leaped across the bed, and seized her. A slash from her knife slit his arm. Aye, she was quick. He wrapped his arms around her, even then responding to the feel of her naked flesh. He quelled her, still without anger or the desire to cause hurt, and breathed into her ear, "Drop the knife."

She refused, and they struggled, Rory striving mightily to keep from harming her all the while.

The knife made no sound as it fell onto the pile of wool that was her gown.

"Where did ye get it? Where did ye get the knife?"

She made no answer. She'd gone perfectly still in his arms.

"From Rhian?" He hoped it was her sister and not Leith. He wanted very badly to be able to trust Leith.

Could he trust no one? No one for whom he'd ever cared during his life?

He lifted Saerla with ease—she was but half his size—and turned her in his hands to face him. Glared into her face. The anger had begun to seep into him now, burning its way through the icy pain.

"Who ga' ye the knife? Was it Leith?"

"Nay."

It must have been her sister, then. She'd had contact with no one else.

"Ye will no' see yer sister again. Ye ha' earned yoursel' confinement." If she thought him a monster, he would live up to it. She could be shut into a cell in the depths of the stronghold like any common prisoner. Away from everyone.

Including him.

He let go of her, then bent and snagged the knife, which he turned between his fingers. Backing off farther, he stalked around the bed to his own clothing.

The wound at the side of his neck still trickled blood—he could feel the path it made running down. Trickled, not gushed. He would be dead by now had she succeeded in her intention. Her plan for his death.

Leith would have become chief. And his son after him, if Rory could believe Leith's story. The child who bore half MacBeith blood.

He backed off yet another step, never taking his eyes from the woman who continued to stand facing him. He gathered his clothing, making sure of the weapons he always carried as a matter of course.

He felt for the bar on the door, lifted it by touch, and hauled open the panel. Tossed his clothing out into the corridor ahead of him.

Still she had not moved. She stood with tears on her cheeks, her hair a wild tangle. Grief filled her eyes.

Swiftly, swiftly now, he stepped out after his clothing. Shut the door and replaced the bar.

He stung as if he'd been thrashed from head to foot. His neck, his arm. The hole in his back. His heart.

Alone in the hallway, naked as he was, he leaned against the wall. The cold from the stone seeped into him but failed to quench the flames of anger that had begun to roar through him.

Magic? Had he truly begun to warrant its existence for a few short moments in her arms? She was a witch, and he was a fool.

With no one there to see him, he hastily dressed and took himself away. From the chamber that had once been his. From the lie that was the light.

INSIDE THE CHAMBER, Saerla crumpled to her knees. She went down atop the soft fabric of her gown, where she huddled, naked, shaking.

She had made her bid, aye. She had failed. *Failed*. Now he knew—knew she wanted him dead.

Did she?

His hands moving over her. The gentleness as his fingers found the secret place she kept for herself alone. The fire and splendor of it when he'd entered her still gently, and freed her from all earthly bonds, setting her in flight.

They had flown together.

He'd been vulnerable. As vulnerable as this dangerous man would ever be. She'd taken her chance, but the powers had not been with her.

They had been with him.

That hurt almost more than the rest of it and felt impossible to accept. She had given up her virginity to a monster. Found a foreign, savage joy in it. A part of herself she never knew existed. She'd offered herself up in order to save her clan. Magic should have assured her success.

The magic had sided with Rory MacLeod.

What, then, had the Vision meant? Was she not intended to be the catalyst to end this war, and preserve what she loved? Save all the light and beauty that dwelt up on the rise?

Aching, all her tears dried, she knelt and refused to rise.

Chapter Thirty-Two

RORY DID NOT intrude upon Leith and his woman in their chamber the next morning. He preferred to speak with his cousin alone, and anyway, he did not wish to gaze upon Rhian if he could help it.

He had not slept after he left Saerla. It seemed an impossibility. Instead, he'd called for a guard to station at her door and then paced until dawn. The battlements. The forecourt. The grounds beyond.

At dawn, when dark began to leave the sky, he at last went to his study, where he swabbed away the dried blood on his neck and looked at the wound in the scrap of mirror he used for shaving.

Another inch—another half inch, he decided. Another flick of the blade and she would have had his life.

And what would she have done then? What, after his life's blood pumped out all over her where she lay? Would she have fled? Taken refuge with her sister? Aye, for surely they had schemed together in this.

Only Rhian could have given her the knife. Saerla had denied it, and he refused to believe his cousin would have done such a deed.

In the early light flooding the windows of his study, he changed his clothing, making certain his jerkin and his hair covered the wound. He felt hot and cold by turns—anger alternating with a far more dangerous and hurtful emotion.

Half his anger centered on himself. He should have known she would betray him if she had the chance. She was the enemy. How could he have imagined differently?

Bitterly he thought about it. This, *this* was why he never dealt with women. Last night, out of desire, he'd stepped onto unknown ground. Desire, quite clearly, was a weakness he could not afford.

Better to get a son, or a crop of them, with some woman with whom he was honest. Ratha, quite likely. Best to tell her from the outset there would be no emotional ties. No love.

He returned to the training field and, when the men showed up, worked them hard. He worked himself harder, and if they looked at him from the corners of their eyes, they made no protest. Likely they supposed he prepared for the battles to come. If Moira MacBeith did not cede him the glen.

They had nine days. Nine days were all Saerla had left before he made good on his threats.

Could he kill her? He'd been certain he could not harm one glorious hair on her head. Now…

He became aware that Leith, who numbered among the men at training stood beside him, eyeing him dubiously.

Rory swung around and glared back at his cousin with renewed ire. Had Leith known? Would he betray Rory to such a degree?

"Get back to work," Rory told him, "if ye ha' the backbone for it."

Leith flexed the fingers of his right hand. He'd been working hard and could now hold a sword, though without much authority. Doing so caused him pain. Rory did not, at the moment, feel sympathetic.

"Ye be in a vile mood this morning, cousin." Leith's blue-gray eyes watched him carefully. "D'ye mean to work us till we drop?"

Rory sneered. "Will ye behave like men and no' wains? We ha' no long before we will be at war in earnest. I wish to end it then." He would deal no more with MacBeith. With mercy.

"I thought, perhaps"—Leith lowered his voice to a rumble—"ye were upset about the child."

The child, the heir with which Leith's treacherous woman would supposedly present him. Rory tossed his head and said savagely, "I care naught for the MacBeith brat. It may no' survive by any road. Many bairns do no'."

Leith's eyes widened, and he took a step backward. "Is this what it has come to, cousin? That ye wish my child ill?" Ire bloomed in his eyes. "Mayhap I should tak' Rhian and go."

"To MacBeith? So ye might harbor the heir to MacLeod there? Aye, and would ye turn yer coat like Farlan?" Rory had no one he could trust. No one.

He rarely saw Leith suffused with rage. It happened seldom, but it happened now. He drew himself up and regarded Rory as he might a stranger. "At least there at MacBeith we might feel welcome."

"Aye, they will tak' ye in with open arms, these fine, upstanding MacBeith clansmen, who want ye dead."

"As do ye, cousin?"

"I do no' want ye dead." Rory wanted Leith back. His loyalty, his laughter, the times that used to be when they fought and ran and played together. When loyalty was not a gnarled tangle, and he knew without doubt who cared for him.

"Only my son?" Leith threw the words at him and began to turn away. Rory snagged his arm.

"One thing before ye go," he snarled. "That woman o' yours, Rhian, will no' see her sister again."

"Eh? Why no'?"

Because they scheme together. They scheme against me. Rory did not say that. Leith might not know that Saerla planned to kill him. The scheme might have been hatched between the two women.

He hoped so.

"Saerla MacBeith is a prisoner. She has forfeited any and all privileges."

Leith's eyes narrowed. "Rhian is tending her. That wound on her head—"

"No more. The prisoner shall have no visitors."

"Rhian—Rhian will no' like it."

Rory spat, "I do no' care what Rhian likes."

"Wha' has happened? Rory?"

"Ask yer woman."

"I am asking ye, cousin."

"I went to see the prisoner last evening, to tell her that her fate and her life lay in her sister Moira's hands. When I did, she drew a weapon on me."

"A weapon!"

"Aye." Rory bared his teeth. "She could have come by it only one way. Talk to yer bitch o' a woman."

He stalked away before Leith could reply, or strike him for the slur. But not before he saw the desire to do so in his cousin's eyes.

⇢⟫⟩⟨⟪⟵

SAERLA DID NOT weep once Rory left the chamber. Not after those first few tears, the ones she barely knew she shed. For many long minutes she huddled there on the floor and listened to her body, what it told her clearly.

She was no longer a maid. She had given that to him. She had done so not out of an attempt to render him vulnerable, out of obligation, or by force. If she were honest with herself, she must admit that.

She had wanted him. There, for those moments lying beneath him, receiving his touch, kissing him, tasting him, feeling his heartbeat, she'd wanted exactly what they had shared.

Now he'd been inside her—inside her where no one else had been—and it had not hurt, no. All the hurt had come after.

Despite that, despite the unexpected gentleness of his touch and the way he'd made her feel, she was wounded to the heart. As if the blade of the knife she turned on him had sunk deep into her own breast.

What would he do? He'd been angry. *Angry.* He was a dangerous man at the best of times, and such anger could push him to any number of terrible deeds. He might move to attack MacBeith straight away. He might haul her out of this chamber and slaughter her in retaliation.

After a long time, when her legs grew cramped and the cold air from the window crept into her bones, she got up and crawled back into her gown. She felt better dressed but still vulnerable. Going to the basin, she tried to take stock of herself.

Hair in a tangle. His fingers had been there. Stroking. Burrowing. Lips swollen. He had crushed them beneath his. He had sucked on them one after the other. Body tingling in places previously untouched. She could still feel him inside her. The thrill and the splendor of it, his strength becoming hers as he became hers. Light and darkness coming together in something so powerful it defied description.

He would never touch her so again. Not even if she wanted him to. But she'd known that. Known it the instant she put the blade to his skin.

She crossed to the window and gazed out, unseeing. Ever since she'd been small, six or so, she'd lived in the company of Visions. Dreams. Visitations. She'd learned to accept their manifestation, glean the wisdom they brought. Follow where they led.

Now that wisdom had betrayed her, she'd acted in belief. Perhaps even against her instincts.

Because at that moment—at the moment when Rory Mac-Leod lay in her arms, closer to her than anyone had ever been— she had not wanted to kill him.

What if she'd had it all wrong? What if Rory wasn't meant to die at her hand?

What if the light, her constant companion, had deserted her?

Chapter Thirty-Three

NO ONE CAME near Saerla's prison that morning. She had hoped—prayed—Rhian might arrive. She'd debated what she might say to her sister, who was so wise.

Would she confess all? Throw herself upon Rhian and confide that her body no longer felt completely her own? That, having shared it with Rory, she could still feel his touch? That—worst of all—she longed for him to touch her again?

But Rhian did not come. No one did for the longest time. Saerla paced the chamber from the door to the window and back again, and struggled to think.

He had taken the knife. She still had the wee sgian dubh, not that—not that she could ever attempt anything like what she had done, ever again.

Around noon, so she figured, a rattle at the door heralded the arrival of a guard carrying a meal on a wooden tray. He departed before Saerla could finish saying, "I wish to see my sister. The healer—"

Her only answer came in the form of the barred door.

She did not want to eat. She felt far too ill. She returned to her pacing and her questioning until the light began to fade, and, exhausted, she took to the bed.

Not a good idea. When she curled up tight with her arms wrapped around her body and her cheek against the bolster, she could smell him.

His black head with the hair like silk had touched just here. His forearm here beside her when he'd looked down at her, green eyes gleaming, just before he breached her. Entered her. Asking. Asking a question.

Please.

Which of them had uttered that word? Her need had been just as bright as his.

It had not been her heart that tripped her up so much as her desire. She had not counted on that, had not expected it. She'd thought herself far more a Seer than a woman.

Rory MacLeod had proven her a woman after all.

Perhaps, she thought lying with her cheek on the bolster and breathing in the scent of him, he brought out the woman in her precisely because he was so much a man.

A beautiful man. Because he was—*he was*. The sharp angles of his face. The sculpted expanse of muscled chest. The broad, lithe shoulders. Those rough, calloused hands that were so gentle with her. The strong column of his throat—

The bright trickle of blood.

Now he would hate her with a fervor unrivaled. Rory Mac-Leod did not forgive. He had cast off his closest friend, Farlan, shunned and humiliated him for a breach in loyalty.

He would desire vengeance against her, and no doubt planned even now the best way to get it.

She knew the best way—harm someone she loved. And Rhian was here in his power.

Leith would never let Rory harm Rhian. Would he? Not if he could prevent it.

How could she have forgotten she risked not only her own safety but Rhian's?

She fretted over it a while longer until she lost her battle with exhaustion and fell asleep.

And dreamed.

In the dream, she once more saw the three lads, the one with hair like flax, the one with a head of rich brown, the other black. They ran out on the green sward like wild things, ignoring the calls that came from the distant stronghold. Leaping and tussling together as wolf cubs might, they appeared completely in tune with each other and the glen. The loch stretched behind them, and the glen dozed in a summer haze.

They laughed. They hollered. They brandished their swords, either borrowed or stolen from the armory, and played at being warriors.

Until the boy with the hair that gleamed like the feathers of a blackbird turned and faced the other two.

"Come on, then. Which o' ye wants to challenge me?" He raised the tip of his sword. "See if ye can tak' me down."

The other two boys exchanged glances. Suddenly all the fun had flown as their companion's mood changed.

"Nay, Rory," called the fair-haired lad. Leith. "Ye always best us."

"And will"—Rory tossed his head—"until ye learn to fight back. 'Tis as Master Murgor says—a man does no' ken wha' he can do till he has a sword in his hand."

Farlan spoke up. "And yer father, Chief Camraith, says we are no' to fight each other again. No' after the last time."

"He is no' here, is he?"

The lads peered around. No one was there save the three of them—and Saerla, who watched silently.

Rory's green eyes gleamed wickedly. "Are ye afeared, Farlan?"

Farlan said nothing. He did not raise the sword in his hand.

"If ye be afeared now, what when we are grown and tak' the field in earnest, to win all Glen Bronach?"

"That is a long way off," Leith cried.

"'Tis no'. 'Twill be here in the blink o' an eye, and we will be men." He took a step toward Farlan. "Face me!"

"I do no'—"

"Face me! First to knock the other down is the victor."

He did not wait for Farlan to agree or otherwise. Instead, he came in for the attack.

Clearly startled and on the defensive, Farlan raised his sword and fought back.

No coward, Farlan MacLeod. Saerla had seen him face rampant hostility with quiet strength. Rory's ferocity, though, drove him back. Nearly of a height, the two lads contested while Farlan lost ground step by step.

Until a vicious strike from the black-haired lad's sword got under the brown-haired lad's guard and laid open the skin of his arm.

Leith cried out then. "Stop. Stop, cousin!"

But Rory did not stop. Rather, the ferocity of his blows increased until he took his friend down into the grass.

"Stop!" Leith threw himself between the two of them. "Rory, for God's sake!"

Both lads breathed hard. Rory's chest rose and fell violently. His eyes had cooled to green ice.

"Ye will ne'er make a warrior, Farlan MacLeod, lest ye stop being afeared."

The dream fled like wisps of mist, driven by a chill wind. Saerla awoke to find herself still in the bed, exactly where she'd been.

She remained there with her eyes wide, wondering. Which? Which was the true Rory MacLeod? The man who had made love to her so sweetly, or the lad who refused to show mercy even to his best friend?

Morning came gray with rain that matched Saerla's mood. Yesterday's meal sat untouched on the table where the guard had set it. She felt far too sick to eat. No other food or water was brought.

Around noon she caught voices, the sound of an argument outside the door. Someone demanding to be let in.

Her sister, Rhian. Struggling against the guard.

"Nay, mistress. I ha' orders. I canna let ye in."

Rhian threw herself at the door. "Saerla? Love, are ye hurt or harmed?"

Saerla was both hurt and harmed. She ached for the refuge of her sister's arms but could not let Rhian risk herself.

"I am well enough. Please, Rhian, go."

"Wha' has he done to ye?"

"Naught." She'd done this to herself.

"I will no' rest till he lets me in."

But Rhian left. With a hearty curse for the hapless guard, she did. Saerla caught the sound of her footsteps fading away.

She wanted to weep then. She wanted to sob, but would not let herself. She must be strong like her sisters. She must make Da—and Alasdair—proud.

She must harbor what magic she could, because therein lay her strength. But it seemed most of the magic had fled her.

If the powers wanted her here—and it seemed they must—then they had to restore that magic to her. The magic, the light. Her strength.

She sat beside the window where so little radiance could be found and imagined herself on the rise at the far side of the glen. Among the stones. Gathering the light.

Chapter Thirty-Four

MOIRA MACBEITH'S REPLY to Rory's letter arrived not long into the afternoon, brought by the party he had sent accompanied by the original messenger, whom Moira, the accursed council, or all of them together had seen fit to release.

He felt both glad and surprised to see Kevan among the other men and beyond anxious to get his hands on the letter. This could well be it. Surely Moira would concede. The fight would all be over and the glen would be his.

He could send Saerla home. Be rid of her once and for all.

"Wha' happened?" he demanded of the clearly exhausted band of men.

Bodach rolled his eyes. "Meetings. We were held wi'out harm while the bitch o' a chief made up her mind. And wrote yon letter." Rory already clutched the sheet of foolscap.

He glared at Kevan. "And ye? Did they hurt ye?"

Kevan shook his head. "Nay, chief. I was but penned up. Treated neither badly nor well. The worst o' it was no' kenning wha' was happening all the while."

Rory clapped the man's shoulder. "Go ye to yer quarters and rest. If ye ha' any information for me, come to me later wi' it."

Kevan snorted. "All I saw was the inside o' a cattle pen."

Bodach, who had led the returned party, narrowed his eyes. "They are preparing for war, chief. Mustering and strengthening their defenses. That much was plain to see."

"Aye, so." Rory's fingers contorted on the letter. He needed to read it at once.

He hurried to his study, a chamber he'd begun to detest, and found Leith waiting outside the door.

"Come awa' in." He gestured to his cousin. Leith wore a mutinous look on his face and no doubt wanted to petition for his woman to see Saerla.

Not yet.

Leith paced in a manner utterly unlike him while Rory unfolded and read the letter, which he saw, with a spike of ire, was once more written in Farlan's hand. The anxiety inside him cranked up a notch. Holding his breath, he began to read.

He got to the end, and read the whole of it again, then cursed bitterly, causing Leith to cease his infernal pacing and stare.

"Wha'? Rory, wha' does it say?"

Rory answered him in a growl. "Mistress—Chief—Moira tells me she canna accept my offer and cede her lands to me. No' even to ransom the life o' her sister. She says should Saerla's life be forfeit, I should prepare for war."

The chamber went so quiet, Rory figured neither of them so much as breathed. He certainly did not. The breath had frozen in his chest, unable to compete with his thundering heartbeat.

Refused. The damned woman had refused.

Och, and he could scarcely believe it. No warrior—not even one as fierce and undoubtedly twisted in her sensibilities as Moira MacBeith—could let a one of her blood, her sister, languish and die in the hands of her enemy.

Especially a woman such as Saerla. Fragile and strong. Gentle and fierce, earthy and otherworldly. Almost too precious for this realm to hold.

She had tried to kill him.

Now he would have to take her life.

He stared at the sheet of foolscap, no longer truly seeing the words written there, feeling only the pain inside. He ached. He did, from head to toe. All he contained seemed to be pain. The hole in his back. The prick at his neck. His heart...

His accursed heart.

At that moment, he hated the world and everything in it. He hated Farlan and he hated Moira MacBeith. He hated himself most of all.

Leith asked, "Rory? Wha' will ye do?"

Rory turned on him savagely. "Wha' the letter tells me to do, o' course. Moira MacBeith has made her choice. In return, I will tak' her sister's life."

"Ye will no'."

Only a day ago, Rory might have agreed with that. He'd believed he could not harm so much as one curl on the woman's head. Saerla, with her actions, had made it easy for him.

Perhaps that was fate come into play. Removing another obstacle. Proving all the glen should belong to him.

"Watch me."

"But Rory"—Leith appeared beyond stirred—"she is but a woman." He lowered his voice. "We do no' harm women."

Aye, so Rory's father had hammered into all of them. A man protected women. With his life, if necessary.

Especially, he thought again, a woman like Saerla.

Who had tried to kill him.

He snarled, "She is no' just a woman, is she? She's a prisoner. A warrior. Sister to their chief."

"Rhian says—Rhian says Saerla is touched by the gods. Special."

"She would say that, would she not?"

"Saerla walks only lightly in this world. She receives Visions—"

"All the more reason to eliminate her, lest she offer undue advantages to our enemies."

"Rhian—"

Viciously, Rory interrupted him. "I do no' care wha' Rhian says. Yer woman has ye wrapped around her finger. I will no' listen to ye."

Pure anger shone from Leith's eyes. "Then I will no' stay here. My woman and I will leave at once for MacBeith."

Pain tore through Rory once again, transmuting to the pure flame of anger. Would Leith turn on him also, as Farlan had done? He gritted his teeth, and his hand flew to the hilt of the sword he wore. "Try it. Ye be my heir. Ye will no' leave."

"Aye, so? I am a prisoner here now, am I? Mysel' and Rhian?"

"She may go anytime she chooses. As for ye, cousin, ye ha' made yer bed. But"—he lowered his voice to a growl—"if ye wish to protect yer woman as Da always said, ye will step carefully around me."

"D'ye threaten Rhian in order to coerce me? Big, strong man ye are! If ye harm Saerla, Rhian will go mad wi' grief. She will turn wild."

Rory gestured at the letter still spread on the table. "Moira MacBeith had only to agree wi' my terms. She had only to cede her lands, and Saerla would be goin' home today."

Away from him. Out of his life.

And good riddance.

A storm of agony looked at him from Leith's eyes. "Do wha' ye will, cousin. And turn on me as ye may. I will ha' no part in it. Slaughtering that brave wee thing—"

"So ye turn on me instead, d'ye? Just like Farlan."

"If I must."

"Ye swore fealty to my father, and to me. Ye and Farlan both did. If yer woman has stolen yer balls, 'tis no' my fault."

"Ye bastard!" Leith thundered.

And there it was. The breach that had no doubt begun to widen the first time Rhian MacBeith smiled at him. The first time she crooked a finger and took him to her breast.

Fool.

Aye, so, Leith had come back from MacBeith with his loyalty already fractured. Now the rift was wide.

"Get out o' my sight."

"Rory—"

"I said go."

Leith did not stir. "How will ye do it, Rory?" One corner of his mouth twitched in a bitter grimace. "How does a great man like yoursel' go about slaughtering a woman?"

"Slit her throat." Just as she would have done to him.

In a flash, one powerful flash, he was back in the bed—his bed—with Saerla lying beneath him. Safe and warm. Sheltered. *His.* And his heart, his heart was at peace as it had never been.

The feel of her. The taste. The heat that had convulsed and quivered around him, half stealing his soul.

The prick of cold metal at his neck.

Had she succeeded, had she pushed the blade home, his blood would have showered upon her, hot and vital.

Only right that his hands should be the ones to slit her throat and feel that heat.

"'Tis Moira MacBeith who has chosen her sister's fate," he told Leith. "And 'tis I that will make good on it."

Chapter Thirty-Five

ORY MORE THAN half expected a visit from an enraged Rhian. Leith had already proven incapable of controlling his woman. Since she carried his child, Rory supposed Leith would not use force to keep her in line.

He did not expect her to attack him in front of his men.

They had mustered out in the green sward in front of the forecourt. The rain had stopped, though clouds still hung low over the glen. Rory wanted MacBeith to see that he prepared for war, if they were looking.

And they would be looking.

He'd made a speech, a braw one, to his warriors. All about how these would be the last battles of this campaign. How by the end of summer, all of Glen Bronach would belong to MacLeod. They would all be rewarded by expanding their holdings, as would their sons after them.

He did not intend to march out and attack MacBeith, not this time. No more scurrying across the loch in wee boats and arriving at a disadvantage, nor making the perilous trek over the high country to cross the burn.

Moira would have to come at him if she wanted revenge for the death of her sister. Let her arrive at a disadvantage. Let it end here on MacLeod ground.

He was indeed giving directions for defense when Rhian

came storming up—with Leith, damn him, in her wake.

"Rory MacLeod!"

She called him out there before all his men. And she looked magnificent, her blue eyes glowing with rage and the cloud of her auburn hair spilling loose from its plait down her back. Leith appeared grim, and Rory supposed he had argued till he had no breath.

It might have been laughable had he not been so angry, and had the woman not looked so dangerous.

He turned, sword still in hand, and shot her a forbidding look. "Mistress MacBeith, this is no place for ye. Pray, go back inside."

"I will no'." Of course she would not. If it were possible, Leith would have kept her from creating this shameful scene.

"For yer own safety, get back inside."

She drew up in front of him, eyes glowing and bosom rising and falling. He saw no weapon on her, though that did not mean she had none upon her—like her sister. Quite clearly, she wanted to kill him.

"Why? Will ye harm me if I do no' cower and obey yer orders? 'Tis what ye do, is it no', Rory MacLeod? Threaten and harm women?"

The warriors surrounding Rory made a ring, giving the woman plenty of room. Not a man of them, so Rory figured, but had seen an angry woman before, though perhaps not one so angry as this.

"I ha' no wish, Mistress MacBeith, to harm ye." He flicked a look at Leith. "Take her inside." If Leith needed help, Rory would assign a couple of men to carry the wench.

"Coward!" she cried at him.

Not what he wanted to hear. Rage poured through Rory in a drench that turned him cold. "Wha' did ye say to me?"

"'Tis what ye be—a coward. Holding a woman hostage—"

"She is a warrior. One who faced me on the battlefield." Rory waved an arm. "Like all these men."

"—and threatening to take her life!" Rhian went on as if he

had not spoken. "A life blessed by the powers o' earth and sky, fire and water. One worth far, far more than yours will ever be."

That might well be true. Saerla's life might be worth ten of his. He could not let that sway him.

"Your sister, Moira, had the chance to ransom the prisoner and chose her death instead."

"She likely did no' believe even ye," Rhian spat, "would be despicable enough to slaughter a woman."

"Then she will learn her error, will she no'?"

"Farlan said—"

"Just as she will learn the error o' listening to a traitor turn-coat."

Rhian shuddered. "Ye would no'. 'Tis an empty threat. Even ye will no'—"

"Nay?" Inflamed, Rory tossed his head. "Would ye ha' me prove it to ye?" He turned to the two men nearest him. "Go and fetch the prisoner from my quarters."

"Eh?" One of them gaped at him.

"Fetch her now. We shall have it over and done."

The men exchanged a look and went.

Rhian cried out and flew at Rory, hands made into fists. Leith caught her back and cradled her in his arms.

"Ye need to learn," Rory snarled into Rhian's face. "Ye and both yer sisters do. I mean—and do—wha' I say."

He watched horror bloom in her deep blue eyes, replacing some of the anger. She had not believed it, nay. But she would.

Mayhap it needed to happen here and now, the letting of Saerla MacBeith's blood. Quite possibly he would not be able to do it otherwise. But in the heat of this moment, before so many eyes and to prove a point, so he must.

WHEN THE DOOR of the chamber burst open, Saerla stumbled to

her feet. She'd been sitting at the window while the rain cleared, yearning for home—reaching for it with her mind and spirit.

She did not recognize either of the men who stepped into the chamber, big, heavily armed men damp with sweat. Not her usual guards, though she could see one of those behind them, looking alarmed.

Her fear spiked up through her, raw and bright.

"What d'ye want?"

"Come wi' us."

They left her no option. They seized her by both arms, one on either side. She struggled the way a hare did in a snare, thinking of her sgian dubh, which she'd hidden in her soft leather shoe. No chance of reaching that now. The man on her left, who reeked of sweat, shook her.

"Come along and we will no' ha' to hurt ye."

"Where?"

"Be silent!"

Her guard, eyes wide with shock, backed off and let them pass, then followed. Saerla, continuing to struggle, felt her feet leave the ground. She gasped, "Why ha' ye—"

"Chief's orders," grunted the man on her right.

Rory. Ah, so he'd decided on his revenge. As she'd known he must.

They dragged her through the stronghold and out the main doors to the forecourt. So it was to be public, then. Her punishment.

Her murder?

Her heart pounded so hard that she could not breathe. She looked to the sky, to the lowering clouds. At the colors she loved and the ever-present light trying to break through.

They hauled her out to the forecourt, and the world opened.

What looked like a small army had gathered, splotches of dark against the field of pure green. Beyond...

The glen. Her glen. The loch stretched wide, gray as the sky. And the hills opposite, where lay her heart.

Returning her gaze to those gathered, she saw Rhian among them, held in Leith's arms. And *him*. Rory MacLeod.

He'd run his calloused palm over her skin, up her leg. Urged her to open for him, and she had. With abandon.

Now, as his men deposited her in front of him, she stared into his green eyes, wild and spilling over with emotion. Rage? No doubt.

"Saerla!" Rhian cried.

Saerla looked at her sister. A thousand memories came tumbling. She and her sisters giggling together when they were young girls. Tending Ma together when she was so ill. Standing over Da's grave. Poised hand in hand as Saerla called a Vision while her sisters' strength held her down. Rooted. Strong.

By all that was holy, she needed to be strong now.

Here in the open, she could feel it all. The ground beneath her feet. The kiss of the air on her cheek. The flowing water and the flame that was the light.

She returned her gaze to Rory MacLeod's, holding him. Challenging him.

Well? What is it to be?

"Saerla MacBeith," he pronounced, "your sister the Chief MacBeith has refused to ransom ye. Your life is now forfeit."

Chapter Thirty-Six

S HE WOULD NOT, could not, allow herself to fall. She refused to display any weakness here before this man. She commanded her legs to hold her up, even though they trembled and threatened to give way.

She had more dignity than that. More endurance than that. She would not allow this monster—Rory MacLeod—to see her crumble.

The guards had let go of her and backed off. She stood alone on the green turf, about three paces from Rory and another five from her sister and Leith. Rhian wanted to fly to her, she could tell. But Leith held Rhian fast.

That the monster intended to end her life here in front of everyone, she had no doubt. Mayhap he would do it because Moira had, aye, rejected his offer of ransom. She did not know. Perhaps he would act out of revenge for what she had done. He certainly appeared angry enough.

At least she'd been able to see the glen she loved one more time before she died. How much worse to die enclosed by the stone structure behind her, shut away from it all. She raised her eyes to the distant rise across the way—there behind the MacBeith stronghold. The slope was swathed in cloud, but her heart knew what lay there.

She had to believe. Only when one stopped believing did all

hope die.

She regretted that Rhian would have to witness this. Naught would ever be the same for her sister. It would change her beyond measure.

Sister, hold fast. No matter what happens, be strong for your child.

Rhian did not cry out again. She did not weep. She stood silent in the circle of Leith's arm.

Saerla felt rather than saw Rory move. He stalked behind her, and it was as if she could feel the breath in his lungs and the blood in his veins. Just like when they lay together.

She had not expected that. It shocked her so that when he laid hold of her by one shoulder and drew her against him, her back hard up to the muscles of his chest, she did not struggle.

He drew not his sword but a knife. With a second spear of shock, she saw it was the same weapon she'd drawn on him.

Ah, so it was revenge he wanted. Blood for blood.

Had he told anyone what had taken place between them in his chamber? She thought not. Far too humiliating. Only they two knew he'd been inside her. That she'd tried to kill him after.

Her knees threatened to fail her then. It did not matter, because his left arm, like an iron bar, held her fast, trapped against him. His right hand brought the knife to her throat.

Rhian gasped. Not another sound broke the stillness.

Let me fly home, Saerla prayed. *Let me return to the light.*

She could feel the blade pressing but lightly against her flesh. Pain would come. It would be swift.

Please.

She turned her gaze on her sister's face once more. The last person of her blood she would see. Rhian's face twisted with distress and her eyes burned with agony.

Nay. Saerla could not bear to look at Rhian as she died. She instead sent her gaze off far. Beneath the gray clouds, over the loch and the green turf to the distant rise.

She would will herself there as she died. She would dwell as a spirit among the stones. She would spend eternity in this place she loved.

Welcome me.

On the far-distant rise above the glen, the clouds parted.

The light broke through. In a spear of brilliance, it found Saerla's eyes, traveled to her carrying a Vision.

She had no defense against the power of its coming and little warning. The images possessed her, and she collapsed in Rory's arms.

Rhian screamed. The scream traveled with Saerla into the Vision, where she found herself hovering above a battlefield.

I must be dead, she thought even as she soared above the noise, the blood, the figures struggling together. *Rory must have employed his knife to slit my throat.* But she had felt no pain.

She felt none now while soaring. She did not bleed. She had no flesh and existed only in the Vision.

What the light wanted her to see.

A battle it was, aye, one fought here in the glen. It took Saerla only an instant to get her bearings and see the truth in the faces, in the tartans below her. The MacBeiths and the MacLeods fighting here on the MacLeod side of the loch.

Moira must have attacked, something she did but rarely.

Saerla Saw her then, at the head of a surging tide of MacBeith warriors. Her face ran with sweat and blood, the scar on her cheek standing out like a brand. Her blue eyes looked fierce. Determined.

At her shoulder, Farlan fought, long brown hair flying, muscles bunching as he swung his great sword. Blood splashed one arm. His or that of an opponent?

Alasdair—she knew very well Alasdair should not be fighting at all, given the last wound he had taken. Yet she Saw him now, there in the forefront of the fray, roaring as he battled through a sea of MacLeod men.

Alasdair turned to face a warrior whose hair shone like the wing of a blackbird.

She wanted to holler then. She wanted to scream. She wanted

to place herself between the two of them, because at that moment she knew with a great tearing of her heart that she could not bear for harm to befall either of them.

She could not intervene. She was no more than a spirit, a receptor of a Vision she did not want to see.

Amid the horror, the blood, and the clamor of the battle—one that had not happened yet but surely would if her sister swore vengeance for her death—she spiraled higher, desperate to escape. Unable to flee. The two men fought, great, sweeping, vicious blows from swords that screeched together as if wailing their own anger and grief.

Alasdair had already lost his shield. While Saerla watched, he knocked Rory's from his hand with a great, crashing, double-handed blow and came for the MacLeod chief's head.

Rory too gripped the hilt of his sword with both hands and set himself, green eyes glowing and feral as those of a wolf. He met Alasdair's mighty blow, lost his footing on the bloodied grass, and almost went down. Alasdair struck again, aimed high, and very nearly took off his head.

Alasdair bellowed something—Saerla could not tell what for the surrounding noise. He hollered, rushed in, all might and power—

And took a blow from Rory's blade right above the heart.

It was a sure blow. Leather armor sliced open, along with the flesh beneath. Alasdair went down like a felled stirk even as a cry no one could hear tore from Saerla.

That cry came echoed an instant later, and Moira, seeing Alasdair fall, rushed forward to face Rory in turn. Saerla could see the agony in Farlan's face as he failed to catch her in time.

Farlan knew how well Rory could fight.

Moira still had her shield. She rushed Rory from behind it, battering him and making a blur of her sword, striving to get in against him with the blade. The contest was sharp, short, and brief. For it was Rory who darted his blade in behind the pressing shield.

And ran Moira through.

Saerla heard Farlan's cry that might be her own. Protest rose within her, so strong it tore apart the fabric of the Vision. It broke up into separate, blinding shards of light.

Leaving Saerla alone and grieving in darkness.

Chapter Thirty-Seven

RORY CAUGHT SAERLA more closely against him when she abruptly sagged in his grasp. At first he thought—feared— the blade he held against her throat had moved without his intention. Cut her. For whatever he threatened and whatever he claimed, he could never harm this woman. Startled, he gazed down into her face as she lolled against his shoulder. Eyes closed. Not so much as a drop of blood marking her skin.

Rhian screamed and charged him, evading Leith's clutches.

Rory, stunned, lowered the woman in his arms to the ground, going down with her so she lay half across his knees.

Rhian threw herself down beside him, making a heap of her skirts in the grass. Rory cast the knife aside and spread his hands. "I did no' touch her."

"Nay. 'Tis a Vision." Dark blue eyes seared him. "She is a Seer. Did ye no' ken that?"

"This? This is a Vision?" Rory stared down at Saerla, sprawled in his lap. She looked dead. Did she breathe? For the life of him, he could not tell.

"'Tis no' always like this. Sometimes when the power o' it overtakes her." Rhian's hands moved even as she spoke, loosening the front of the drab gray gown.

No color whatever remained in Saerla's face. Rory had seen dead men with more health to them.

"Will she die?"

"Nay, she is but…stricken. We maun get her awa' out o' here. Inside." Rhian looked around for Leith. "Can ye lift her, my love?"

"I will carry her." Rory gathered Saerla up like a child and climbed to his feet. The men standing around them, his warriors all, fell back and opened the rough ring to allow him passage to the fortress.

They hurried, Rhian at a near trot and Rory following. By the time they traversed the forecourt and got inside, he was quite certain Saerla did not breathe.

Gone from the world. All her beauty, all her brightness. The warmth of her, the light. A loss beyond imagining.

The world would dim if she left it, nevermore to brighten again.

"Where?" Rhian asked when they got inside.

"My chamber."

He led the way now. Climbed the stairs as if they did not exist, as if his feet did not touch the stone.

The door of his chamber stood open. The attendant guard had gone. Och, by God, he had sent men to drag her away out of here. What harm, what terrible harm, had he done?

"On the bed," Rhian barked, and ducked past him to rush ahead. Rory set Saerla on the bed with infinite care. The place where he'd kissed her. Tasted her. Where, for a few brief moments, she had been his.

Only then did he realize Leith had followed them. His cousin closed the door and came to stand at Rory's side.

"Can ye save her?" Rory asked Rhian.

She went down on her knees at the side of the bed and reached for her sister. Seized her hands and chafed them. Rubbed her arms.

"Does she breathe?" Rory demanded.

"Aye."

He nearly fell down, so relieved was he.

"She has been taken hard by this Vision," Rhian said. "It happens so but seldom."

"But she will recover?"

"Aye. Aye, so I hope. She always has before."

"Can ye no' bring her round?"

Rhian shot him a hateful look. "How?"

"A draught or somewhat." Rarely had Rory felt so helpless. Aye, when his ma had died. And his da. Still, he had no hand in either of those occurrences. Even though he'd dealt Saerla MacBeith no actual harm, he felt he'd played a part in this terrible outcome.

Leith stepped forward. "Leave us, Rory. Let Rhian do her work."

Rory did not want to leave. He needed to stand here, make sure Saerla came back to herself. Witness that her glorious eyes opened once more.

Yet he had no legitimate reason to stay. She was a prisoner to him, naught more. A valuable prisoner, aye, but that was all.

"Mistress Rhian, if ye need aught, just send word. Send it by Leith. I will be in my study."

He turned on his heel and left.

⫸✦⫷

MADNESS, HE CONCLUDED during the time that followed, consisted of not knowing. He'd never been good at waiting. Impatient, so Ma used to claim. From the moment of his birth, the urge to do, to accomplish, had driven him. Patience made a poor servant to such impulses.

Now he paced beside the cold hearth in his study. Too warm for a fire, but the chamber felt clammy and a chill struck at his bones. He should go back out and return to mustering the men. He told himself over and over again that he would do that. After a few more moments waiting. To see if word came.

He tried to fathom what had happened out there in the glen while he held the knife to Saerla's throat. Aye, Leith had told him she was a Seer. And by God, he'd tasted the magic in her when he kissed her. When he was inside her.

He hadn't begun to comprehend what that meant.

If a Vision could come upon her that way without warning and steal her life—how could anyone protect her? How, in the name of God, could *he*?

She was not his to protect. No more, he acknowledged grudgingly, than she was his to threaten or slaughter.

He'd been a fool. A fool. *A fool.*

All women, as he saw it, deserved protection. A woman such as she—

He paced and pondered it. He wondered, and he cursed himself.

Why had he thought—imagined—he might lie with such a woman even once and then walk away from it? Such a woman might require a man to devote his entire life to her. To guarding. To cherishing.

He had other matters to which he must attend. Conquest. The glen.

Those things had been everything to him for so long that he could scarcely remember a time when they had not driven him. Even as a lad running half wild with Leith and Farlan in the glen, he would raise his eyes amid some game, gaze at the water, the rock, and the sky, and think, *All this shall be mine. I will be the one— the one to make it mine.*

He was so close to achieving that dream. To holding it in his hands. He could not let one small woman stand in the way.

No matter how extraordinary she might be.

He wondered suddenly what his da might have said. Though Rory had often denigrated Camraith for what he privately considered his lack of ambition, he'd adored his father. Always good-tempered and patient, even as Rory was not, and apt to choose kindness, Camraith had been one of the wisest men Rory ever knew.

What would he make of Saerla MacBeith? A creature touched by the gods, naught less. One who lived in constant risk of losing all or part of herself. Would Da condemn him, Rory, in turn for holding such a woman hostage? For trying to use her in order to further his own goals?

He knew without question that Camraith would have refused to keep her. He would have sent Saerla home to her sister. He would have looked for a way to sue for peace without surrendering any strength.

Rory did not think he could do that, if he even wanted to. He did not know if he could bear to send Saerla away.

But how did a man keep light trapped in his hands?

Late in the afternoon, when he was already half mad, a knock came at the door of the study. Leith stuck his head inside.

"She has come awake. Regained her senses, more or less."

More or less?

Rory stared at his cousin, who entered the chamber and shut the door behind him. "Rhian remains wi' her. I recommend ye leave them together for a time."

"Aye, to be sure." Saerla needed her sister. "Will she recover completely?"

Leith shrugged. "Cursed if I know. I do no' think even Rhian is sure. She has seen Saerla suffer Visions all her life. I gather few ha' ever taken her as hard as this one."

Leith studied Rory carefully before he went on, "I mysel' ha' never seen the like."

"Nay."

"Ye stood there holding her, just, and she was gazing across o'er the glen. Then her eyes rolled back in her head, and she— Well, 'twas like she was no longer there in her body."

Rory went and sat on the settle before the cold fire, rubbed his hands across his face. "I thought for an instant I'd killed her. That my blade had somehow moved of its own and slit her throat. The manner in which she collapsed against me—"

Leith said nothing. He paced to the table, poured a dram, and thrust it into Rory's hand.

"They are close, these sisters. Rhian is beside hersel', and if Moira believes some harm has come to wee Saerla, she will come seeking vengeance."

Aye. As he would, in her place.

Rory raised his face and regarded his cousin. "Wha' d'ye suppose she Saw?"

Leith shook his head.

"She has no' said?"

"Nay, and I think Rhian fears to ask her."

"It maun have been somewhat dire, to seize her so."

Leith's eyes looked grave and cold. "Her own death, mayhap? The death o' someone she loves?"

A shiver took Rory from head to toe. The desire to protect Saerla, to keep her from all harm, blazed within him again. But how could even he protect a woman from what was foretold?

Chapter Thirty-Eight

SAERLA AND RHIAN lay in the big bed, Saerla with her sister's arms wrapped around her, just as they had when they were very small. She could not tell when Rhian had gotten up from the floor where she'd been kneeling and climbed in under the counterpane, but the reassurance of it, the sense of belonging, helped ground Saerla after that terrifying flight.

All she found missing now from the comfort of it was Moira, who had always cuddled up on her other side.

Moira. She had Seen Moira fall. Run through by Rory Mac-Leod's blade.

When Saerla thought on that, the whole of the Vision came roaring back at her again. The clamor and the screaming. The crashing of weapons. The blood. Alasdair going down. Moira with bright courage in her eyes.

Moira had always been the courageous one. The defender. Not to say she did not become afraid. She did. Saerla had seen stark terror in Moira's face many times. She had on the night Da died. But Moira was able to put that fear aside for the sake of others.

For the sake of MacBeith.

Even though Moira was a defender more than anything else, Saerla could not doubt she would march out and attack Rory if, say, he took Saerla's life.

Indeed, what she'd Seen might have taken place after she, herself, was dead.

Was that why this Vision had affected her so drastically, had taken her down so far? Because she'd been a dead woman—would be a dead woman when it took place.

She drew a deep breath, lying there with Rhian's arms around her, warmth seeping into her, and stared into the room. She breathed, aye, yet. And she tried to remind herself that a Vision was not destiny. It but revealed a path where life might or might not lead.

There could be other paths. But she had not Seen those. She had Seen this. Alasdair lost. And Moira—

Moira did not deserve to be cut down that way. She deserved a life with the man she loved, Farlan of the staunch heart and unfailing strength. And he deserved that time with her.

Just as Rhian, who gave so unstintingly of herself to everyone around her, deserved the peace of receiving that love back again. From Leith. From the child they had created together.

And what did she, Saerla, deserve?

Nothing. The answer came softly and tugged at her heart. She was, and had always been, an instrument of the gods. What had just befallen her proved it.

Perhaps, as such, she had no claim on a future of her own. To be sure, she'd never reached for one. She'd never dreamed of a love or a family. There was the magic for her, in her, and naught more.

A sudden image of Rory MacLeod appeared in her mind, blotting out the other images, the horror and the blood. Green eyes blazing. Not with vengeance or with anger, but desire.

Would he have killed her out there on the green sward? Would he, after having held her in his arms? After being inside her?

But mayhap she had destroyed any soft feeling he might have harbored for her. With her blade, she had. She could not possibly still want him—that man among all others. Just as she could scarcely believe she had offered herself to him so eagerly, joined with him so avidly. Flown with him.

Two souls together, rather than one. One alone, as, despite all the presence of the gods and despite her sisters' love, she had always been.

He stood alone, did Rory MacLeod.

That thought startled her, because it was true. He had lost many who had been dear to him and had cast off his closest friend. Put conquest ahead of human decency and love.

Was Rory capable of love?

And why should that matter to her? She'd lain with him, aye. She'd seduced him so she might put her blade to his throat. He knew that. He hated her for it.

She had been unable to press that blade home. When it came to it, with the blood pumping through his veins and hers, she'd had an instant before he reacted, when she might have killed him. She had failed.

She closed her eyes for a moment, lying there beside her sister, acknowledging it. How could she kill a man who had kissed her so sweetly? Who had touched her so gently?

He was a monster.

He was not.

He would never forgive what she had done. And if, out of vengeance, he took her life, then would the terrible Vision unfold. She would lose Alasdair and Moira. And the light.

Rhian stirred beside her, awakened and brushed Saerla's cheek with careful hands.

"Sister, do no' weep."

Saerla said nothing.

Rhian shifted and half sat up. But one taper burned in the chamber and night had fallen outside the narrow window. Saerla could barely see the expression in Rhian's eyes.

Love. And concern.

"Saerla, d'ye want to tell me wha' ye Saw?"

"Nay." *Nay.*

"Sometimes if ye recount it, that helps ye recover. So it has been in the past."

"Aye." But she could not speak the words. That might make it real. "No' this time."

"But, my love—"

"Nay, Rhian. Do no' ask me."

Rhian went silent. Saerla could feel her thinking. Not a stupid woman, she leaped to it. "Ye ha' Seen—Seen the death o' someone ye love."

Saerla stopped breathing.

"Who, sister?"

"Please do no' ask."

"But I need to know."

"Please."

"Saerla, if ye ha' Seen somewhat terrible, we may be able to send a warning."

"How? I am a prisoner, and ye, in truth, little more."

"Leith will help if I ask. Send a letter to Moira."

"How?" Saerla asked again. "How might he get that to her?"

Rhian went suddenly still.

"Rory MacLeod," Saerla said in a rush. "He bade me send a letter to Moira—one urging her to accept his terms for my release and surrender to him all our holdings. I might tell him, now I am willing to tak' him up on that."

Rhian drew a breath. "Ye would no'."

"Nay, but if I could include some hidden message, one only Moira would understand—I might prevent her attacking." She might prevent what she'd Seen in that terrible Vision ever happening.

Another path for her to choose.

"Sister, ye maun tak' a message to him for me. To Rory Mac-Leod."

"Saerla—"

"Bid him here to me."

"Nay." Rhian sat upright, tears standing unshed in her eyes. "I want him nowhere near ye."

And what would Rhian say if she knew Rory had been as close to her as any man could be? Right here in this very bed. Too many secrets for her to keep.

"Rhian, 'twas no' Rory who felled me out there on the grass, but the Vision."

"He had his blade to yer throat! He hauled ye out o' here like—like a common thief. My sister!" Rhian struggled visibly to get hold of herself. "I thought I would see ye die."

"I ken. I ken." Now Saerla comforted Rhian with her arms fast around her.

"I do no' want him in the same chamber as ye."

"No' even if it might save the lives o' those we love?"

Rhian raised her head from Saerla's shoulder. They gazed into one another's eyes.

"Those we love?" Rhian repeated the words, horror-struck. "More than one?"

"Aye, sister. I pray thee, tak' him the message."

"Ye be no' strong enough. No' strong enough yet to face that monster. Ye ha' no' even been up on yer feet."

"Help me, then."

With Rhian's support and moving like an old woman, Saerla rose from the bed. She felt like she'd been thrashed from head to foot. The Vision had stolen all her strength.

"Please, Saerla, rest a bit longer before ye ask me to send for him. Regain yer strength. Let me mix ye a draught—"

"Will that help me feel stronger?"

"It well may."

"Verra well, then."

"And wait another day—"

"Rhian, I dare no'."

"But—"

"I dare no'. What if Moira should muster out today?"

They stared once more into each other's eyes. Rhian nodded. "Aye, sister, as ye wish."

<hr>

Chapter Thirty-Nine

"MY SISTER ASKS to see ye."

Rory, hearing the words, rose from the bench where he sat, as if drawn up by strings. The night had been endless, and he'd known no sleep. Even after Leith left, he'd paced his study while pain from the hole in his back gnawed at him with sharp teeth, and the hole in his heart…

Now, when he could pace no longer, Rhian MacBeith appeared at his door standing like an avenging angel with her head high and her eyes fierce and bright.

She hated delivering the words, that was evident. She did not want him anywhere near her sister.

Let her try to keep him away.

"Mistress Saerla—she is recovered?"

"She will no' be recovered for some time. She asks to see ye regardless."

"Has she said what knowledge it brought to her, this Vision?" He'd pondered that all night also. Terrible, heavy knowledge it must be.

"Nay. She will no' tell even me." Rhian's chin jerked up another notch. "Will ye come?"

"Aye, I will."

He trotted after her, new emotions replacing those that had dogged him all night. Doubt and regret were pushed out by a measure of hope and an unreasonable euphoria. She wanted to see him. *Him.* But why?

His chamber lay not far away. He'd traveled the distance many times in his mind during the night. Imagined himself demanding entry to the chamber where Saerla lay. Being sent away again in disgust.

No guard stood outside the door. He'd forgotten to assign one. Not even Leith was there. Rhian turned and faced him, her expression fierce.

"Ye will no' harm her. Lest ye will deal wi' me." Not an avenging angel, nay, but a protective mother.

"I will no' harm her."

"And ye will no' try to send me awa'. I stay wi' her, aye?"

"Aye."

Satisfied, she opened the door.

Light flooded the chamber, glorious morning light. Rory had to narrow his eyes against it. From out of the radiance stepped Saerla MacBeith.

She looked pale and quite tiny, clad in her dull gray gown—likely the only garment she possessed. And she shone. Her hair made a nimbus of red-gold around her head. Her eyes looked clear and solemn.

She stole Rory's breath.

He'd imagined her all night lying near to death—or already dead. Stricken down as he'd last seen her. Now gratitude shook him to the root, a humble sort of thankfulness he'd never before known.

"Mistress," he breathed out in a voice he barely recognized.

"Chief MacLeod." She inclined her head at him as to a stranger. Impossible that they had moved in the bed together. Held one another with tenderness. That he'd tasted her pure sweetness.

Desperately, he called on his self-control. "I trust ye are re-covered from yer—fit?" He did not know what else to call it.

Rhian, behind him, began to speak. Saerla directed a look at her.

"Leave us, sister."

"I will no'."

"Please wait outside the door."

"I will no' leave ye alone wi' this—this—" Apparently Rhian lacked a word terrible enough to describe him.

"Please," Saerla said again.

Rhian looked at Rory. "Touch a hair of her and I promise by everything I hold dear, ye will live to regret it. And 'twas no' a fit but a Vision, ye damn idiot."

She crashed out, leaving the two of them—Rory and Saerla—facing one another in the bright sunlight.

And he…

He wanted to throw himself at this woman's feet—he did, just as when he'd come to her last time. He wanted to declare himself her protector for all time.

A man did not do that. A chief did not. Instead he asked, "Should we sit?" She appeared so frail standing there. In his mind he saw her going down once again into the green grass. Lashes closed on pale, freckled cheeks.

Ignoring his suggestion, she lifted her chin a notch, achieving a resemblance to her sister. Her eyes did not avoid his.

"I wish to send a letter to my sister, Moira. Ye suggested I should do so before. I would do it now."

Rory's mind raced, or tried to. He rarely acted without due thought for consequences, except when he lost his temper. Or when he'd succumbed to passion. With this woman.

"Might I ask, mistress, why ye seek to do this now?"

"Moira has no' agreed to your last offer. She sent back a refusal with your men, instead."

"She may still change her mind—"

"I believe ye have had her answer." Slowly, Saerla shook her head. "She will no' ransom me. That means she will attack in an effort to tak' me back. It is a war I would prevent, if I can."

Looking into her eyes, Rory beheld only truth. Was this what the Vision had brought to her? A warning of war?

Or had she Seen her sister failing to rescue her? His heart began to beat hard. If he might keep her here, hold her always, somehow win her favor, make her his own…

"Is that what ye Saw, mistress, in that dire Vision? This coming war?"

She began to sway on her feet. He reached her in two strides and caught her hand.

He half expected Rhian to burst in through the door and behead him with a stolen sword. It did not happen. Instead, he guided Saerla to the settle in front of the fire.

"Here. Sit."

His fingers tingled where he touched her. A warmth traveled up his arms and through the rest of him. An ache, replacing all the others, filled him.

"Can ye write, mistress?" he asked gently.

Again her eyes found his. Clung to them. "I can. We were all taught, and I sat in sometimes on my brother Arran's lessons. Since I was youngest, I learned the least. I canna write so well as Moira, or even Rhian. I can puzzle it out."

Rory nodded. Naught about this woman should surprise him. Fragile and strong. Magical and fierce. Possessed of unearthly talents. Had there ever been a woman to match her?

"I shall have ink and parchment brought. If ye like, I will mysel' write whatever ye wish to tell yer sister. Ye may read it after to make certain I ha' copied it out true."

She shook her head. "It should be in my hand. Moira will know."

"Aye, so. Are ye strong enough for the task?" He could feel her fingers trembling in his.

"I will mak' myself strong enough."

"Aye, then." He rose, went to the door outside which Rhian lingered, looking anxious, and bellowed for a servant. When the girl came, he bade her fetch the required elements from his study.

Then he looked at Rhian. "Ye may as well go. She wishes to

write a letter. It might tak' a time."

"I—"

"I will no' harm her. Ye ha' my word."

A sneer crossed Rhian's full lips. "The word o' a man who held a blade to her throat." But she took herself off, if not without another warning glare.

Back inside his bedchamber, Rory rearranged some furniture and brought a small table to the place where Saerla sat.

He said, "Mistress, I want ye to know I would no' ha' slaughtered ye out on the sward."

That made her gaze return to his, startled. "Ye were verra angry."

"I was."

"Ye wanted revenge. For what I ha' done." She blinked at him.

"I did."

"I tried to let your blood. Ye would ha' cut my throat. Tit for tat."

"I would no'."

"Yet—"

"Saerla! I would no'." He tried to convince her with the truth in his eyes. He willed her to believe it. In a whisper, he added, "I could ne'er harm so much as a hair o' ye."

Her lips parted. Could she believe him? She considered him a monster.

"Then," she said slowly, spreading her hands, "how will all this end? I in your hands. And Moira unable to betray MacBeith in order to ransom me."

He did not know. Perhaps she could stay with him.

Forever.

Chapter Forty

RORY MACLEOD WAS not a patient man. Saerla could feel him chafing as he paced the room behind her, waiting for her to finish writing her letter.

It would doubtless have been much easier for him to take the quill from her, nudge her aside, and write the letter himself than watch her struggle over it. She had not lied about her abilities in the schoolroom. What had seemed a good idea when Moira was young had dwindled to less than important by the time Saerla became old enough to learn.

Not only did she labor over the script itself, but the content of the missive. Rory could—and undoubtedly would—read this letter when she finished it. She needed to pen a warning Moira would understand, but that he would not.

She began by begging Moira not to ransom her. *Our lands and what dwells upon them are far too precious to sacrifice for one life. As I belong to what exists at MacBeith, preserving it will preserve the best of me.*

Likewise, I beg ye do not launch an attack to try to regain me. I would not have ye risk yourself. Do not, I pray, allow others I hold dear to risk themselves either.

Allow me, sister, to make this sacrifice for those I love. The gods will guide me to the destiny I have earned.

Would Moira listen? Her sister was a protector to the very

heart. Her first instinct, just like Rhian's, had always been to look after their small sister.

Could Moira leave her to her fate, even for the sake of all they loved?

And what of the man pacing the floor behind her? He doubtless thought she would beg Moira to save her and would not like what she had written. Beyond that, was she to believe he had forgiven her for raising a blade to him? For attempting to kill him? He was not a man who forgave easily, if at all.

He insisted he would not have cut her throat out there in the glen. He claimed he would not harm her now. She did not know if she believed him.

When she finished the letter, she spread her hands and directed a look at him.

He might have been a caged beast, green eyes aglow in the sunlight that streamed through the window. Muscles tense.

"Wha' ha' ye told her?"

"To abandon me to my fate. Ye will no' ha' what ye seek, Chief MacLeod, no' by threat. Ye will either ha' to battle for it or negotiate a peace." But if Moira did not bring the fight to him in an attempt to ransom Saerla, at least the terrible Vision might not come true.

A muscle jumped in Rory's cheek. "Negotiating a peace, Mistress Saerla, will no' gain me ownership o' the glen."

"Nay, but it could bring ye somewhat much more valuable."

"There is naught more valuable to me."

"Perhaps then you will refuse to send this letter to my sister after all. For when ye suggested I write to her, you thought I would urge her to succumb to your demands in order to save me. I ha' done just the opposite. Glen Bronach—and what lies up on the rise—mean more to me than my own life."

For several moments he continued to gaze at her while a pulse—the very one she'd thought she could still—beat at his throat.

Raggedly he said, "Yer life, mistress, is in no danger. I ha' said

I will no' harm ye." His eyes narrowed. "Ye do no' believe me."

She shook her head.

"Saerla, I will no' harm ye." He reached down, seized her hands, and drew her up into his arms. He did it gently, as he always touched her, and yet her pulse jumped as it might in response to great fear.

Or passion.

She could not let him touch her. She could not let him caress her. Again.

And yet she said nothing when carefully, almost tenderly, with his hands lodged at her waist, he drew her in. She fought the impulse to rest her hands upon his chest.

"Saerla. Wha' if ye do no' return home, ever? If ye stay here wi' me? Wha' then?"

His lips swooped in to meet hers, as inevitable as the coming of spring. As the rising of the sun, as the onset of a Vision. She could not refuse it. She could only lift her face to him and part her lips.

Och, and it felt wondrous, breathless, and as if every separate part of her had been waiting for exactly this a long while. It opened her, sheltered her, and called up the light. She felt that light bloom inside her as it did when she stood on the rise back home. When she gave herself over to something far greater than herself.

Was this, that which existed between her and Rory MacLeod, greater than herself?

She did not know, but her hands did come to rest on his chest before creeping up around his neck. She did stretch up on her tiptoes, the better to feast on his mouth. She did open to him, granting him admittance. And when the kiss ended at last, when he buried his face in her neck and clutched her as if he would never let go, she trembled violently.

With need.

"Saerla. Saerla."

A man who did not bend. A man who sought and gave no

mercy. Yet now he lowered her back down onto the bench and came down with her, to kneel at her feet.

She stroked his hair, the feelings that flooded her—the tenderness—too strong to bear. All hesitation had flown from her. She could only *feel*.

"Will ye send the letter?" she asked with her fingers still in his hair.

He raised his face and looked at her, wonderment in his eyes. "I will."

"Even though—"

"I ha' given ye my word. It means something, Saerla."

"Aye." Her mind raced, searching out ways it could all go wrong. "If Moira imprisons the messenger—"

"I will ask if Leith will tak' the letter. She will no' harm Leith."

"She will no'." Not with Rhian awaiting his return.

"Saerla. Tell me somewhat. These Visions that befall ye…" He touched her cheek softly. "How, by God, d'ye endure it?"

"'Tis no' always like ye saw out on the sward. There are times it comes gently. Sometimes even in dreams." She thought of the three lads running and chasing through the glen. "Other times, aye, it is harsh and brings me things I do no' want to See. But I ha' received such Visions for as long as I can remember, almost." She shook her head. "I do no' ken why I was chosen for such a fate."

"'Tis a curse."

"And a blessing." For with the Visions so often came the light. And when the light possessed her…

Could she explain that to him? Could she say that being possessed by the light felt as strong and wondrous as the passion when he touched her?

Nay. He was her enemy. Perhaps not the monster she'd once thought him, but her enemy still. And making herself vulnerable to him could not possibly be wise.

He gazed at her with those intense green eyes, beseeching

and demanding in equal measures. Nay, but she did not make herself vulnerable to him. The feelings that unfolded inside when he touched her did. When she touched him. A separate kind of power and magic.

Did he feel it too? Was it possible?

To test it, she stroked her fingers through his hair there where he knelt at her knees, and the spark in his eyes flared. For an instant, to the exclusion of everything else, they were all that existed, united in that radiance.

"Saerla." He leaned in he kissed her again. She joined her lips to his, her breath to his, her heart—

He gathered himself and got to his feet. "I will send the letter. Saerla…" New emotions broke through the passion in his eyes. So strong were they, Saerla came to her feet.

He clutched her hands. "After, when the letter is sent, whether we receive an answer or no'—tell me. Tell me, Saerla, I may return here at nightfall. To spend the night wi' ye."

He stood and waited for her answer, this man who believed he could own the world. She could see the need in his eyes, the same that filled her, raw and urgent.

Need. It was all about need.

She bowed her head, knowing very well she should deny him, but unable to make the words come.

"Go send the letter. See to your defenses. Then, aye, ye may return to me."

Chapter Forty-One

HE RETURNED AT nightfall just as the birds began to sing their evening songs outside the window. He came with his head bared and with open hands, wearing no weapons. What, Saerla supposed, was a show of good faith.

She herself had put the sgian dubh away, hidden it inside the chest at the foot of the bed where she'd found it. This, whatever it was that existed between the two of them, was not about hurt or harm. Not about distrust or anyone getting the upper hand. Not even about being a MacBeith or a MacLeod.

Rhian had been with Saerla much of the afternoon, and in a tizzy, worrying about Leith and what might happen at MacBeith. Worrying about what might happen to Saerla also. Worrying about what the Vision had shown her.

Saerla had said nothing to Rhian about Rory or his promise to return. Rhian did not know Saerla had already lain with the man, their enemy.

That she would do so again.

It was almost a relief when Rhian left, when Saerla heard the guard step into place outside. Only then did she, alone, begin to doubt her choices. Begin to wonder if, when Rory appeared, she should send him away again.

She'd almost determined upon doing just that, had fought her way back to a measure of sanity, when she heard his voice outside the door. His voice, which seemed as changeable as the man himself. Harsh or violent. Cold or rumbling with sweet tenderness.

He dismissed the guard. She heard that clearly even as the door opened. "Ye may go. I will no' need ye back here tonight."

What would the guard think? Would he speak of this?

Did she care?

Rory stepped in and stood with his back against the closed panel while they gazed at one another.

And Saerla's resistance crumbled. All the sanity she'd worked so hard to gain flew away in a rush.

This man. This man, with his bright green eyes and his glossy black hair and his battered body that spoke of pain, with the emotions that fair tore him asunder, had come to her without weapons. Without disguise.

"I ha' sent the letter wi' Leith. I do no' expect him back before morning. Mistress, am I still welcome here the night?"

Ah, so he gave her one last chance to refuse him. This monster who never lent power was laying it squarely in her hands.

She should tell him to go. She should not muddy the waters that lay between them, a barrier as big as the loch that divided the glen.

At this moment, if ever, she should seize her own power.

The concept, though, was an odd one because she'd never felt she owned herself entirely. She'd always followed her sisters, who kindly told her what to do. Her da, in all things. Alasdair, while training for the field.

And when the Visions came—she had no power whatsoever then. They claimed her, used her, and brought both darkness and light.

For Rory MacLeod above all others to offer her autonomy seemed strange. She needed to seize that measure.

So she lifted her chin and met his gaze. Her heart beat in her breast, making its own demand. But she must think clearly on this. Let the light show her what was true.

He was a man and she a woman. Perhaps for this night, in this place, they could be nothing more.

She held out her hand. "I would be pleased for ye to stay."

He crossed the floor slowly, silently, as if afraid she might startle and change her mind. When he took her in his arms, he did it tenderly, as if he feared she would break.

She knew once he kissed her, she would be lost. So she raised her fingers to his lips and said, "I ha' one request."

"Name it and 'tis yours."

"For this night, we are no' enemies."

Light flared in his eyes. "I agree. By God. Saerla, I agree." He lifted her in his arms and carried her to the bed.

Even there, he did not hurry, though she could feel the urgency in his body and see it in his eyes. Laying her down, he leaned above her and gazed into her eyes. It felt as if he searched her, and she could feel all he desired, both of body and mind.

It was she who reached for the front of her gown and began to unlace it. She had not finished before he touched her hands gently and completed the task for her. He still gazed into her eyes when he opened her bodice, and did not break that speaking gaze until he lowered his mouth to her breast.

Saerla had never considered herself a woman of fire—that was Rhian's provenance—but she felt the flames flare then. Or perhaps it was the coming light, that which lifted her up. Lifted both of them. Rory's lips seemed to tug upon her very spirit. She wished with a sudden, overwhelming desire to gift it to him. To take his in return.

"Och," she murmured. "Och, Rory."

With strong hands, she drew him up, bringing his mouth to hers. She needed to breathe of him, to taste of him. She stroked his tongue with hers and felt the desire break inside him. Madness. Och, sweet, sweet madness.

He trapped her face between his hands and kissed her. Kissed and kissed her. She broke the contact only to beg that he might remove his clothes, and to wrestle out of her own. Better, much better when he came down upon her then, naked flesh to naked flesh. Heat to heat, and light to light.

No words were spoken. They needed none. She lifted him, caught his desire, and shared her own. Took him for flight. When he slipped inside her, set the rhythm and began to rock the two of them together, it was like the beating of wings. She could almost feel the blessed air flowing through her hair and catch the shadows of the clouds above. Sense the glen she loved so well beneath them.

"Do no' stop," she begged him in a whisper then. "Do no' leave go of me."

"Ne'er," he whispered in return.

NEVER BEFORE HAD Rory experienced bliss. Och, he'd come close to it the last time he and Saerla had lain together, when he'd been inside her and found an inexpressible sense of completion. But even that had not been like this.

Perhaps he'd never before been completely satisfied. Wanting for naught. His mind lost in a haze and even his body no longer his own.

It belonged to her, to Saerla MacBeith. Whatever she wanted to do with it, he would respond. Whatever she asked of him, he would give.

Had done. Would do again.

At the moment he lay on his back in the bed—what had been his own bed—floating. They had not lit a fire, the night being mild, and all but one candle had gutted out. His body, for the first time he could easily remember, had stopped hurting. Even that damned hole in his back.

He opened his eyes when a touch feathered across his skin and saw Saerla leaning over him, eyes soft and wide. It had been her hair—that glorious mane—he felt trailing across his chest.

And he could feel her breath on his lips, so close was she.

He smiled at her because he could do nothing else. He'd been inside her repeatedly. She'd opened herself to him like a flower to the sun. She'd also wrapped herself around him; she'd given and demanded. He knew how she tasted everywhere, and she him. He had never in his life been so close to any person.

Now when he smiled at her, she smiled back at him. A smile in the eyes of Saerla MacBeith was a defense against the darkness. It shone with light.

"Beautiful lass," he murmured.

"Ye mak' me feel so."

He became suddenly serious. "Ye be the most beautiful, the finest thing ever to set foot upon the face o' the world."

"Is it so?"

"It is."

"Such a compliment deserves a kiss." She gave it to him, and her lips molded to his in that way they had. Whenever and however she touched him, she became instantly a part of him.

He opened to her helplessly. *Drink me dry, lass. Take all that I am.* But she did not. Not his Saerla. She was too merciful. Instead, she ran her soft lips over his cheek, down his neck to his chest, and kissed him there. Just over his heart.

The heart that hammered with equal helplessness for her. Only for her, from now on.

"Lass, I am spent."

"Are ye?"

"Aye. Come and lie in my arms. Sleep for a time." He could think of very little better than waking tomorrow morning with her there.

She came down to lie against him without protest, cuddling tight. He fished for the counterpane, displaced during their lovemaking, and pulled it up over the both of them.

"Should I dream—" she began.

"Do ye, often?" Not ordinary dreams, he would wager she meant.

"Aye. My sisters used to hold me when we were small, and the dreams came."

"I will hold ye now. I will hold ye. Do no' fear."

Be safe in me. He wanted to add that. He did not.

"I ha' dreamed o' ye, Rory MacLeod."

That startled him half-awake. "Have ye?"

"Aye. Of ye as a lad. The three o' ye, Farlan and Leith."

Days long gone. The trust between himself and Farlan, now broken. Those careless times would never come again. "Why would ye dream o' that?"

"I do no' ken." She sounded sleepy.

"It has no importance." Or did it?

Nearly asleep, she whispered, "Ye always led the way. And looked down on them for following."

Had he? But Farlan followed him no more. And Leith—who knew what Leith truly thought?

He lay and pondered it for truth and wonderment while Saerla slept in his arms.

Chapter Forty-Two

"MAY I RETURN tonight?" Rory stood looking at Saerla, his green gaze hard-held and serious.

The night had flown like one of her dreams, not founded in reality. And the early morning, for they'd awakened only to make love again. Only then had he climbed back into his clothing, affording her another look at the terrible wound in his back, as had she.

Now they must return to the events that crowded the day—he to his plans to devastate her people and she to her efforts to thwart him. The night over, they must return to being enemies.

Until, perhaps, tonight.

She should tell him nay. She knew that quite well. For he was still asking, not taking. And one night's escape into an agreed-upon madness did not warrant another.

Did it?

Last night had been a time apart. She had understood that even when embarking upon it, and if she'd lost track of the transient nature of the experience while caught up in it, who could blame her? When Rory touched her, when she so much as thought about him touching her, she lost her mind a little. The fact that he became similarly affected when she touched him only added to the depth of the spell.

But it was just that—a temporary madness. Today, with the

rising of the sun, they returned to being enemies, separate and apart.

So she held his gaze, sharp as a weapon, and though every part of her longed for another night with him, said, "I do no' think it wise."

He took the refusal stoutly. He did not flinch or waver, but she thought she saw disappointment flash in those green eyes.

His angular jaw jerked upward. "As ye wish."

"Ye will tell me, though, as soon as a reply to my letter arrives? Send word?"

"I will. Better, I will ha' ye brought forth."

"Eh?"

He glanced around the chamber. "There is no need for ye to remain imprisoned here."

"Is there no'?"

Slowly he shook his head, his hair falling forward. She remembered the feel of it between her fingers, and her knees went weak.

"Nay. Ye are no' longer my prisoner, Saerla MacBeith. So long as I ha' yer word ye will no' try to escape, ye may come and go from this chamber as ye will."

"But—" Her beleaguered mind tried to make sense of it. Failed. "If I am no' allowed to escape, how is it I am no' your prisoner?"

"I prefer to call ye my guest."

"Your guest. For how long?"

He shrugged. "That depends on wha' your sister decides to do."

"Chief MacLeod—" Just last night she'd called him Rory. She'd breathed the name into his ear and over his skin. "My sister will ne'er surrender our lands."

"We shall see."

He strode out before she could form a reply. He left the door half-open, and no guard stationed outside.

Saerla stood there struggling to decide what that meant, and what would happen if she walked out and across the glen.

He would stop her then. He would not let her go.

And *could* she leave him?

That question, appearing in her mind, stopped her cold. Aye, they had shared a lot during the night just past. More intimacy than she had ever imagined might exist, not only of the body but the mind, the soul. But she would return home. To be sure she would—go back to her family. Back to the light that dwelt on the rise.

Before she could ponder it farther, Rhian arrived, puffing up the corridor with an anxious look on her face. She glanced at Saerla before giving her a sharp look and asking, "Where is the guard?"

"I am no' certain." Saerla could not explain to Rhian what she herself barely understood.

Rhian's eyes narrowed. "Ye can scarcely escape now. Half the warriors in the stronghold are out on the sward awaiting Leith. He maun return this morning."

The night past could not have been an easy one for Rhian. Despite the bloom her pregnancy had lent her, she appeared strained, and clearly had not slept.

"Wha' if he does no' return, Saerla?"

"He will."

"Ha' ye Seen—"

Saerla shook her head. "I've Seen naught more."

"Wha' if Moira or the council decide this is a good thing, having the heir to MacLeod once more in their hands? There were those who disagreed with ever letting Leith go."

"Rhian, Moira will no' keep him fro' ye."

"I could no' live without him, Saerla. I for certain could no' live here without him."

A slow ache started in Saerla's heart. She would have to do just that—manage to live without Rory. That day would come.

And, she assured herself swiftly, what she felt toward Rory MacLeod did not approach what Rhian felt for Leith. That was love. What she felt for Rory was, at best, lust. Need.

Rhian remained with her until word came, brought by none other than Leith's sister, Aisleen, that Leith had been spied by watchmen on the ramparts, returning across the glen.

Rhian caught Saerla by the hand, and they followed Aisleen from the chamber, down through the corridors and out into the light.

A glorious morning it was, the sun already well up and sending shafts of radiance over the hills. Saerla had not been outdoors since being stricken by the Vision. Now, even though she viewed it from the wrong side of the glen, from a place she'd never expected to stand, she was nearly overcome with love for this place she adored.

Surely any price asked would be worth paying for its preservation?

As Rhian had said, they found a large number of people out beneath that sun. Guards ranged across the turf and on the walls. Warriors bound for the practice field. Ordinary people awaiting their fate.

They found Rory standing at the forefront with his war chief, Murgor. Rory's eyes were narrowed against the glare from the loch as he stared off toward MacBeith. Home.

He glanced at Saerla and Rhian when they took places beside him, their hands linked.

To Rhian he said, "He has just rowed across the loch and pulled his wee boat up on this side. See?"

Saerla could feel Rhian trembling through their linked hands and knew she longed to run and meet Leith. Knew she would not allow her composure to break, here before so many eyes.

"He is safe," Saerla whispered to her sister, and Rhian nodded, some of the terrible fear leaving her face.

And aye, Saerla could see him now, a large figure—for Leith MacLeod was not a small man—moving steadily across the brilliant green turf. She lifted her eyes farther. Above the glittering water of the loch. Up the rise, opposite till she found the place where perched the fortress made of pale granite.

Home.

And farther still.

Even on this bright morning, mists gathered on the rise, obscuring the stones that had occupied that place for so long.

Although she could not see the stones, they endured. And when she died, even when she passed from this world and flew to the next, when she surrendered the path of light she kept, the magic would continue on.

Comforting. And, in a terrible way, quite terrifying.

She withdrew her gaze to find Rory watching her, his eyes as green as the turf. A strange thought found her. As she was part of this glen, stone, water, wind, and sunlight, was he not also? Part and parcel of this place, this beautiful place where they'd both been born.

They stood so, Saerla's and Rhian's hands linked and sharing strength, until Leith drew near, coming at a steady jog. Then Rhian's will broke and she ran to him.

She did not embrace him, not there in front of so many people, but they stood looking into one another's faces, exchanging words no one else could hear before they joined arms and came on.

Rory quickly stepped forward to intercept Leith, and they spoke in turn. Leith, seeing Saerla standing waiting, looked surprised.

"I ha' spoken wi' yer sister," he said, "as well as given her yer letter. Let us speak o' it somewhere private."

He glanced at Rory, who nodded.

They went, the four of them, to a room that might once have been a solar. Now, though flooded with sunlight, it had a forsaken air of neglect. They sat down around a table, and Rory laid his large, scarred hands upon it.

"Well? Speak, man."

Leith looked at Saerla, not at his cousin. "Moira read your letter quite carefully, mistress. *Quite* carefully." Was there an added message in Leith's voice? Did that mean Moira had understood the warning Saerla had dared not put into words? "She did no' write a letter in return, did no' wish to tak' the time. But I spoke wi' her about it at length." Leith glanced at Rory. "Wi' her and Farlan both."

Rory's expression tightened at the mention of his former friend, but he said nothing.

"Her answer?" Saerla asked softly. Her heart had commenced beating hard in her chest.

Leith looked at her kindly. "She bids ye ken she understands yer message. But that ye be loved quite dearly there at MacBeith, and she is no' certain she can hold her people, or even the council, from making war on yer behalf. Yer people want ye back, Saerla. She bade me tell ye, it may be out o' her hands."

Rory clenched his fingers atop the table. Saerla bent her head, not wanting to see what lay in his eyes.

She'd meant to save those she loved. She feared she would instead be their doom.

Chapter Forty-Three

A FTER THE FOUR of them left the solar, Rory retreated to his study, where he brooded for several hours. Rhian and Leith had gone away back to Leith's quarters—to provide one another comfort, he did not doubt.

Saerla had returned to his chamber.

He debated reinstating a guard there, at her door, and decided against it. Aye, she still made a valuable hostage, as much as ever she'd done. But he had trouble now with treating her as one.

Because he'd held her in his arms. Tasted her. Been inside her. Felt the light that lay within the fragile shell of that outer beauty. He knew, now, what she was.

Not just a woman.

It would be wrong to pen her. It would be disrespectful to steal her will. Anyway, no man could imprison the light.

Not even him.

He'd seen the look in her eyes when Leith gave her Moira's responses to her letter. Pain, regret, terror—all standing clear in those beautiful, mist-blue eyes. He'd read the letter she'd written Moira—of course he had—before he sent it with Leith. And he could only wonder why she wanted so badly for Moira to abandon her to her fate, here at MacLeod.

He wondered at the fate she'd Seen while stricken by the Vision.

He did not know what he should do next. His threat to harm Saerla if her sister did not surrender MacBeith's lands to him was entirely hollow. He'd threatened Saerla's life, and she'd threatened his. It meant nothing when they touched one another.

But what did that make of him? A man who backed down from his intentions. His sworn purpose.

Moira did not know he wouldn't slit her sister's throat—unless Farlan, traitor that he was, had given that as his opinion. Saerla's letter had begged Moira to refrain from a rescue. Had, in essence, begged her to let Saerla die here.

Rory could quite see how Moira would be unable to do that. How her folk, including that monster of a war chief, Alasdair, could not allow it. They, even more than he, knew what Saerla was.

But neither could he back down in front of his own people. He could not surrender this fight. What kind of chief would that make him?

He wished suddenly he could speak with his da, if only for a short time. Camraith MacLeod had been a very different sort of chief than he. Strong he might be, but he could show love—to his people and particularly to the young son of his slain comrade, whom he'd taken in and raised as his own. Da had loved Farlan full well.

What would he say about Rory having cast him off?

Nay, perhaps Rory did not want to hear what his father might say.

For a good portion of Rory's life, he had looked down on what he considered his da's weakness. He knew full well that Da, with the stronger tribe, could have crushed MacBeith any time he chose over the years. He couldn't understand quite why he had not followed through with the intentions of their ancestors who came to claim this glen so long ago.

Glen Bronach. The glen of sorrows.

As soon as Da died, before Rory had even resolved his own grief, he'd determined to accomplish what Da had not.

Was his grief resolved even now?

Nay.

What would Da have made of Saerla MacBeith? Ah, he would adore her.

He remembered Da throwing back his head and laughing right along when Leith would crack some joke. He remembered the fondness in Da's eyes when he looked upon Farlan. He would doubtless consider Saerla MacBeith to be one of the most precious beings he'd ever beheld.

As did Rory.

But he'd set himself up as a strong chief. A man who did not bow or bend. He had more or less promised the people who followed him a victory. He could not back down.

For the sake of a woman.

Not that she would ever have him.

That thought followed so swiftly on the heels of the other that it near ran him over. Aye, she'd *had* him. But their physical union had been a thing apart. An agreed-upon setting aside of differences. Lust.

He'd wanted her beyond all reason. She'd wanted him. What followed had been as inevitable as his next breath.

He argued it with himself until dark. He went out and spoke with the guards, climbed up and stalked the battlements. There was no sign of movement from MacBeith.

Yet.

He was beginning to understand Moira MacBeith as he understood Farlan, who advised her. A woman of some deliberation, she would act with care. But she *would* act. And it would come before the ten days he had set for Saerla to live expired. For she could not be sure he would not harm her sister.

Even if Farlan told her so.

Before dark fell, he took himself to Leith's quarters and pounded on the door. When Leith admitted him, he could see Rhian sitting on the side of the bed refastening her gown. Had the two of them been in each other's arms all this while?

The thought made him surly, and he scowled into his cousin's face. "I ha' a question."

"Aye?" Leith looked cautious. Rory wondered what had happened to the old sense of camaraderie between them. The ease and the laughter. Leith had been one of the people with whom Rory had been most comfortable.

What had become of his life?

He glanced at Rhian, and she turned away as if she pretended not to listen.

"When ye spoke wi' Moira MacBeith, did ye tell her Saerla's life would no' be forfeit?"

"Eh?" Leith blinked at him. "Why would I do that?"

"Because 'tis true. I ha' no intention o' taking her life."

Rhian spun around and faced him. Her eyes went wide.

"B-but…" Leith said, "that was no' my understanding. Neither was it Moira's. She believes she has but days to save her sister's life."

Rhian rushed up to them. "Ye do no' intend to kill her? But ye hauled her out onto that sward and put a knife to her throat!"

"Aye. Things ha' changed since then."

Her blue eyes narrowed. "Changed how?"

"I ha' rethought the wisdom o' taking her life."

"Och, God," Rhian breathed. She swayed, and Leith put an arm around her. "Och, God!"

Reaching out, she seized Rory's forearm. "Ye maun tell Moira this. She will be in agony thinking she has left Saerla to die."

"But, mistress, that is just what Saerla's letter begged Moira to do."

Rhian, stricken, fell silent.

"Rory," Leith said. "Rhian is right. Ye maun be the one to tell Moira ye ha' removed the sentence o' death from that lassie's head. Let me write a letter to Farlan."

"So ye and Farlan can scheme against me? As ye did when ye were there at MacBeith?"

Leith's expression went tight. "I—and he—seek only for a

resolution that will prevent an unholy battle, one in which those we love may well fall."

"That is where ye be wrong, Leith. There *needs* to be an unholy battle. Since Moira MacBeith will no' surrender her lands to me even to buy her sister's life, there needs to be a battle in which she goes down to defeat." Into Leith's face he declared, "It needs to be done and over, once and for all."

"And if ye lose this grand battle?" It was not Leith who asked the question but Rhian. "The great Rory MacLeod, ye ha' no' won a battle against my sister yet."

"'Twill come, Mistress Rhian. It must. It is my destiny."

That made the two of them exchange a look. "It is *a* destiny," Rhian returned, less aggressively now. "As Saerla herself always says, destiny opens paths before us. It's we who maun choose among them."

Saerla. The very sound of her name started up a powerful longing.

"Excuse me," he told them. "I ha' somewhere to be." Or so he hoped.

Again, Rhian caught his arm. "Saerla kens ye do no' mean to kill her?"

"She does."

That seemed to strike Rhian hard, and render her silent.

Rory went straight from Leith's quarters to his own. No guard stood there. Nor was there a bar on the door. It struck him that Saerla could have walked away any time this afternoon. Returned home. To the light.

She must, however, remain still inside. Someone among the guard would have told him otherwise. The question that possessed his mind was:

Why?

He stood there trying to keep himself from knocking at that door. He paced the corridor; he turned and paced again. She had told him it would not be a good idea for him to return here tonight, and he agreed. He fought impulse and desire alike.

At last, while still he warred with himself, the panel swung open. Saerla stood there looking at him, her hair a nimbus of red gold.

"Please, mistress," he said hoarsely. "Please let me in."

Wordless, she seized him by the hand and towed him into the chamber.

Chapter Forty-Four

ALL AFTERNOON, SAERLA had waited for Rory to arrive. Just as if he'd announced it, promised it, she'd known he must come despite her having refused his request for another night together. No words had declared it, only the look in his eyes.

The longing.

She told herself over and over that if he did arrive, she must send him away again. Because anything more between them was impossible. What had already occurred should never have happened. A woman of intelligence did not surrender to desire.

Not even when the day grew old and the sun went down, and the longing became unbearable. She knew then she never should have touched him. Because once touched…

The intimacy and the desire for it became a thing of its own.

How she knew he stood there outside the door of the chamber, she could not say. Mayhap she heard him. Mayhap she sensed him.

She'd lifted the bar from the door—for och aye, she'd kept it barred for her own safety—and swung the panel wide. Admitted the monster. And then—most significant of all—she replaced the bar behind him.

He'd come to her once more without weapons. He'd come this time without his leather jerkin and wore a soft woolen sark, a kilt, and leggings. That the kilt bore the MacLeod tartan did not escape her.

Had he come to speak with her, or for something more?

She turned from the door to look at him and beheld a storm of emotions in his eyes. A man who felt deeply, was Rory MacLeod. A man who could not always control his emotions, or express them.

A man often misunderstood.

"Saerla," he said, and something flared inside her at the sound of his voice. She saw all at once the young lad with his black hair shining in the sun, running wild in the glen he loved. The glen she loved.

He seized her hands and sank to one knee before her, pressed her hand to his lips. "I ken fine ye ha' refused me already, but ask I may stay wi' ye the night."

She knew what he meant. He did not mean to stay and sleep beside her in the bed. Nay, he wanted it all again. The fire. And the wild flight.

She should, aye, deny him. Once again, he gave her that opportunity. She could hold fast to the decision she'd made and send him away.

She should.

Instead, she knelt down also in a billow of gray wool, trapped his face between her hands, and gazed into his eyes. "We should no'."

"I ken."

"There is no answer in it. No solution for the tangle in which we find ourselves."

"Nay. But there is salvation. For just this one night, Saerla. Let me love ye."

Sorrowfully, she shook her head. "'Tis wha' ye said before. For but one night."

"I find I need another."

As did she. Saerla closed her eyes for a moment, fighting the knowledge that she needed, even more than wanted, him inside her.

Opening her eyes once more, she looked at him with severity. "And wha' about tomorrow? Wha' when this night, in turn, is no' enough?"

"Then I will come to ye again. And beg, if I must."

"Rory—"

"Saerla, let this chamber, this one enclave, be a place apart. Where MacLeod and MacBeith do no' exist."

Was that possible? Could they take it back, back to a time before the hate and strife began? Could he be a wild lad once more, and she the lass who gathered the light?

Almost as if he heard her thoughts, he caught her hands again, this time against his heart. "Please, Saerla, shed your light upon me."

If she were to give to him, so Saerla decided, she would do it unstintingly. Without question. Without restraint. For a gift given in obligation was no gift at all.

So she arose and cast off her gray gown and what lay beneath while he knelt at her feet and watched. She took down her hair, which had been held back in a plait, because she knew—she knew by then—how he liked that. And when she stood bare from her head to her feet, she held out a hand to him.

"Now you."

He was already hard for her when his clothing came away. The sight made her go hot and boneless all at once. Weak and strong with the power of it. She could feel his fingers upon her even before he lifted her up and carried her to the bed.

She had turned it down because she'd hoped—hoped he might come to her, aye, even though she'd forbidden it and did not know whether she would let him in. Now she stretched her body atop the linen sheet, ready to let him into her body just as readily, an invitation.

He knelt between her thighs, caught her legs, and lifted them to tilt her toward him. Without hesitation, in a move that stole all her breath, he slid into her the way a sword slides into its sheath. The sound that came from his throat might have been a sob or a groan of satisfaction hard won. She reached for him, curled her legs around his waist and her arms around his neck, drew his mouth to hers, and kissed him as the fire built and built.

The light kindled inside her and spread to him. It traveled along their tongues that meshed and tangled. Along her limbs that held him and all the places where their bodies met. It shone the brighter for illuminating his darkness.

They moved together, thoughtless, heedless, helpless. When he came, she did also, the waves of pleasure lifting her into flight. Once again he flew with her on strong wings, and she could not tell which of them carried the other. In those glorious moments there was no past, no future. Only the feel of him, the heat, and the inexpressible sense of completion.

"Saerla," he whispered as he eased down upon her. He kissed her all over her face with palpable tenderness. "Saerla, och, God."

She captured his mouth like a starving woman, opened to him once more.

"Lass, I canna stop touching ye. Wanting ye."

"Do no' stop."

"D'ye give me leave—"

"I give ye leave. Anything."

He kissed her throat, her shoulders, her breasts. He trailed caresses over her belly and onto her thighs. When his breath whispered across the place between them, she offered herself readily, and time itself stood still while she tangled her fingers in the silken black locks of his hair.

She flew again, racked by the pleasure that was also somehow pain. This he gave her, even as she gave to him. Equal. Unstinting. A form of worship.

After, when he stretched his body beside hers in the bed and held her, he still could not keep from touching. His hands slid everywhere, smoothing her skin. Palming her breasts. Twining through her hair.

Neither of them spoke, Saerla because she had no words, and even if she had, she would not seek to break this spell. Instead, she kissed him over and over again, conveying with the caresses what mere words could not.

Eventually he slept, and after a time, so did she. She dreamed.

She saw the three lads running on the green turf, the brown head, the yellow and the black. They laughed and tumbled as they played together. They should be back at their lessons, but instead they had escaped, at large in the glen they loved. They made their way down to the loch, where, as always, a few wee boats lay drawn up on the shore.

Looking across the loch, Saerla could see the opposite shore. Three girls stood there all in a row. Holding hands.

"'Tis magic over there," Leith breathed, serious for once.

"I do no' believe in magic," Rory declared.

"How can ye fail to believe," Farlan demanded, "when ye can look across and see it?"

The three lads gazed across the loch. They saw the three lasses. One had hair of copper red. One's locks were darker, a rich auburn. The last—the smallest—had a halo of red-gold.

"I want to row across." Farlan moved to the nearest boat. "To live there."

"Ye canna," Rory hollered. "That land does no' belong to us, no' yet. Ye belong here."

Farlan turned and looked at Rory, brown eyes wide and grave. "I belong here in Glen Bronach. And there—that side—is the same. Rory, why canna all be one?"

Leith stepped up and gazed at Rory also. "Home is home. Home is where yer heart longs to be."

The black-haired lad tried to scoff. He squared his shoulders and fisted his hands, and glared across the waters.

All he could see was the smallest lass's hair, a nimbus of light.

Chapter Forty-Five

Rory woke slowly by inches, the dream falling gradually away from him. He could tell where he was by the bliss that held him fast. His own chamber. The warmth of Saerla's arms.

Even the troubling dream could not serve to destroy his sense of well-being. The peace of it ran far too deep.

He lay there thinking about that word. *Peace*. Both Farlan and Leith had refused to cease tossing it at him. As if it were some valuable commodity worth pursuing.

Naught could mean more than this woman in his arms.

That thought shocked him, because he'd determined long ago that naught could mean more than possessing all the glen.

Before he could hope to make sense of it, Saerla stirred against him. The air filling the chamber was not yet light, but he could see her, a small crease of a frown dancing between her brows. Trouble in her face.

He did not want her to wake so. He did not want her ever to know a day of trouble. Sadness. Distress. It was not possible, though, and not reasonable to hope he might keep her from it.

Her eyes opened, mist-blue as the sky over the loch on a rainy day, and she regarded him gravely. "Rory."

Did she too seek to orient herself upon waking? To remember all they had shared together last night? To make sense of what had become of their world?

Nay, but there was no sense in it. He would never have believed a single person, a woman, could change everything.

She whispered, "I had a dream. About the three o' ye—yoursel', Farlan, and Leith. As young lads."

Amazement touched him. "As did I." But why should he be so surprised? He had breathed her air all night. Lived upon her heartbeat. Why should he not share her very dreams?

"We ran together in the glen. Down to the loch. Farlan—Farlan wanted to row across."

"And I and my sisters stood on the other side."

"Aye."

"We could see ye. But we did no' fear ye then. There was no hate in it." She repeated, almost under her breath, "There was no hate in it."

He did not want her to fear him now. He certainly did not want her to hate him. It struck him that he'd done all he could these past months to ensure she did both.

He said, telling himself as much as her, "'Twas but a dream."

"Was it?" Soft with mist, her eyes met his again. "There are dreams, and *dreams*. Surely one shared maun mean something beyond the ordinary."

"Nay," he said shortly. Even though Farlan had grown up to make the passage across the loch and not come back to him. Even though Leith had opened his heart and admitted a part—the very center—of that place.

"Nay," he repeated, and sat up, even though leaving her arms was the last thing he wanted to do. Though he wanted to kiss her soft lips, touch her tender breasts, and start the lovemaking all over again.

Lovemaking.

"I maun go." He swung his legs over the side of the bed. It would not do for anyone to see him leaving here early this morning.

Yet he could not make himself move any farther. He sat there seeking to convince his muscles to act against his longing, and felt her fingers on his back.

They brushed his skin gently, like the touch of a warm breeze, and circled the hole there, the one that would not quite heal.

"Such a dire wound," she murmured. "So deep inside ye. It maun ha' near pierced your heart."

She touched him. She not only touched him, for the linens rustled as she leaned forward, and he felt her lips on the ugly wound. "Bless. Bless and heal."

He sprang up and turned to face her. There she lay, half sprawled to reach him, her hair a wild tumble his fingers had made. Temptation beyond measure, yet still she retained an unfathomable innocence. A magic he could not resist.

"Do not touch me," he told her raggedly. "Ye should no' touch such ugliness."

"But I ha' been touching ye all the night long."

"No' there." That wound represented, for him, something he did not even want to contemplate. A failure. A near defeat.

Here in the privacy, the sanctity, of this chamber, he might share with her the best of him. Not the worst.

He turned back and scrambled into his clothing while she watched. Only when he finished did she gather the sheet and half rise from the bed.

Would she ask him to stay? What would he do if she did? He might bring himself to say no. But if she touched him—if she laid her fingers on him again with such stunning tenderness, he feared he might fall to pieces.

All the same, when he was fully clad, he looked at her standing beside the bed. She barely came up to his chin. A mere wisp of a lass.

How could her hold on him be so powerful?

"Mistress Saerla," he asked, even though he hated himself for it, "may I return to ye tonight?"

She closed her eyes for an instant as if she too fought a battle. He could not let himself forget that she, just like him, was a warrior.

She opened her eyes and said, "If I say nay, if I deny ye—"

Agony ran him through, pressing deep like that arrow in his back.

"—would ye respect it? Would ye keep away?"

"To be sure," he told her swiftly, before he could catch the words back. "Wha' ye give to me here, Saerla, is freely given, or…" He struggled to finish the thought. "It means naught."

"Aye." She nodded. "If ye come to my door, Rory MacLeod, I will let ye in."

Suddenly he could breathe again. He could live through this day, whatever it held, till the sun tumbled from the sky once more.

"But, Master MacLeod, I would ha' ye think carefully before ye return." She nodded at his tartan. "About wha' ye are, and wha' I am."

"I scarce ken wha' ye are," he admitted. An angel, perhaps, if he believed in such. A witch, if they commanded the light. Hell, he scarcely knew what he was when with her.

She lifted her chin a notch. "I am one o' the three sisters MacBeith and will always be."

Not here. Not here in this chamber. Here, she was his.

He did not say so. He but inclined his head to her respectfully, as to a queen. This woman he had tasted. She who had rocked in his arms.

"I will, wi' yer permission, mistress, return tonight."

And every night until her sister came to destroy him.

He went out of the chamber and away as swiftly as he could. Not many were about so early, only a few servants. But their heads turned at seeing him hurrying along the corridors.

He headed not for his study but out into the open air.

And there, the glory of Glen Bronach opened before him.

Bonny place, and all he'd ever desired. The love of his heart, if he could be said to have one. But what of the woman inside? Was she not still more beautiful?

More, was she not the very embodiment of this place? The cool mist, the water, the freckled granite stone. The light, the eternal light that illuminated it all.

He must put such fancies away from him. Go and look to his defenses.

Breathe, until he could be with her again tonight.

Chapter Forty-Six

"**I** NEED TO speak wi' ye, sister. A matter o' great and terrible importance."

Saerla looked at Rhian, who had just burst in through the door of the chamber, and a pinprick of doubt stabbed her. Doubt and dread. For days she'd been able to feel this coming.

For nights she'd pushed it away from her.

How many nights had it been now that Rory MacLeod spent in her arms? Quite truly, she had lost count of them.

He always came humbly, his hands bare of weapons. She always thought about refusing him admittance. She never did.

She never could.

She had left the sgian dubh in the chest where she'd found it, because the thought of harming him—one black, silken lock of hair, one beat of his heart—had become as foreign to her as setting herself afire. She did not understand what he'd come to mean to her. She worked hard at keeping the time they spent together here in this chamber separate from the rest of her life. From reality.

One thing only she knew—when he was with her, when he was inside her, nothing else mattered.

To either of them.

Yet the instant Rhian came bursting through the door, the dread she'd harbored for days rose up to swamp her.

"Wha' is it, Rhian?"

Rhian shut the door carefully behind her, staring as if she'd never seen Saerla before.

"I canna warrant what has just come to my ears. I will no' warrant it."

"Wha' has come to your ears?" Saerla asked, though to be sure, she already knew. She had feared all the while it would get out, even though Rory always left her, early before many in the stronghold were astir.

Just like at home, someone was always watching.

"I should say," Rhian babbled on, sounding like a madwoman, "it came first to Leith's ears. On the training field, of all places. And then again in the warriors' hall. In whispers, o' course. Wha' could he do but come to me?"

"Wha' is said in these whispers?"

"That Rory has been spending his nights here. With ye."

Saerla might seek to lie about it. She could deny the truth to her sister, but she'd never been good at lying. Rhian always knew.

Besides, there was a part of her, a fierce, secret part, that did not want to deny the beauty of those moments she and Rory spent together.

She looked her sister in the eye. Should Rhian, of all women, not understand? She, who had given her heart to a MacLeod and forsaken MacBeith to come here and live with him?

Rhian continued to regard her, eyes wide. Shocked. Beseeching. Saerla had never seen her look so.

"Saerla, tell me it is not true."

Saerla said nothing.

"Tell me these are but vicious rumors Leith has brought to me."

"What, just, has been said?"

Rhian's face became grim. "Rory has been seen leaving here early of the mornings. By the guards on duty about the stronghold. More than once!"

Saerla did not speak, though dismay washed through her.

"The first time they thought no' much o' it. Then they began to watch for him. They gossip about it like old women. Their chief, having his way wi' the MacBeith captive."

Saerla did not know what to say, how to admit this truth or explain even to Rhian what she herself did not completely understand.

"Saerla?"

"Aye, Rhian, 'tis true. Rory has been spending the nights here wi' me."

"Spending—" Rhian's stunned gaze moved to the bed and back to her sister. "Wi' yer permission? He did no'—no' force ye?"

Saerla's cheeks flamed. "He did no' force me. I welcomed him."

"But—" Rhian's legs wobbled visibly. She crept to the bench and sat down. "But ye be an innocent. My wee sister." Unsullied and untried, her tone insisted. "Ye be un-breached!"

"I was."

"Saerla!" All Rhian's shock lay in the word. All her horror. "How could ye?" It was a wail.

A spear of anger pricked Saerla. "Ye ask me that? Ye, o' all women?"

"But—but Leith is gentle, beneath all his brawn. He is kind. He loves me. He is no' a monster. He is no' Rory MacLeod, o' all men!

Of all men.

Not giving Saerla a chance to speak, Rhian hurried on. "How did such a thing even come about? How could ye let him touch ye? He being what he is—" Bright anger flared in her eyes. "Ye say he did not force ye?"

"Nay."

"If he did, I will kill him."

"Sister, listen to me. It was I who began it. I thought—I knew I must get near him if I were to use the knife ye brought me."

Horror appeared in Rhian's eyes. "But I thought that knife

would defend ye! I—"

"And I thought the best way for me to get him close enough to me that I might use the knife was to seduce him." Color stained Saerla's face, but she held her sister's gaze. "I ha' never done such a thing. I did no' think I could. But it worked all too well. Rhian, I seduced him and mysel' as well."

"What are ye saying?"

"That I desired what passed between us. I wanted it. I wanted him. I still do."

Rhian seemed to shrink where she sat. She looked at Saerla with doubt. With…was that disgust?

Saerla clenched her fists, turning sick inside.

"Saerla," Rhian whispered. "He is Rory MacLeod."

Not when he is here with me. He is the young boy who ran wild in the glen. A man who touches me so tenderly, it melts my very bones. He who allows me to fly. But that was not completely true, for he remained the conqueror also, deep inside. She had felt that in him. The sense of dark purpose remained always. When he left her, no doubt it flared to life again.

"I maun confess, Saerla, I canna imagine ye doing such a thing. Taking up a sword on the battlefield, aye, though even that was difficult for me to accept. But this—"

"I ken. I did no' expect it to happen either. I thought when I laid my blade to his neck, it would be over—"

"Ye laid yer blade to his neck?" Rhian's eyes narrowed. "And he still lives?"

"I failed, Rhian. I failed."

Rhian clearly did not know what to say.

"Since then, he has continued to stay the nights wi' me."

"Och, Saerla! The warriors are saying that he has taken ye even as he might take all our lands. That he has raped ye, and by doing so rapes all MacBeith."

"That is no' true. Wha' I give to him, I give freely." Leave to touch her with those calloused hands that nevertheless remained ever gentle. Leave to run his hot mouth everywhere over her skin. To fly with her over the glen and into the light.

"Men, being men, want it to be so. They are frustrated that the conflict has gone on so long. That Moira, a mere woman, has stood against Rory MacLeod. That Rory has no' kept his promise and conquered the glen."

"I canna help what others think."

Rhian's eyes glittered. "Wha' about what ye think? Ye feared him, Saerla. He was a boogeyman. The greatest monster in our world. Ye saw wha' he did to Farlan. How he treats Leith, when he argues for peace. How could ye place yoursel' in the destroyer's hands?"

A fair and goodly question. Before being captured and brought here, Saerla had received a Vision back at MacBeith, one so terrible she'd been willing to share it with no one. She'd Seen herself in Rory MacLeod's hands. Being, as she'd believed then, aye, forced by him. *Ye will be mine,* he'd said.

It had not been what she imagined, the truth behind that Vision. That, she now realized in full. The Vision she'd feared so terribly had turned into something else entirely.

Rhian leaned toward her and lowered her voice. "Listen to me, Saerla. I understand the power o' attraction. O' passion. I ha' experienced it wi' Leith, and aye, 'tis a force that can sweep a woman awa'. But Leith—Leith is no' Rory MacLeod. He is the man I love."

"Aye, so," Saerla murmured, beginning to feel distraught. Would her own sister deride her for surrendering to carnal pleasures? Could she bear that?

"For me to give mysel' to Leith," Rhian hurried on, "I maun trust him. Trust him wi' all my heart, and all I am."

Saerla bowed her head.

"My lass, my dear, ye canna possibly trust Rory. And if ye canna trust him, ye can never love him!"

"There is love," Saerla said raggedly, "and there is need."

"Aye, so. But, Saerla, ye ha' never been a woman who gave heed or notice to things o' the flesh. Your calling has always been to higher matters."

"So because the gods speak to me, I am never to have aught else? I am never to be a woman?"

"Aye, lass, to be sure. But no', by God, Rory MacLeod's woman!"

Saerla wanted to weep. Was she not, as she'd begun to believe, meant to be here? Had the Vision she'd Seen and feared not preordained it? Was she to deny what had taken root within her?

Her sister—one of the people she loved most in the world—condemned her for those feelings. She could see that in Rhian's eyes.

"Saerla, ha' ye thought where this will end?"

Nay, she had not.

"Do ye no' want to go home?"

She did, aye, more than anything. More than *almost* anything.

"Wha' if ye go home wi' his babe in yer belly?"

That made Saerla stare.

Rhian's lips twisted. She put a hand to her own stomach. "Believe me, it can happen. And do no' tell me ye ha' no thought o' it."

She had not. Not in so many words.

"Ye be a right clever lass, Saerla. Ye maun have considered—"

When he touches me, I can think of little else. When he is inside me, there is no past or future.

She did not say that. She struggled to form other thoughts instead.

Often—usually—Rory withdrew from her before he spilled his seed. There had been times when they were so deeply joined, when they climaxed at the same instant, that he'd left it with her instead.

Grief now looked at her from Rhian's eyes. "I always thought, sister, ye would find someone special, a man who would understand the beauty that is inside ye. Who would join ye inside yer world. I hoped ye would ha' bairns o' yer own—"

"And I always thought I would live my life alone." There had been no place in what Saerla gave to the gods for a man. Or for that kind of love.

She did not love Rory MacLeod. She was not at all sure what she did feel for him. It could not be love.

"Sister, ye maun put an end to this madness. Should he come to ye again, ye maun send him awa'."

Send him away.

"We maun get ye home to MacBeith, where ye belong."

But that was not fair. Rhian was not at MacBeith, but here with the man she desired.

"Saerla"—Rhian leaned forward and touched Saerla's hand—"naught is more important than the powers that ye serve. Naught can ever be."

"Aye, sister." Mayhap Rhian was right. But when Rory came to her door, would she be able to send him away?

Chapter Forty-Seven

"A WORD, COUSIN, if ye will."

Rory glanced at Leith in surprise. The man looked unaccustomedly grim, and Rory could feel the uneasiness coming off him. In truth, all the warriors with whom he'd worked this afternoon had seemed out of sorts.

To be sure, it had been a hard training session. Rory had spared none of the men, nor himself. They had only a few days left before the sentence he had laid on Saerla's head would expire.

Her sister and the whole MacBeith army would be coming.

It had not happened yet. Rory felt as if he spent half his time, though, in keeping watch for them. The first thing he did every morning after leaving Saerla was climb to the battlements and look toward MacBeith. Most often, it being very early, the only people astir were the guards. They always assured him all was quiet.

Even while he worked at training, he cast glances toward the loch, interrupting his own concentration. And before he went to Saerla of an evening…

His thoughts fractured there, caught upon the image of her. The idea of her. Misty blue eyes, soft lips. Strength and vulnerability. Beautiful, beautiful woman filled with light.

He eyed Leith and assessed his condition. His cousin worked determinedly to win back the full use of his arm, and it was coming along. He did better now than he had.

As did Rory with the wound in his back—which, he came to believe, had begun to heal at last. It no longer pained him as deeply or as fiercely. No longer interfered so drastically with his movements.

That too must be down to Saerla. She had taken to caressing the wound—the flesh around it—when they lay together after coupling. And she'd put her lips there in that kiss of blessing.

By God, he wanted her. He could not wait to be with her this night.

He tossed his head at his cousin. "I suppose ye think we are training too hard?"

"'Tis no' that. I am that glad to win back the strength in my arm." Leith twitched. "But can ye no' feel the discord?"

Rory could. "The men are on edge. They ken an attack can come at any time."

"I do no' think that is all." Leith glanced around. "We canna speak here."

Aye, so, the warriors watched him all from the corners of their eyes.

"Come to the study." Rory wanted a drink anyway. One that would hold him till the sun went down and he could be with Saerla.

They went swiftly to the study, where Rory shut the door behind them and poured two drams before he sat down.

"Wha' is it, then, Leith?"

Leith remained standing, his broad shoulders braced and his forehead creased in a frown. He eyed Rory doubtfully.

"Ha' ye no' heard what the men are saying?"

Rory shook his head. He had, to be fair, not kept an ear to the ground so far as the clan was concerned, not the way he had previously done. "Wha' are they saying?"

Leith swallowed and shook his head. His gaze did not waver from Rory's. "Ye ha' been seen leaving wee Saerla's chamber. Early o' the mornings."

Wee Saerla. Aye, she was tiny to contain so much strength. Delicate limbs. Narrow hands moving over him.

"Impossible," he barked. "No one saw me." He'd left her far too early. Had he not?

Leith snorted. "Ye think the men on guard at the doors o' this fortress are fools? Ye think no servant, up early, but has seen ye creeping awa'?"

He did not creep. He was Rory MacLeod. He went where he chose. Did as he intended.

He lifted his chin and narrowed his eyes at his cousin. "And, so?"

"Ye ha' been spending yer nights wi' her. Sleeping wi' her."

Aye, they had slept between bouts of joining and togetherness so fierce and tight that his mind even now stuttered over it.

"Surely, Leith, 'tis my business, and Mistress Saerla's, whether I spend my nights wi' her."

"She's had a sentence o' death on her head!"

"No longer."

"So ye ha' said, though mere days ago ye hauled her outside and put a blade to her throat. And I ken fine how much you desire ownership o' this glen. Wha's to keep ye fro' changing yer mind?"

"I will no' harm Saerla MacBeith."

Leith blinked at him. A new look invaded his eyes.

Unable to face that expression, quite, Rory poured himself another drink and tossed it straight down. Despite the numbing effect of the liquor, dismay began stealing over him. He'd meant to keep his association with Saerla secret for her sake as well as his. Now the men knew.

No wonder they'd been stealing glances at him from the corners of their eyes.

"Are ye in love wi' her, Rory?"

The question caught Rory like a hard blow to the jaw. He stiffened. Few people in the world would challenge him on such a matter—Leith was one of those few. But it was a question he himself did not want to consider.

He laughed harshly. "Do no' be a fool."

"Love is but foolishness, is it?"

"Aye, to be sure. Can ye imagine me in love?" He spoke the word mockingly. "I ha' important matters to which I maun devote mysel'. I ha' no time for such nonsense."

"Then why spend your nights wi' her?"

"Ye, of all men, would ask me that? The man who got her sister ripe wi' child while a prisoner?" Rory leaned forward. "Hear me and hear me well. Mistress Saerla and I both wanted what passed between us."

"Ye did no' force her, then?"

"To be sure, I did no' force her!" Rory surged back to his feet. "Is that wha' ye think o' me? Am I a man who forces women?"

Leith's eyes narrowed. "I would no' ha' said so. But Rhian insists her sister is an innocent, and no' the sort to succumb to the pleasures o' the flesh. Saerla is only lightly o' this world and has ne'er shown interest in any man."

That made Rory's chest expand with sheer euphoria. For, aye, she showed interest in him. Every inch of him.

Precious lass, to give herself only to him.

But another point overshadowed his gratitude. "Ye ha' told Rhian wha' the guards and such ha' been saying?"

"Aye, so."

"Ye did no' think it better to keep such gossip from yer woman's ears?"

"Rhian and I keep naught from one another."

Sanctimonious bastard.

"And she needed to know lest ye did force the lass and she needed rescue from yer—yer—" Leith sought a word.

"Lust?"

"Aye."

Christ Jesus! All he needed was Mistress Rhian coming at him like a mother wolf on the defense. This was why he'd thought to keep it secret. But all had broken apart, so it seemed.

"Well now, ye ken I did no' force the woman, and ye can tell Rhian the same."

"I imagine if 'tis true, Saerla will tell Rhian hersel'."

"What?"

"Rhian will be with her sister by now. Ye did no' expect me to keep her awa'?"

Rory supposed God himself could not do so.

"She will tell Saerla to ha' done wi' ye. Surely ye ken that."

And would Saerla listen? She had told Rory how close the sisters had been all their lives, and how she, the youngest, let herself be guided by both Rhian and Moira.

If he presented himself at her door this night, would she allow him in? Mayhap not. Quite possibly stern words from her sister would destroy the spell that had been woven between them.

Pain seared through him at the thought. A sense of loss most terrible.

He thrust it away from him. He was Rory MacLeod, a strong man, full grown. Chief of a powerful clan. Would he let the desire for a woman bring him to his knees?

He had seen what such weakness had done to Farlan. To Leith, for God's sake.

He did not need Saerla MacBeith. In truth, he must have been mad to go to her all these nights past. What he should do was keep away from her now that their trysts had come to light. Be a man. Deny the desire.

He nodded at his cousin. Leith had woken him up right well.

"I will do wha' is wise, cousin, and keep awa'."

Chapter Forty-Eight

TWILIGHT CAME DOWN softly outside the window of Saerla's chamber. She had sat there long after Rhian left, trying to occupy—or distract—herself by keeping her hands busy on the spindle. She had long cast the instrument aside, though, after the thread broke time and time again.

She sat instead watching the light and thinking about her life. It had been an odd enough sort of existence for a young woman. Daughter of a chief, born to a loving home with many advantages. The darling of her family and gifted with a rare ability to See beyond the confines of this world. She had stepped from that after losing her adored big brother and trained as a warrior. Successful at that also.

It should be enough for any woman.

But then she'd encountered Rory MacLeod.

She'd seen him on the battlefield, to be sure, including the first time he'd captured her. And she'd Seen him in that terrible Vision—the one she'd dared confide to no one—of her being in his power, when he'd said, *Ye will be mine.* She was sure, having received that Vision, he meant to capture and rape her.

She knew better now.

There had been no rape, no forcing. She wanted the man with a strength she'd never imagined. Indeed, she scarcely recognized herself when she was with him. She was not the same woman she had been.

She lived always in her mind, in her spirit. Not the flesh.

But she had been a long time away from the sacred ground on the rise back home. The place where the Visions so often found her. Where both the spirits and her ancestors spoke to her.

Where she lost herself in the light.

That must explain it, how she was able to turn to Rory, who carried so much powerful darkness. He had vowed to destroy her clan and claim the lands she loved. He had spread death with a merciless hand. So determined and ruthless was he, he'd cast off his dearest friend.

And yet…*and yet.*

When he came to her, he did it softly, gently. And the darkness in him somehow called up the light in her, and transformed into a powerful passion.

Her eyes widened as she realized what that meant. She had not left all the light back home.

She kept it inside her, even here.

The realization made her want to weep. It meant she had not lost herself completely to what lay between her and Rory MacLeod. She remained Saerla MacBeith. He would not change that. Not even her feelings for him could.

What *were* her feelings for him?

She leaned to rest an elbow on the edge of the slit window embrasure and thought about it. Desire, aye—that went without saying. Everything about him, from the set of his shoulders to the gleam in his green eyes, appealed to her. More than that, his mind—clever and quick and devious, the opposite of her own— seemed somehow to reflect and complement all she thought. The need in him—for aye, Rory harbored a deep need, even if he did not acknowledge it—called up her own need.

Aye, she needed him. That was it. She craved not only his touch but his company. His presence. The way she felt when they lay together, replete, as if neither of them required anything more from the world.

She could, at those moments, feel his sense of completion as much as her own.

Need, though, was not love. She did not love Rory MacLeod, could not permit herself to love him. For beneath it all, he remained the monster. Her enemy.

Rhian said if he appeared at her door this night, she should refuse to admit him. And outside the window, night swiftly approached down the glen on velvet wings. No doubt, as so often, Rhian was right.

Did Saerla have the strength to turn Rory away?

Perhaps he would not come. If rumors about the two of them flew, he would have heard them. He could not allow himself to appear vulnerable. Unable to turn from a woman.

Nay, he would not come.

Could she bear it?

Aye, for there were greater matters here than her longing. The love for her clan. Her people. Her duty as a possession of the gods.

This—this had been but a mad interlude. One meant to teach her something. That Rory was, beneath it all, just a man.

He would keep away from her this night. She felt sure of it, and she beat back the grief while the moments stole by and the gloaming fell across the land outside her window.

She believed it, right till the moment she heard his knock at the door.

She leaped to her feet.

It had grown late—later even than he usually came to her. Perhaps after all it was not him but Rhian, returned to make sure she did nothing foolish.

But nay, she knew even before she hauled the door open. Before she saw him standing there.

He waited quietly, his black head bowed, his hands empty. His gaze found hers the instant the panel swung wide, asking a question even before his lips found the words.

"Mistress, may I come in?"

All the breath left Saerla in a rush. It felt precisely like she'd been struck in the gut during a battle and she could not speak.

Nor did she move, digging her fingers into the oaken door as if she'd score it. Leave her mark. For an instant her life reeled before her eyes, all the glorious days leading to this one moment. The two paths offered by destiny lying before her. Shut the door. Allow him in.

The moment seemed to stretch out forever while she sought words that would not come.

He spoke before she could in, a harsh whisper. "I should no' be here. Word has got out that I ha' been seen coming awa' fro' yer door—"

"Aye."

"Yer sister told ye?"

"Aye." Was it all she could say? Saerla closed her eyes for an instant, clinging to the door. "I should send ye awa'."

"Aye. Ye should." She counted her heartbeats up to ten. "Will ye?"

She opened her eyes and looked at him. Monster. Destroyer. A danger to her people and her peace of mind. The man who had worshiped her in his arms.

If she shut the door upon him now, it would be done. He would not appear here again. She need only shut the door.

Her nails dug more deeply into the wood of the panel. Her bare toes curled on the stone of the floor.

"Saerla." He whispered it, the voice she heard in her ear when he breached her and made her complete. The plea he gave to her when he knelt at her feet. The music she heard in her dreams.

Who was he? That man, or the one who would wrest away the glen she loved?

Sometimes—sometimes a woman had to act on faith.

She swung wide the door.

❧ ⸎ ☙

Chapter Forty-Nine

R ORY HAD BEEN sure she would deny him. He told himself—had told himself repeatedly—that it was her right. She could send him away if she thought it best.

The expression he saw in her eyes when she opened the door declared she thought it best.

And aye, he had prepared himself for the humiliation of it. The frustration. The disappointment. He'd prepared to commit himself to the bleak pit of despair that awaited should she reject him. One so deep he might never crawl up and out of it again.

It might be for the best, if she rejected him. If it ended here. The desire. The madness. He could answer those looks his men had started tossing at him. Get back to the task of conquest.

But she stood there on her little, bare feet with her eyes full of mist and considered him. He could see that, feel it.

Was he worthy of Saerla MacBeith?

Nay, not by a long way. His mind knew that. His heart…

His heart whispered, *Please, lass. Please let me in.*

As if she'd heard his heart, she suddenly drew wide the panel and did invite him in.

He strode into the chamber that was no longer wholly his own. If she left here, if she went from him, he would not be able to use this place. He would have to find other lodging.

He turned and faced her even as she carefully shut the door

behind him. Words needed to be said. Decisions must be made.

He wanted only to hold her.

"Saerla."

All at once, she was in his arms. She trembled. She pressed against him and stretched on her tiptoes so her lips could reach his. He drew her in tight, tighter. The yawning darkness inside him retreated a few steps so he could breathe.

"Och, lass. Darling." He spoke between the small, fervent kisses she showered upon him.

He captured her face between his hands, his fingers in the wild tumble of her hair, and kissed her more deeply.

Naught could be deep enough. Not until he was inside this woman. *Inside her.*

"Och," he babbled when the kiss ended. "Och, Christ."

They needed to speak together, so he told himself again. Make those decisions. But she twined her arms around his neck and wrapped her legs around his hips. He carried her to the bed.

"I should no' be here," he told her as he unfastened his sark.

"Nay, ye should no'." She watched him, quiet now as he shed the garment and the others he wore, her eyes filled with wonder. When he stood naked before her, he had nothing. No rank. No ambitions. No clan. He was a man breathing only for her.

"Since word has got out—" He stopped speaking because she held out her hand to him, one small hand, and then all words fled. He climbed onto the bed and gathered her, still clad in the gray gown, into his arms.

Nothing had ever felt so good. Nothing in his life. He'd feared he would not hold her again. Inhale her breath. Crush her mouth beneath his.

She wiggled away from him, freeing herself just enough to remove her clothing. Once she did, it got even better. Skin against skin. The heat and taste of her. The madness that took hold of his head when they began to move together, softly at first and then with an abandon that gripped both of them equally.

But this was no longer merely about a need of the flesh. The wanting went far deeper, and when she opened herself to him, when he slid into her and the light came out to embrace him, obscuring everything else, he wanted to sob. He, a grown man. A warrior.

She was filled with beautiful light, his lass, his darling, his love. When they lay entwined so, she beat back his darkness.

They flew together on the wings of the light, he inside her, she resting safe in his arms.

They flew high over the glen, brushed the tops of the braes and the sky, their hearts beating as one.

After, she lay quietly beneath him with tears on her cheeks. And he…he knew the truth.

It had come to him while he soared above Glen Bronach with her, the place they both loved. He felt what was inside her, this strong and fragile woman he held for the time. For a time only.

For one could not imprison the light.

Lying with his cheek against hers, he felt that full well. The light came where it chose, blessed as it chose. Saerla possessed a beautiful spirit. Her body might be his for a short while. To claim that spirit required far more arrogance than he possessed.

She had stripped all his arrogance from him. He came to this woman humbly, begging her presence, unsure even now why she let him in.

"Rory." She turned her face on the bolster so her lips slid across his cheek. She kissed the corner of his mouth, and tenderness for her once more swamped him. "Ye left me your seed."

Had he? When he was inside her, he could not think clearly. Only feel. He blinked. In the beginning he'd been careful about that, tried to be careful. Everything about her, though, seduced him.

"Aye, so," he breathed raggedly.

"Rhian has reminded me I might well conceive your child."

He propped himself on one elbow and looked down at her. With infinite care he ran a finger down her cheek. His child, conceived in such light?

But she said, "'Twould be a terrible, hard thing."

"Would it?" Would it truly?

"Aye."

"And, bonny lass, ha' ye conceived my child?" He laid a broad hand on her belly.

She shook her head. "Nay. At least, I do no' think—I ha' no' Seen so. Still"—she studied the expression in his eyes—"ye need an heir. One no' of MacBeith blood."

A great heaviness descended upon Rory. The dark yawned at his feet. But he, aye, knew now what he had to do. "Saerla—" he began, and paused, devoid of words. He'd never been good at expressing his feelings. Easier to act and let the pieces fall as they may. And his feelings for this woman—well, they went beyond expression anyway.

"Listen to me. Tomorrow is the tenth day."

"Eh?"

"O' the number I gave to yer sister. I said if she did no' yield her lands to me I would tak' yer life on the tenth day."

Saerla's eyes widened.

"To be sure, I will no'. I could no'." Again he struggled for words. "I could sooner place a blade into my own heart as harm a hair o' ye."

"Moira does no' ken that."

"She does no'. Ye sent her yon letter asking her no' to spend hersel' on a rescue. She refused."

"Aye, she did."

"Aye," he agreed softly.

"Wha' will ye do?"

"I ken fine wha' I maun do. Come first light tomorrow morning, I will send ye home."

"Eh?" She struggled to sit up. He kept her where she was with a hand at her breast.

"Saerla, listen to me. 'Twas wrong ever to keep ye here, a prisoner. Nay man can imprison what ye be." He said what he did not wish to. "I maun mak' it right and send ye back."

And what did he see in her beautiful eyes? Surprise, surely. For all her Sight, she had not foreseen this. Did he see sorrow also? Regret? Och, God, let him see at least a hint of regret. Because it would tear him asunder to watch her go from him. No matter that he knew to his very soul it was the right thing to do.

"Rory." She laid her hand against his cheek and studied him. "Ye would do this for me?"

"I would." *Tell me ye will no' go. Say it will break your heart to leave me.*

But she did not. Even though her eyes filled with tears and her lips trembled, she did not offer to stay with him.

And that was only right. How could he hold such a creature in his scarred and bloodied hands? Miracle enough that he'd had her for a time.

"Wha' will happen after that?" she asked.

"Eh?"

"Once I am returned home."

He did not like to think. When he looked beyond this moment while still they lay together, when he peered at the prospect of her leaving him, he saw only the darkness.

She rushed on, "Will ye seek to forge a peace? Ye and Farlan—"

"Nay."

"But, Rory, 'tis possible—"

"Nay. I maun go on wi' my plans. I ha' sworn that to my people. Farlan and I—that breach canna be healed."

Now he saw sorrow in her eyes, a depth of it that matched his own.

She whispered, "Surely it can. Once, ye were so close wi' him and Leith. As close as my sisters and me. I ha' Seen—"

"Once. Long ago." And would he one day look back on these moments with her in that same way? Aye, for he must wed a good woman of his own clan, beget an heir. Live the life that lay—should lie—before him.

Could a man live so, without a heart? Because she would take his heart with her. He loved her as he would never love anyone again.

Yet he could not tell her so.

If he loved her, he must do what was best for her. Send her back where she belonged.

"Saerla, promise me something."

"What?"

"That ye will no longer tak' the field in battle. If yer sister fights on—"

"So she will. She will never yield to ye, Rory."

"Ye will no' march out. Ye will no' don yer armor or tak' up the sword. Ye will hold fast to yer magic."

Barely a breath away from him, she gazed up into his eyes.

"I canna mak' ye that promise. Och, I will hold fast to my magic, aye, till I die. But"—she hesitated, tears once more flooding her eyes—"so long as ye wage war against us, I maun march out against ye."

"Nay." His entire being cried it.

"Rory, I can no more gi' up fighting for what I love than ye will stop this campaign and let Glen Bronach lie in peace."

It would end badly. It would all end in terrible sorrow. He suddenly knew that as if she had whispered the truth of it in his ear. As if he himself had Seen.

Even though he did right by her, it could only end in grief.

The tears in her eyes spilled over, ran down to wet the bolster. "I am to leave ye, come morning?"

"Aye. I will send ye safe wi' Leith—"

"Then mak' love to me. Mak' love to me one last time."

With all of his heart, he did.

Chapter Fifty

SUCH A MORNING should not look so bright, Saerla decided as she stood gazing out on the sward at the front of MacLeod's stronghold. The sky should be dark with cloud, a storm boiling up the glen from the direction of the sea. The loch should be tossing, and the hills scowling.

Instead, the beauty of it all fair dazzled her eyes. The turf shone brilliant green in the new light, and the loch glittered with a thousand shards of radiance. The sky stacked blue upon blue, and the smallest details stood out in stark relief. On the far side of the glen she could see…

Home.

MacBeith's keep stood out glowing whitely. Above it, the rise of granite and turf seemed to beckon her. There did mist gather still, a cauldron of magic.

She longed to be there, so much she ached with it. She did not want to leave the man who stood at her side.

He had done as she asked last night and made love to her one last time. That it was love and no longer just lust, her heart was now certain. At least on her part, her heart was fully engaged.

She'd known that full well as she tasted him for the last time. Opened herself to him for the last time. Inhaled his scent. Plunged her fingers through his black hair. Taken him inside her, deep inside.

What he felt, she could not tell. A man such as Rory MacLeod might be incapable of love as she understood it. So they, at MacBeith, had always believed. He was, aye, tender with her. Inexpressibly tender. And he was sending her home.

She turned and looked up at him. His black hair shone in the sun, and his face, set in an emotionless mask, might have been carved from the same granite that formed the glen. He did not look at her, had refused to look at her since they'd risen and dressed this morning, and he'd left to make the arrangements to send her home.

Now he still gazed anywhere but at her. At the loch, at Mac-Beith's fortress beyond. At his own stronghold behind them. At the two who stood here in their company.

It was just the four of them out here on the sward—Saerla, Rory, Leith, and Rhian. Leith would accompany Saerla on her journey, ferry her across the loch and leave her on the other side. She would make her own way from there, every step taking her from the man she loved, while Leith rowed back.

She could not bear it.

She could not do anything else. For her arrival back home might stay the battle she'd Seen, the one in which both Alasdair and Moira lost their lives.

Though only the four of them stood out in front of the stronghold, Saerla did not deceive herself. Scores of others watched them from behind and atop the walls. Guards, others of the warriors, servants, MacLeod clansfolk.

She could not touch Rory as she wished. Lean up and kiss him one more time. She would not so embarrass him, nor impugn his dignity. Even though it seemed everyone knew already where he'd been last night.

Even Rhian, who'd rolled her eyes at Saerla when they met this morning.

"Did that monster force his way in upon ye again last evening?"

"There was no forcing, sister. I let him in."

Rhian had not been pleased. "Aye, well, the gods be praised he is doing the right thing and letting ye go."

They were both doing the right thing. How, then, could it feel so wrong?

Leith stepped up to Saerla and looked at her kindly. "Ready, mistress?"

"Sister. Call me Sister."

He tried to smile. Leith ordinarily had a very engaging smile. It failed him now. Did he understand in part what it took for her to leave?

Rhian came forward and embraced Saerla hard. It felt like being held once more in Ma's arms. "Sister, be safe."

"Ye also." When would she see Rhian again? "Tak' care o' the bairn."

"I will."

Saerla turned to Rory. He still gazed off across the glen, over her head, green eyes narrowed, as if nothing more concerned him. The planes of his face had gone tense and stern.

"Chief MacLeod."

He focused on her at last. The cold in his eyes flared into something else that encompassed despair.

Should she tell him how she felt for him? Lean up close before they must part and whisper the words for his ear alone? *I love ye, Rory MacLeod. I love ye right well.* She might never have another chance. Might never see him again.

Except on the battlefield. In her dreams. Rory running wild with two other lads.

"Mistress." He gave her a jerky bow. "A safe journey."

"Look after yoursel', and please, please consider achieving a peace."

His lips twisted in a bitter grimace. It was the last sight she had of him before she and Leith started away.

RORY STOOD AND watched Saerla out of sight. He could see a great distance, so clear was the air. That meant he stood there a long while following the progress of the two figures. Leith, so large and broad, Saerla looking terribly small at his side. When they reached the loch, Leith drew up a wee boat and prepared to help her in.

Once she crossed the water, she would be lost to him.

But nay—she was already lost to him.

At his side, Rhian babbled something. Telling him he'd done the right thing. He barely listened, all his being focused on the woman with the crown of red-gold hair.

Just before Leith helped her into the boat, she turned and looked back at him. And it was as if—almost—he touched her again. As if they flew together once more.

If only they had wings. They might meet on the updrafts. Soar above the glen, over the hills and into the light.

He was earthbound without her. Sworn to this land, to this granite, to his intentions.

She got into the boat. Leith rowed away.

He could not bear it.

Mayhap he should have told her early this morning in his chamber before they parted. Told her that he loved her. But nay, love did not adequately describe what he felt for her. No words could describe.

He lost sight of them as they crossed the water. Coming to himself, he realized he stood alone. Mistress Rhian had gone.

Savage emotions arose and gripped him. He wanted to destroy something. Rend someone limb from limb. Assuage this grief in violence.

But it could not be assuaged, this hurt. It had no limits. He had done the right thing, aye. But by God, he would pay a price.

He marched back into the forecourt, no longer letting himself gaze away across the glen. She was gone. Her soft lips, her fragile fingers, the great and splendid wealth of her. Worse, the magical refuge that was her heart.

He would never again know joy. Aye, but a man could carry on without joy. He had done so before. He could see to his duties, mind his defenses, plan for conquest. For he could not let something so weak as feelings for a woman interfere in the achievement of his lifelong plan.

Ah, but what he felt for Saerla MacBeith was not weak. It was by far the strongest thing he'd ever known.

Strong enough to make him let her go.

On his way through the forecourt, he bellowed to his men, "To training! Wha' be ye waiting about here for? We ha' battles to fight!"

He would lose himself in drilling, in the sweat and the pain of it. And perhaps, for a few short moments, he could dismiss Saerla MacBeith from his mind.

Chapter Fifty-One

"S HE WILL NO' eat. She's taken precious little to drink, and I do no' think she's slept at all. She has no' even been up on the rise since she returned home. Farlan, I do no' ken wha' to do."

Did Moira not realize that Saerla could hear her speaking to Farlan, there outside the door of her chamber? Did she think Saerla deaf? Aye, but the worry in her voice went straight to Saerla's heart. Not enough, though, to rouse her from the depths of her sorrow.

"Nay," Farlan murmured unhappily in reply. Seeing Moira upset worried him. Besides, Saerla believed Farlan too cared about her welfare. He was, at the heart, that kind of man.

Saerla had to admit, Moira had chosen well in her mate. Though she'd once had her doubts about the MacLeod prisoner, she saw now the depth of Farlan's character, steady as the rock beneath the glen they all loved.

As had Rhian chosen well. Saerla liked Leith very much. On the trip across from MacLeod, he had been infinitely gentle with her, almost as if he understood.

Only she, of the three sisters MacBeith, had chosen poorly. The marauder. The monster. He who would steal from them all they cherished.

How could she have given such a man her heart?

Four days had passed since she'd returned to MacBeith. Four interminable days. Four endless nights. Saerla had to admit, the nights were the worst, because she'd become accustomed to spending that time in Rory MacLeod's arms. Now she could not so much as place her head upon the bolster without thinking of him. Longing for him. So she refused to lie down and instead paced the dark hours away.

"She is no' our Saerla anymore." Tears half choked Moira's voice. "Wha' did he do to her there, when he held her prisoner?"

What had he done to her? Run his big, calloused hands all over her body. Bestowed kisses like blessings. Brought a sleeping part of her to life.

Moira knew none of that. Saerla had barely spoken with her sister before retiring to her chamber. She'd not told Moira that she'd gifted Rory with her virginity. That she might even now be carrying his child.

No Rhian here, to advise her as to that. Only time would tell, and she grieved over time.

"He did the right thing in the end," Farlan rumbled, "and sent her home."

That was Farlan all over—defending his former friend, who had cast him off and deprived him of his birthright for the sin of disagreeing with him. Farlan of the great and generous heart.

All at once, Saerla wanted to weep. She had not yet, save those few tears at the parting. Now she wanted to weep and weep.

Her chamber door opened. "Sister?" Moira stepped in with Farlan like a rock at her back. "I am that concerned for ye. Ha' ye taken aught to eat this day?"

Saerla shook her head. She'd not eaten nor combed out her hair. Worse, she'd refused to let Moira persuade her into clean clothing and still wore the gray gown she'd inhabited at Mac-Leod. Rhian's gown.

"My love." Moira came farther in and hunkered down by the bed where Saerla sat. Stark concern sat plain to see in her beautiful blue eyes. "Ye maun eat something. I fear ye will sicken, and then what? Wi'out Rhian here—"

"I am well enough, Moira." An outright lie. "If ye would do somewhat for me, pray, leave me be."

"I canna do that. I want my wee sister back." Moira seized both Saerla's hands in her own.

"I am right here, Moira."

"Ye are no'. That monster may ha' sent ye back home, aye, but the Saerla I love is no' inside the lass he returned to me."

I am here she wanted to say but did not. *I am merely hiding like a beast hurt past enduring. And he is no' a monster.*

"Come out and get some air," Moira urged. "'Tis a beautiful day."

"Ha' ye been watching from the walls? Do the MacLeods prepare to attack?" Would Rory mobilize soon? Would he go back to making war on them as if nothing had ever happened between them?

Moira shook her head. "No' sign o' movement yet."

"And ye?" Saerla searched her sister's eyes. "Do ye muster for an attack?"

"No' yet. Alasdair—Alasdair says to wait. He is very nearly well enough to tak' the field after his sore hurt. He says once he is able to march out beside me at the head o' the men—"

Then the fighting would recommence. She had done nothing to prevent that, or the possible outcomes she'd seen in her Vision.

She seized Moira's arms. "Sister, ye maun no'. I ha' Seen terrible losses if ye return to the fight." Her life and Alasdair's.

"Ha' ye?" Grief flooded Moira's eyes. "But if he attacks us, we canna refuse to fight. I will no'—can no'—surrender our lands."

"Och!" Saerla raised her hands to cover her face.

Moira, distressed, glanced at Farlan, who had stepped up behind her.

Farlan sent a look of concern to Saerla. Did he guess at what she'd Seen? That he might be going to lose the woman he loved?

From the depth of worry in his brown eyes, she gathered he

might. Then again, the concern might still be for her, Saerla, because he said, "Moira has the right idea, mistress. Come out and tak' the air."

"Aye," Moira said in agreement, and urged Saerla up. As soon as Saerla stood, her legs failed her and she went down again onto the floor.

Terror flashed in Moira's eyes. "Saerla!"

"Shall I carry her to the healers?" Farlan asked.

"Nay. That is no' wha' she needs. Pray, Farlan, carry her up the rise."

⟫⟫⟫⟪⟪⟪

IT WAS A steady pull up the skirt of the mountain to the rise, and a long way for Farlan to carry Saerla, but he did so without apparent effort. Not until they'd nearly reached the level place that overlooked the glen did the breath come more quickly in his broad chest.

Moira had not come with them. Though she had indeed set out with them, she'd been called away to some problem with the defenses. So it was just Saerla and Farlan when they reached the cairn that marked Da's grave.

Farlan set Saerla down carefully but kept an arm around her lest she fall. She stood and gazed out over the glen.

Moira had been right—it was a glorious day. Clouds flew fast from the west, driven by a steady wind, and everything below her glittered, from the stones of the keep to those embedded in the turf, to the broad waters of the loch. Everywhere, everywhere lay glorious light.

She drew a breath and then another deeper one. They felt like the first she'd taken in far too long.

Beside her, Farlan said nothing. He was a quiet, restful sort of man withal. But he kept his broad hand planted against Saerla's back, and she could feel his strength just as she could feel the strength pushing up through her feet from the granite beneath the soil.

Och, aye, she'd needed this.

She raised her eyes to the fortress across the way, the one made of dark stone. It looked so small from this distance, too small to contain someone of such vital importance to her.

Aye, Moira was right, it lay quiet. Like a dark jewel in the gods' hands.

"'Tis a bonny place when ye see it fro' up here," she said to Farlan. "And all of a piece. 'Tis a sin to war over this."

"Aye, so."

"Ye would think all the love, Rory's for his side and ours for this, would bind it together."

"Love is a strong enough force."

Saerla turned her head and looked at him. "Ye believe that, do ye?"

"'Tis the strongest thing I ha' ever known." Strong enough to take him from his home and bind him to Moira's side.

Suddenly she wanted to confess all to this calm, steady man who had hitched his star to love. Surely, he would understand. But she could never forbid him from speaking in turn to Moira, and she was not ready for Moira to know what she had done.

Lain with the monster who beleaguered them. Given him her heart.

Instead, she stepped away from Farlan and laid her hands on the stones of Da's cairn. Warm from the sun. Full in the light.

Da? Be ye here?

The answer came swiftly, a deep throb of reassurance in her mind. *Aye, daughter. I am here and everywhere.*

Saerla's eyes filled with tears. *Do ye condemn me for what I ha' done?*

Love, daughter, should ne'er be condemned. It is never wrong. Did I no' bid ye tell Moira so, back when she fell for this man who stands beside ye?

He is a good man.

He is. And so is Leith MacLeod, for whom yer sister Rhian traveled awa' from us. Why should it be different for ye?

'Tis different because Rory MacLeod is different. He is the darkness that brings our pain. If he costs us Moira's or Alasdair's life—

Darkness, daughter, can be battled only by light. 'Tis that ye carry within ye. Gather it, Saerla. Gather it and make o' it yer weapon.

Saerla nodded. She stood for many more moments listening for further wisdom before she walked from her father's cairn and into the waiting circle of standing stones, cloaked in magic.

Chapter Fifty-Two

"HOW FARES THAT arm o' yours, Leith? Be ye ready at last for the fight?"

When Rory asked the question, his cousin turned and directed a searching look at him—wondering, no doubt, how best to reply. They had just ended another grueling training session. Rory had been driving himself and the men hard. He'd been able to see, during training these days just past, that Leith swung the sword with more power and control than at any time since his injury.

Rory wanted him to admit it. He wanted a reason to attack MacBeith.

Four days had passed since Saerla left him. Since he'd sent her away. He knew very well he'd been in a foul mood. Nay, that did not describe it sufficiently. He'd been in a savage mood. Harsh, unsparing, impatient, and constantly on the verge of losing control of himself.

Such befitted a man living in darkness.

Leith did not want to return to the fight, as Rory knew very well. His woman did not want it either, did not wish the battles against her folk to resume. Leith had no doubt surmised that if he admitted he was ready for the field, the campaign would restart.

But Rory needed to prove something to himself, if not to his people. He needed to prove he could wage war upon Saerla's clan without a qualm. He needed—

He needed to see her, to touch her, to inhale her scent. He needed her warmth and the mist in her eyes.

All the magical light of her had fled him. And aye, he remained mired in darkness.

He knew very well that Leith's arm was better. He left off waiting for an answer. "When we go to battle, ye will tak' the place at my side."

Leith's lips twisted. The look did not suit him. His should be an open, sunny face. "Ye mean Farlan's place?"

Farlan, aye, had always fought at Rory's side, ever since first they'd entered battle together. After Da died, Rory had trusted Leith with one flank, and Murgor with the other. All that must now change.

Farlan would be standing against him, not with him. As might Saerla.

She was a warrior. She went to battle with a sword in her hand. He had met her so before, and if he did again…

Suddenly he could not breathe.

Leith stared at him. "Cousin, what is it?"

"Naught." *Naught.*

"Rory." Leith clapped a hand on his shoulder. "Will ye no' at least consider—"

Rory turned on him. "If the word 'peace' crosses yer lips, I swear I will out wi' my dirk and stab ye through the heart."

"All right. All right!"

"I ha' made a promise to our people. Is that to mean naught? Did my da no' keep his promises, always?"

Leith said nothing.

"Wha' sort o' chief would I be that did no' follow through on his word? I want all o' Glen Bronach in my hands by the end o' this season."

"Aye, so ye ha' said."

"So"—Rory whirled to face Leith full-on—"will ye tak' the place at my side? And do no' say ye maun ask yer woman first.

Has she got yer balls hanging fro' her belt?"

A rare spark of anger took light in Leith's eyes. "My balls are where they belong."

"Then gi' me yer vow o' fealty."

"I ha' already sworn fealty to ye!"

"Then best show it. I need ye and yer sword at my right hand. 'Tis where ye will be."

Leith's head came up. "Ye offer me no true choice, then. Rory, only think. If we march out, I may well be killed. My arm is better than it was, aye, but I ha' no' the strength I had in my hand before, and 'tis no' yet completely healed. If I fall, where will that leave Rhian?"

"Wi' yer brat in her belly, it seems." Had Rory given Saerla, tiny Saerla, his child? Did she even now carry a part of him?

"She will be alone among strangers."

"Will yer mother and sister no' look after her, and the brat?"

"My son is no' a brat." Leith grew angry, and no mistake.

Rory spat into his face, "Ye ha' a choice, Leith. Ye can answer my call upon ye for service, or ye can abandon yer clan as Farlan has done."

"Ye would let me leave? I might tak' Rhian and go?" A new light took hold in Leith's gaze.

Once more, Rory felt as if he could not draw breath, though for a different reason. He'd been socked in the gut. *Would* he let Leith take his woman and leave? Turn his coat and fight for MacBeith, against him?

He could not do that.

"'Tis yer loyalty holds ye here," he sneered, unable and unwilling to display the depth of his hurt. "If ye have no' the honor to uphold that—"

"Ye are no' an easy man to serve, Rory. Especially since ye sent wee Saerla awa'."

Do not speak her name. But Rory did not say that. He could not.

"Speak wi' yer woman," he growled instead. "Get her permission to fulfill yer vow. We will march out tomorrow."

"Tomorrow?" Leith looked stricken.

"Aye, why wait? Every day we tarry gives that war chief o' theirs time to grow stronger."

"Can ye muster the men so quickly?"

"Aye, so. They ha' been ready for days. If they are no' prepared to fight after these last days spent drilling, they will never be."

And he, Rory thought, marched to battle and possible death—for that was always and always a possibility—without an heir. Only the lad that Rhian supposedly carried. Or did he? Could it be, after all, that Saerla did carry his bairn?

He had not meant to give her a child. But there had been times—she had claimed him, milked him so he had given his all.

He might be waging war on his own son. For an instant, terror gripped him, so bright it seared his senses. He wanted to protect Saerla, and any child—lad or lass—she might carry.

Och, he was sworn to ruin, and there was no way out.

"MY DEAR ONE, I was hoping for a word wi' ye."

Saerla turned her head when the kind words sounded behind her. She and Farlan had come down from the rise earlier, she trailing a measure of magic. Being there had partially restored her. And now she sat out front of the stronghold in the quiet, watching the gloaming come down. Wondering…

What if this were the last peaceful gloaming she would ever know?

Why she should feel that, she could not say. She had received several messages while up among the stones. None said she would die.

In truth, most had concerned life. Aye, Moira and Alasdair's lives still hung in the balance. But it seemed love could save them.

She smiled at Fiona, who approached her across the green turf. Fiona had been Da's lover at the time of his death, a big, rawboned woman so different from Ma, it was almost ludicrous.

Perhaps Da, knowing he could not have Ma again, had merely accepted love where he found it.

As had she.

"I feel much better, Fiona."

"Good, that. Yer sister was gey worried about ye. As was I." Fiona perched beside Saerla on the rock where she sat. "Poor Moira was half frantic when that beast held ye in his hands."

Saerla's body twitched.

"She wanted to march out and wage battle to win ye back. Alasdair was all behind it, though he was no' fit to fight. Far from it. Farlan tried to discourage Moira, and the council came down on him for a traitor."

"Farlan is no traitor."

"Is he no'?"

Saerla shook her head. "I ha' scarcely known a truer heart."

"Aye, well, then yer letter came. Fair forbidding Moira to attack. Lass, why did ye send that? We feared ye were being bullied into it. Were ye?"

Saerla hesitated. Fiona was the last person in whom she should confide. The woman, God love her, was constitutionally incapable of keeping a secret.

Yet kindness shone from her hazel eyes. Love lay here also.

Carefully, Saerla said, "I feared, Fiona, that the consequences o' such an attack on Moira's part could outweigh what might be won."

Did Fiona understand? She blinked at Saerla and said quietly for her, "Wha' could be more important, wee lass, than restoring ye to us?"

"Keeping all who bide here alive and safe." Saerla looked away from Fiona's troubled face. "Now, the battle will come anyway, and I hate to think—"

A loss might well be had on either side. Alasdair would have to fight with a half-healed wound in his gut. Moira always marched out in the vanguard, first targeted to be struck down. And Rory, Rory with that ugly hole in his back.

She could not bear to lose any of them.

"Lass, ye seem overwrought. Come back to my quarters wi' me. We will sit quiet. I will mak' ye a wee bit o' supper. Just the two o' us, aye?"

"That does sound wonderful. But I—I ha' been unable to tak' much to eat since I returned."

Fiona went quiet, which was so unusual for her, it made Saerla search her eyes. She found great hesitancy there.

"Is it so?" Fiona examined Saerla disquietingly. "Are ye right within' yersel'?"

"I am not sure that I am, Fiona."

"Ye ken fine, lass, we worried about all kinds o' nasty things befalling ye there at MacLeod. That Rory might make a weapon o' ye or an instrument o' revenge. Even though we knew Rhian would protect ye as best she could."

He is not like that. But Saerla could not say so. She said nothing.

Fiona clasped Saerla's hands between her own. "When I was young and first wed my husband, Raef"—a warrior who had died years ago, leaving her a widow—"I knew I was wi' child because I could no' stand the sight o' food."

Fiona stared at Saerla meaningfully. Saerla stared back, mute.

"Lass, if yon monster forced ye while ye were there, ye can tell us. None will place any blame upon yer head."

"He did no' force me."

Fiona drew a breath. "If somewhat else happened—"

"Why should ye think so?"

"Well, he is no' an ill-looking man, withal. And ye ha' a look about ye, lass. One I recognize full well. Have ye had yer courses since ye came back?"

Saerla shook her head. "It has no' been long enough."

"Aye. Well, they may still come—"

Or they might not, for a number of months.

"Fiona"—she clasped the woman's hands in turn—"speak to no one o' this, I pray."

Fiona looked unhappy. "Yer sister should know."

"Know what? I am no' certain aught ails me more than upset and exhaustion." Swiftly, Saerla rushed on, "If Moira thinks— Well, she will ne'er let me march out to battle."

"It might be best if ye do no'. Lass, 'tis no' safe. And do ye want to engage in such a horror?"

She did not. But nor could she stay back. She had to be there if fate ran a sword through her heart.

⁌ ⟐ ⟐ ⟐ ⌐

Chapter Fifty-Three

"To arms! To arms! Clan MacLeod has mustered and is on the move!"

The call came from a ravaged throat before first light. Whoever cried it ran past the door of Saerla's chamber, where she lay awake staring into the soft dark, echoed swiftly by others giving the alarm all over the stronghold.

She'd found no refuge in sleep, only memories of lying in Rory's arms that tormented her.

She sat up now, and the chamber went around slowly, a sickening sensation. When had she last taken something to eat? She'd refused Fiona's offer to feed her yesterday afternoon. She'd sworn the woman to secrecy but did not know if Fiona could hold her tongue.

And now it came. The battle she'd foreseen and dreaded. Prayer had not held it back, nor all her wishing.

Was she fit to fight?

She got to her feet and immediately had to run for a basin in the corner, where she heaved in vain, having little to bring up. She swiped at her face with clammy hands.

Did she carry Rory's child? Or was she just weak and ill from the ordeal she'd suffered?

More and more cries sounded beyond the confines of her chamber. Footsteps pounded. She must pull herself together, don her leathers, and go. Because not seeing what happened out there in the battle would be so much worse than braving it.

Half crammed into her warrior's clothing, she paused and ran a hand over her flat stomach. She could picture Rory's hand there, feel the gentle care with which he touched her with his big, scarred fingers.

"Be safe, wee one," she whispered before she finished dressing, gathered her weapons, and went out.

An orderly confusion reigned out in the forecourt where the clan warriors mustered. Alasdair was there ahead of Saerla, giving no sign he still suffered any pain. He shouted orders, and the men rallied around him.

Where was Moira? Men crowded the battlements, some hanging dangerously far over the edge. No sign of either Moira or Farlan.

Saerla presented herself, her sword and her shield, to Alasdair, whose dark eyes flicked over her and away again. Would he declare her unfit to fight?

But other matters beset him. He gathered the men and told them a force had been spied moving out from MacLeod, like shadows through the dark.

Suddenly, Saerla feared she would be sick again. Rory. The man she loved coming to destroy all that mattered to her.

"Will we defend here, Alasdair?" a man near her cried. "Or march out and meet them?"

"That will be up to yer chief to decide." Alasdair jerked his head, and Saerla saw Moira walking toward them with Farlan at her side. Both were clad for war. Moira was not a small woman, and in her armor with her hair tied back, she might well pass for a slender man.

There were murmurs from those around Saerla at the sight of Farlan. The MacBeith warriors still did not trust him. Saerla wondered what it would take to make them do so.

Before she could imagine, Fiona darted forward and spoke a word in Moira's ear. Whatever she said startled Moira, as Saerla could see from her posture. Moira searched the crowd and located Saerla.

Och, curse Fiona, anyway!

Saerla slipped away between her fellow warriors, hoping Moira would not take time to locate her amid so many distractions.

Moira, with Farlan, marched up and joined Alasdair. When she lifted her voice, everyone quieted to listen, from the walls right down to the turf.

"Rory MacLeod comes to steal what is ours. This is sacred ground! Our fathers bled and died here, as did their fathers before them. We can do no less."

A bird flew out over the glen, giving a cry of heartrending beauty that seemed to echo the words, heralding the dawn.

"We will march out and meet this marauder upon that sacred ground. We will defeat him once and for all. May all the powers and the strength of our ancestors be with us!"

Tears blinded Saerla's vision. How could anyone doubt that Moira should be chief? She had Da's strength and Ma's wisdom.

Alasdair clapped Moira on the shoulder, demonstrating that she had his support and backing. The warriors began to form into lines. They had drilled long and hard for this. Would it be enough?

So distracted was Saerla, she failed to notice when Moira made a beeline for her, without Farlan this time.

"Sister. I would like ye to stay behind." Moira's blue eyes had gone hard, her face tight. At that moment she looked so like Da before a battle, it near stole Saerla's breath.

Saerla shook her head. "Please do no' ask that o' me."

"'Tis best." As had Fiona's yesterday, Moira's gaze slid over Saerla, probing gently. "Stay back and oversee the defense o' the walls."

It was a reasonable request, and a duty Saerla had fulfilled in the past. If things went badly—very badly—in the field, the men on the walls would make a last stand.

"Sister, I pray ye let me accompany ye."

Moira stepped closer, even though the clamor all around assured them no one could hear, and grief flooded her eyes. "Fiona says—" She stopped abruptly.

Saerla said nothing.

"Tell me but one thing, Saerla. Did he force ye? For if he did, I swear I will slice him from stem to stern."

"Moira, nay." Saerla seized her sister's arm. "Do no' get too close to him. I ha' Seen—"

"All the more reason for ye to stay behind."

"Nay! I maun be there if—"

"There will be a reckoning this day for all the past hurts and the harm he has done."

"Moira, nay! I wanted it. I desired to lie wi' him. I love him—"

Only then, belatedly, did Saerla realize Farlan had come to stand beside Moira. He leaned forward and eyed Saerla with compassion.

Moira, though, recoiled. How could she? Should not she, of all women, understand? Yet she spat, "Him, Saerla? Ye be deluded."

"Let her come," Farlan said. "Else she will worry hersel' sick."

Saerla shot him a grateful glance before she tightened her grip on her sister's arm.

"Moira, if we be separated in the battle, promise me ye will be careful out there. And—and ye will bid Alasdair to be careful also."

A glint in Moira's eyes showed she took Saerla's meaning. She turned and looked at the man at her side.

"Farlan, if this is to be a parting, remember that knowing ye has been worth every moment o' trouble and strife. I will love ye forever, and beyond forever."

And there, in the midst of the hubbub and confusion, they shared a searing kiss.

Out over the glen, the soaring bird cried again—a sound of sorrow.

Chapter Fifty-Four

I T WOULD BE a glorious morning for a triumphant victory. Rory and his warriors had set out well before sunrise when the dark offered them cover, and had gained a lot of distance before dawn broke over the eastern mountains. The air, though, already felt soft. Not so much as a breeze stirred, and no hint of mist or cloud clung to the brae sides. The dome of the sky arched in achingly clear azure, brightening, it seemed, with every footstep.

The only clouds were those that darkened Rory's heart.

So much was wrong with this campaign that should—would—bring him all he'd ever wanted. He never went to battle while filled with uncertainty. It was a fatally poor sort of undertaking. Yet now he worried—worried he would meet Saerla on the field. That in the heat of the fight he might not know her in time. That his sword, driven by a kind of battle madness, might injure the woman he loved.

What a cruel irony that would be. A grief from which he might never recover.

Did he do the right thing in marching out? A man should never ask that either, when he went with scores of warriors at his back and a sword in his hand.

With his cousin at his side. Aye, Leith had taken that place. He was tangibly and vitally unhappy about it, but he was there.

What Leith had said to his woman, Rory could not guess. She

had been there at the leave taking and given Leith the kind of kiss he must have felt to his toes.

Rory remembered such kisses. Given open-mouthed. A claiming and a surrender.

Bright tears had stood in Rhian MacBeith's eyes when Leith walked away from her, but she had not shed them. A strong woman.

Leith must have seen those tears also, and they might account for part of the reason he was so unhappy. It did not really matter, for Leith's unhappiness made another blight on the endeavor. So palpable was Leith's misery, he scarcely felt like Leith. One earmark of Rory's cousin, lifelong, had been his buoyancy of spirit. Always the smile, always the laugh. The amusing quip.

What had Rory done to him? That thought appeared with such stark abruptness, he fair shied from it. He had driven Farlan from him and killed the joy in Leith's heart. The two men closest in the world to him.

But today, so he promised himself, it would be done. The final battle fought. The prize in his hands. *Only, pray do not let me meet Saerla on the field.*

Before they reached the MacLeod loch shore, a runner came with word they'd been spotted from the far fortress and the MacBeiths were mustering.

"She is going to march out and face us," Rory said to Leith, who responded with a look of sheer dismay. It could be bad, or good. He'd had very little success in breaking through MacBeith's defended walls. On the other hand, full-out battle could have twists and disastrous turns, and unforeseen consequences.

Which Saerla might well have foreseen.

He closed his mind, if not his heart, to her and organized the crossing. Since it did not appear they would need it—yet—he ordered the battering ram left behind. While Leith rowed their wee boat across the loch, he lectured himself. Once his foot hit MacBeith soil on the other side, he could think about naught save victory. He must cease to be Saerla MacBeith's lover and become a conquering chief. Nothing more.

The loch, as still as a broad mirror, gave them no difficulty in crossing, and by the time they reached the foreign shore, the sun shone bright. His men drove the wee boats onto the shore, and he saw the MacBeith forces coming.

Suddenly Leith grabbed his arm. His cousin's gray-blue eyes bored into his own, burning with intensity. "Rory, there is still time—talk to Moira MacBeith when ye meet her. Negotiate a peace."

Rory attempted to pull away, but Leith's grip had grown strong. "Are ye mad? Did I no' tell ye wha' I would do to ye if ye used that word again?"

"I do no' care. Stab me through if ye must. 'Twould be better than more wholesale slaughter. Rory, that is Rhian's family. Saerla's family."

For an instant, Rory saw her gazing at him even as Leith did, mist-blue eyes filled with desperation. He did not want to hurt Saerla in any way, by hurting those she loved.

His lips twisted. "Man, I canna change course now. I ha' scores o' men at my back! I ha' made my folk a promise."

Leith's face went tight. Sweat broke out on his brow. He had never looked less like *Leith*.

"So, cousin, this all comes down to saving face? Ye would see Farlan die? Ye would perhaps see Saerla die all for the sake o' yer pride?"

Rory smiled tightly, or perhaps it was a grimace, for the way pain pierced his heart through. Had he lost Leith, also? Had he lost everyone who cared for him?

"I may no' be a worthy man, cousin, but at least I am an honest one."

THE DAY COULD not be more beautiful. Saerla, stationed at Alasdair's back, where Moira had put her—perhaps in the hope the big man could protect her from harm—found herself near dazed by it. The glen she loved so well, like a cupped hand with the loch resting in the palm, seemed to have gathered all the light of the world, a glorious measure of magic. It made her believe that all would somehow come right, for how could it do otherwise on such a morning?

Their company rattled as it marched forth. She could feel the courage of those who surrounded her—feel it like a Vision. Alasdair made a wall of determined valor. And bright, defiant courage fair streamed from Moira, with Farlan at her side. Farlan—Saerla could feel his absolute devotion that would not waver no matter what happened.

What, she wondered, would happen? What to her, if she fell in this battle? She could now see the MacLeod forces up ahead. They'd had time to disembark and form up into ranks. Scores upon scores of blades, any one of which could steal her life.

If she fell upon one of those blades, if it pierced her through and stilled her heart, would she then fly up as she did so often during a Vision? Would she become one with the light that surrounded her? Was that why it had flooded in so strong on this one particular morning?

Aye, so, for at the end of life, did not all return to its source? And had she not always carried a portion of that light? Why fail to believe it would just consume her and carry her to the next life?

But och, och she did not want to leave those she loved. Alasdair and her sisters. Farlan, because aye, she'd come to love him with his deep kindness also, like a brother. Rory—

She caught her breath then because she could see him up ahead. There with Leith close beside him. Leith—och, poor Rhian!—and score upon score of men at his back.

Moira called out, her voice achingly clear in the dancing air, and their company halted. There beneath the blue dome of the sky, beside the sparkling loch on MacBeith soil, the two armies faced each other.

All it would take was one of the commanders, either of them, to give the order, and death would follow.

Moira, there at the front, would face Rory.

Unless Saerla got in the way first.

For she could not see her sister fall. She simply could not—

Quick as the thought, she pushed past Alasdair so she stood beside Moira and Farlan, to one side. Alasdair seized the back of her jerkin.

"Back wi' ye, wee one."

She froze where she stood, directly in sight of Rory MacLeod. Her enemy. Her lover. She opened her very spirit to him and took him in.

A tangle of emotions filled him, not all what one might expect from a chief bent on conquest. There was anger, aye. A wealth of determination. But also deep unhappiness and grief. He would do as he must this day. He did not relish it.

He carried his drawn sword in his hand. His shield, with the MacLeod bull painted on, rested on the opposite arm. His black hair, tied back out of his way, shone in the sun, and his green eyes looked hard as stones as he stared at Moira through narrowed black lashes.

He had not seen her, Saerla, not yet. Did she want him to? Would she be able to raise her sword to this man who had held her in his arms? If it meant saving the life of her sister or this man at her back?

"Moira MacBeith!" he called out, and the sound of his voice made Saerla tremble. It traveled along the course of her very blood and set her soul to dancing. Love and fear and despair all tumbled through her, unbearably bright.

"I give ye here one last chance to surrender all MacBeith lands to me. I offer ye a last chance at ending this strife between us wi'out bloodshed. Wi'out the dead littering this ground when I take it from ye."

Moira's head came up and her shoulders went back. Farlan, at her side, glanced at her as if willing her to accept.

But it was an offer Moira MacBeith could not accept.

"Never!" she called out, just as Saerla knew she must. "'Tis sacred ground upon which we stand. Never will I surrender it from MacBeith hands!"

Both armies stirred, the men shifting on their feet. Warriors eyed one another, choosing their opponents. In a moment, the peace of the beautiful morning would be shattered.

Saerla wanted to scream. She wanted to wail, to do or say something to prevent it all. To throw herself at Rory MacLeod and beg him, for all they'd meant to each other, to turn around and go home.

But she did not. She could not. Alasdair's hand still clutched the back of her jacket.

It was Farlan who stepped forward from Moira's side instead. Head high and his sword in his hand, it was he who addressed his former chief and friend.

"Let us fight it out, Rory! Just ye and me in single combat. To the death, for the fate o' MacBeith lands."

Chapter Fifty-Five

BOTH ARMIES SEEMED to take a collective breath and to shudder. Single combat. It was a deed performed in legends, the colorful, ancient tales told beside a winter's fire. Two warriors fighting to the death with a bright fate of some kind resting upon loss and victory.

Saerla had never seen it done. Not in all her life. She doubted anyone there had.

The idea of it seized them all. So shocked was Alasdair, he forgot to keep hold of Saerla, and she stumbled forward. As did Moira, who caught hold of Farlan's arm.

"Nay," Moira said. "Nay!"

The man she loved lacked her permission to make such an offer. Indeed, the council should have to approve it, for did not ownership of all their lands waver upon it? But none of that made Moira cry out with such passion. It was love that made her do so. Love and terror.

"Ye?" Rory stared at Farlan, the sneer that twisted his lips an insult. "Ye think to best me?"

"Aye." Steady as the rock that lay beneath the green turf upon which he stood, Farlan faced Rory. He heeded not the protestations of Moira, who tried to catch him back, or the rumblings of the men behind him.

"Farlan!" When Moira spoke his name, Farlan looked at her.

In his level brown gaze, Saerla could see the reflection of her Vision. Moira falling. Dead. Farlan would risk his own life a thousand times over to prevent that, even if the bid was a perilous one.

She glanced next into Rory's narrowed eyes and saw the reflection of still another Vision. Three young lads racing on the green turf with purloined swords in their hands. The black-haired lad turning to the brown-headed one.

I dare ye to face me!

Farlan had never beaten Rory in such combat, not in play or in earnest. Never.

"Look here!" Alasdair rumbled. "I ha' a say—"

Rory glared at him, then fastened upon Saerla, who stood at Alasdair's shoulder.

For an instant, the green eyes went completely blank. Then some emotion glinted there—fear, mayhap. Or anger. Either way, he knew her. Even in her warrior's garb, he did. He stared for half a score of heartbeats before he turned his gaze to Moira's face.

And sneered once more. "This is no' up to yer war chief, woman. The man who stands at yer side has issued a clear challenge. Will ye sink so low as to refuse honoring it?"

Moira wanted to say she would. Saerla could see that. Indeed, Moira's lips moved over the words. The MacBeith warriors rumbled behind her. They had, most of them, never trusted Farlan. For the very lands that made up their birthright to rest upon the strength of his sword…

Ewan, who led the council, pushed forward. "I object to this! The man has no authority—"

"Aye, then," Rory interrupted. "Chief MacBeith, does the man who shares yer bed no' ha' yer authority?"

Moira succeeded in forcing out three words. "Face me instead."

"Nay, och, nay." Rory gestured at Farlan with the sword in his hand even as Farlan forced Moira ever so gently behind him.

"'Tis him I am willing to face. This has been a while in coming, Farlan, has it no'?"

"It has," Farlan agreed as he took up a fighting stance there in the cleared space between the two opposing armies. His shield bore no device. He was not entitled to that of MacBeith. But it was clear for what he now fought. He fought for his heart.

Moira began to speak again, and Rory turned on her viciously. "The challenge has been issued and accepted. Ye, mistress, canna gainsay it."

⟫⟫⟫⟪⟪⟪

RORY COULD FEEL as well as see Saerla standing there beside the monstrous MacBeith war chief. She looked as she had the first time he'd seen her, clad for war, armed and determined. But nothing was the same.

The single look he'd stolen into her face had shown him much. Too much. A score of bright images. Her lying beneath him in his bed, passion like smoke in her eyes. Her defying him with a dirk she could not, would not, use at his throat. Her face when they'd parted, contorted by pain and longing.

Now she looked terrified, eyes too wide, mouth held in a grim line. She would have to stand and watch him kill Farlan.

He would have to kill Farlan. His best friend.

Nay. Nay, the man who had once been his best friend. For this was a God-given opportunity. Farlan, though a fine warrior, had never in the past bested him. Could not best him. Would not now. In a few short, bloody minutes, it would be over. All of Glen Bronach would be in his hands.

What was the man thinking?

Rory dragged his gaze from Saerla and looked instead at Farlan. Into the warm, steady brown eyes he knew so well. Farlan gazed back at him, unflinching, without a hint of fear or doubt.

The man had balls, Rory had to give him that. But his woman—the one he claimed to love so well—would have to stand right along with Saerla and watch him die. She would lose her lover and her lands all in one blow.

Should he play the thing out slow, or make it quick and merciful? Single combat happened seldom—they had but played at it when lads—and the warriors on both sides would want something to remember. He should give them that. Beat Farlan back slowly to his lover's feet. End it only then in a shower of blood.

Give them, aye, something to talk of in years to come.

Leith, with horror in his eyes, stepped forward and caught at Rory's arm. Aye, Leith, who had witnessed all those boyhood battles, knew what must come. "Rory, ye canna! 'Tis Farlan."

"Get back wi ye!" Rory shook Leith off viciously. "He will pay for betraying me, for loving her, and she for loving him."

But nay, it was all about the lands. Love did not come into it. Not the love Farlan had broken with Rory, nor what he felt for Saerla.

Again, he glanced at her. His heart protested within him. He was not so weak as his heart.

Somewhere overhead, a bird sang a beautiful song of sorrow, winging down the glen. He gazed once more into Farlan's eyes. "Come on, then. Let us settle this once and for all."

For all time.

Chapter Fifty-Six

SAERLA DID NOT want to watch this terrible combat. But she could not look away. She stood with her hands pressed to her lips and her heart hammering hard enough to shake her whole body.

Beside her, Alasdair straddled the ground, poised as if he would rush in and stop the contest by force. Moira—Saerla could not look at Moira at all.

But Farlan—Farlan went into the battle with his whole heart. That could be seen from the first step, the first crossing of the two swords. He started off better than she had anticipated. Better, mayhap, than Rory had expected. For he pressed Rory hard, bringing blow after blow down upon Rory's shield like a man possessed. Those blows drove Rory back step by step, his sword at times a mere blur of silver.

But Saerla, aye, knew Rory MacLeod. Not defeated, nay, not yet. Too stubborn to give way. To lose.

Even though that hole in his back must be hampering him. Even though the emotions he always sought to hide must be riding him. The man knew not the meaning of *quit*.

Farlan delivered a crashing blow that Rory caught on his shield, and the wood split. Rory retreated another step, tossing the useless remnant aside, and his men cried out. Rory's feet moved in the green turf with the grace of a dancer's, and he delivered an answering blow that took him a step forward again. Both men's gazes were locked on one another to the exclusion of all else.

They rained blows on one another with unstinting might, both of them now sweating in the cool morning air. Farlan repeatedly flung the brown mane of his hair out of his eyes. Rory's green eyes had narrowed to slits. The very hills, the standing stones, and the cairns of Saerla's ancestors waited to learn their fate.

Would Glen Bronach be won this day? Would it be lost?

Rory had stopped retreating. Mayhap he thought he had Farlan's measure; perhaps he thought Farlan began to tire from the furious, relentless pace. Farlan did not *appear* to tire. But aye, step by aching step, Rory fought back and gained ground.

The blows took up a terrible rhythm, splitting the clear air, and Saerla's heart crashed in time. When Rory whirled and used the momentum of the turn to wallop Farlan's shield, the plain wood of it cracked asunder, and it fell from Farlan's hand.

Now both men fought without protection.

Moira gasped—Saerla heard her despite the din. Aye, she knew Rory MacLeod always looked for the chance. For the advantage. Fate had just evened the score and handed him one.

Farlan did not waver. Without so much as glancing down, he kicked the pieces of his shield aside and came on against Rory's whirling blade. Both men fought double-handed, gripping the swords that were all that defended them from death.

Rory looked grim and terrifyingly certain. Farlan, in turn, betrayed no hint of fear. To be sure not. He fought for love, and love even now gathered all around them like the light.

Rory. She called his name in her mind, laid all her own love and faith and belief behind it. And he heard her. His narrowed, feral gaze flicked to her for the briefest instant.

In that instant, they connected. Connected as surely as they had when he was deep inside her, when they rocked together, when they became one being, complete. When they flew with the strength and beauty of a bird.

Saerla. Love.

No more than that, but she saw the thoughts move in his eyes. Light and shadow. She felt his lips tighten. Knew when he weighed love—what they felt for each other—against duty. Against avarice. Against pride.

She felt it when he chose. *For love.* The miracle of it shimmered all around her; it uplifted her. The light around them began to grow brighter and brighter as Rory stepped back.

Back.

He continued to catch Farlan's crashing blows on his sword, but the blows he aimed in return had lost their might. Farlan was able to parry them with his blade. Turn them away and press on.

Was Saerla the only one there out of all those watching so avidly who saw that Rory's foot did not truly slip on the trodden grass? Who saw his toe dig into the turf so he tumbled backward, casting aside his sword as he fell?

Did even Farlan, who fought him, see? No time to decide, for Farlan leaped forward and put the point of his blade to Rory's throat where he lay on his back there on the blessed soil beside the loch.

It went abruptly silent, so silent Saerla could hear both men laboring for breath. She could hear the waters of the loch kissing the shore. And the bird, that bonny bird, crying its song.

"Finish it!" Alasdair called out then.

A fight to the death. One Saerla stood to lose. For though MacBeith would retain their lands, she would lose a great, bloody portion of her heart, torn out by the very roots.

Farlan breathed so hard, the sword rose and fell in his hand. Or perhaps that hand trembled. For he stared down into the eyes of the man who had once been his best friend.

Defenseless. Eyes unreadable. Fingers clenched into the sod of this place—this place they all loved.

Please, Saerla beseeched the light, her gods, and every power that had ever attended her. *Make it right.*

"Finish it!" Alasdair cried again.

But Farlan continued to stand, gazing into Rory's eyes.

The warriors on both sides grew restless. Ignoring them, Farlan called out, "Ye be bested, Rory MacLeod, in fair and honorable combat. Let this be an end to it! Again I say, let it be done. No more battles in this glen. No more bloodshed and strife." He took a single step back. "I let ye live to negotiate a peace."

There were gasps all around. No other sound save the cry of the bird now distant. For one more instant, while Saerla's heart pounded, her life and her future hung in the balance.

Then Rory put up his hand. A gesture not so much of surrender as a bridge reaching. *Reaching.* Farlan accepted that hand and hauled Rory to his feet, an act that, as boys, they must have performed a hundred times.

Saerla had a glimpse then of Moira's face—eyes wide with wonder and relief—before Farlan pulled Rory into his arms. The two men embraced, clapped one another on the back almost as if the breach between them had never occurred.

Moira, with tears standing in her eyes, raised her sword over her head. "I declare the warring between MacBeith and MacLeod done! We shall each hold to our own lands and henceforth defend Glen Bronach together."

The muscles of Rory's back tensed, and he stepped away from Farlan. Would he be able to accept such an abrupt end to his dreams and ambitions? Would he embrace a peace so swiftly forged?

But it was he—he who had gone down in the turf and let Farlan win the contest. Had he not?

The ranks of warriors had broken up into babbling groups, some cheering, some grumbling. For most, battling against one another had been a lifelong endeavor. They might not accept this either.

Including Alasdair, who grumbled in a steady stream under his breath, staring incredulously at the scene before his eyes.

Leith rushed forward, a big grin splitting his face, and threw his arms around the necks of both Rory and Farlan, hauling them together again. Moira stepped up also and embraced Farlan, her relief and joy as tangible as the light Saerla could feel filling her. Upholding her.

She stayed where she was. Waited, waited for the man whose hair gleamed like the wing of a blackbird to look around and search for her.

When he did, when he pulled away from his companions, there was no searching. Their eyes met surely and exclusively. Peace flooded Saerla from head to toe.

She stepped from the unhappy Alasdair's side just as Rory stepped from Farlan's. She wanted to throw herself into his arms but would not, here, before so many eyes.

He caught her hands. "Tha' was for ye, Saerla MacBeith. No' for Farlan, nor even for the glen, but for the sake o' the love between us. I should ha' told ye before ye left me. I love ye, lass. I love ye full well."

"I love ye also, Rory MacLeod. Ye—of all men."

"Of all women." His gaze consumed her, vital as the heat of his fingers on her own. His mouth quirked at one corner. "It seems fate must ha' a sense o' humor, presenting me wi' the one woman I can love, and her a MacBeith."

"Naught else could ha' united Glen Bronach, save love."

He tossed his head, an echo of the arrogant man he had been. "Saerla MacBeith, will ye be my bride?"

She continued to hold his gaze as joy spilled through her, sparkling and bright. "I can think o' naught I want more than to live my life at your side, Rory MacLeod."

She saw his joy take hold from hers and ignite him.

"There will be difficulties," she warned. "A glen that has been at war for generations will no' fall into a state o' agreement wi' out some rumblings."

"So there will." His eyes met hers. "I reckon if Farlan and I can forgive each other, can sit down and talk out a peace, then aught is possible."

"So be it." Saerla bowed her head over their joined hands, and he did also until the black hair met the red-gold. Then, hands still joined, they turned and faced all those who loved them.

Epilogue

Ten years on.

THE THREE LADS ran across the bright green turf with the sun sparkling overhead and the wind chasing them up the glen. It might be seen that one of them had a head of golden thatch with a hint of a red cast to it. A second bore a mane of tumbled brown curls. The third had a crop of hair as black as the wing of a raven.

Though the fair-haired lad was the oldest, it was clear the black-headed boy led the way, his young voice calling out eager commands his companions followed good-naturedly.

All down the loch side they ran and tumbled and contested with one another until they fell into the sparkling green turf precisely like three weary young hounds.

They lay in an untidy row, arms folded behind their heads, and looked up at the achingly blue sky.

"I do love it here full well," declared the brown-haired boy, his dark blue eyes full of contentment. "'Tis a braw place to live, is Glen Bronach."

"A braw place, aye," the other two agreed without hesitation.

"My ma says," the brown-haired lad went on, "the strength o' this place is in the stone upon which it stands, and that will never break asunder."

"My ma says," offered the fair-haired lad, a winsome smile dancing over his face, "the strength o' Glen Bronach comes fro' the fire o' love and loyalty in our hearts."

The third lad said nothing. His green eyes narrowed as he tracked a cloud that looked precisely like a dragon, driven before the fair wind. It took him a moment to think over what his two companions had said. Not quickly or rashly did he give his opinion, for words mattered. That he did know.

At last he declared, "My ma says our strength lies in the magic. And that comes fro' the light."

"Mayhap," said the brown-haired lad, "it comes fro' all three. We maun keep the strength o' the stone and hold to it."

"We maun keep the fire burning," added the lad with the sweet smile, "wi'out fail."

"We maun keep the magic safe always," said the lad with the wise green eyes. "And that will protect the glen."

For one solemn moment, they contemplated it in agreement. As everyone knew, there was power in threes.

The black-haired lad gathered his legs beneath him and, his energy restored, leaped to his feet.

"Race ye to the rise! And the first one to Grandfather Iain's cairn is the keeper o' the glen!"

"Silly." The fair-haired lad shoved him affectionately. "Are we no' all sworn to that?"

They ran off through the sunlight leaving a trail of laughter, with the black-headed lad leading the way.

The End

About the Author

Laura Strickland delights in time traveling to the past and weaving deliciously romantic stories for her readers. Her first love has always been Scottish Historical Romance, and her work has garnered her several awards including a RONE. At home in Western New York, she's been privileged to mother a number of very special rescue dogs. Her lifelong interest in Celtic history, magic, and music, along with her mantra of *Lore, Legend, Love* are all reflected in her writing.

Visit Laura at www.laurastricklandbooks.com

www.ingramcontent.com/pod-product-compliance
Lightning Source LLC
Chambersburg PA
CBHW070524310726
48976CB00002BA/530